In a House Unknown

Books by Dolores Hitchens

IN A HOUSE UNKNOWN
THE BAXTER LETTERS
A COLLECTION OF STRANGERS
POSTSCRIPT TO NIGHTMARE
THE MAN WHO CRIED ALL THE WAY HOME
THE BANK WITH THE BAMBOO DOOR
THE ABDUCTOR
FOOTSTEPS IN THE NIGHT
THE WATCHER
FOOL'S GOLD
SLEEP WITH SLANDER
SLEEP WITH STRANGERS
BEAT BACK THE TIDE
TERROR LURKS IN DARKNESS
NETS TO CATCH THE WIND
STAIRWAY TO AN EMPTY ROOM

In a House Unknown

DOLORES HITCHENS

PUBLISHED FOR THE CRIME CLUB BY
Doubleday & Company, Inc.
Garden City, New York
1973

All of the characters in this book are fictitious, and any resemblance to actual persons, living or dead, is purely coincidental.

ISBN: 0-385-03265-x
Library of Congress Catalog Card Number 72-92221

Printed in the United States of America
First Edition

One

For some miles now there had been no houses on either side of the road. The thick forest had been trimmed back to fence line, but small trees stubbornly advanced toward the blacktop. Most were pines, plumed with tufty needles. The earth was green in all directions, and above was the blue sky with a rim of clouds like blowing minarets. My old car came to the crest of a rise; ahead of me was a long dip in the road, at the bottom of the dip a railroad track. The rusty rails and the warning signs were the only marks of man's presence in all this bird-singing wildness.

I pulled over to the side of the road, parked half off the pavement, and got out. I wanted to stretch the stiffness out of my body. And to look ahead if possible at what I might be going to meet, and to think.

I had left the main northern Louisiana highway, Interstate 20, some ten miles back, passed through the tidy, pleasant village of Moss Corner, with its college, its Confederate monument and white marble courthouse, and its outsized A&P. The roads had successively dwindled to what I was on now.

I stretched with my arms above my head and then rubbed the back of my neck with both hands. I looked at the impenetrable woods, and these at least were what I had expected, and I felt lucky that my destination was not apt to lie in an alligator preserve in the midst of bayou waters. There was a great sense of peace here, with only the sound of the wind and the birds. And this was also most likely the point of no return.

For when I turned the next corner in the road, or perhaps the second next corner, or the one after that, or when I had counted three more dips, or five more, and two more railroad crossings, or six more cows, or twenty-nine fence posts, I would come into sight of the house. And then it would be too late. I would become a part of whatever was going on.

The house. That strange house. From my sister's letters, I knew every detail from the broad front steps to the wide verandas, to the enormous parlor with its oil portrait of General Robert E. Lee on horseback over the mantel, to the tower and the belvedere with its view of the countryside. A beautifully kept and polished anachronism, a showplace, a picture postcard of a southern home, half-burned by marauding Yankee soldiers more than a hundred years ago, then restored, the tower and the belvedere added during a flurry of good fortune during the 1890s. And with every inconvenience of the nineties built in immutably, as far as housekeeping went. I had thought of the house for so long, and wished that Rye were out of it. And she would not go. And now this grisly unpleasantness had started, and she had called me.

The best thing that could be said for me as a mediator of other people's troubles was that I was single and unattached. I was, in fact, a spinster. It was an old-fashioned word but I had begun, in my thoughts, to apply it to myself. During these past few years the stubborn reserve and shyness that had plagued me from my childhood had deepened, and it seemed to me, had grown into a stony detachment. And no act of will nor tears could change this.

No use, I thought, to stand here in indecision—I got back into the car, slowly, reluctantly, and started the motor. I could still, at this point, turn back, to the school job in New Mexico, for one. Or I could keep on heading east on Interstate 20 and turn north after a while and end up in New York. I could do shorthand and typing there, the way I had for a year, when I was twenty-one. I could even probably still do modeling after a fashion, the way I'd begun to do at the end of that year. I was still thin, thinner even than I'd been then, and the advertising people had liked my face. I don't see anything beautiful about my face, but they saw something in it. They said.

The car began to roll forward down the other side of the rise; it wasn't turning itself around. And I wasn't turning it. Rye was waiting for me, anxious for me to explain away her fears. Aunt Wanda was there too, though it was harder to imagine her in the setting. My aunt couldn't be said to have lived the kind of life that prepared one for Larchwood.

The car bumped across the railroad tracks at the bottom of the dip. Some birds rose straight up out of the trees, their wings flickering against the blue sky.

I could still turn around.

But I wouldn't.

The house sat on a great rise, far back off the road but fully visible from it. The lawns were silky, deep green, dotted with magnolias. The driveway meandered, avoiding the trees; it was paved with crushed white gravel that sparkled in the sun. It led to the side of the house where an extension of the veranda roof made a porte-cochere.

I slowed the car to look, to satisfy my curiosity. My sister's description of the house hadn't prepared me for its size. Inconvenient it might be to housekeep in, but beautiful—quite completely beautiful—it was, too. I thought that it looked like a vast confection of spun sugar, too lovely to be real. It seemed out of a dream. And I would, in that moment, willingly have shot any damned Yankee who made a move to burn it.

Whoever had originally designed Larchwood, and whoever had made the additions of tower and belvedere, had been like-minded as twins, completing a symmetrical and elegant whole, something that looked in spite of its size as delicate, as airy as the minareted clouds at the rim of the sky.

"You're beautiful, you Larchwood," I said grudgingly, and let the car swing off the pavement into the drive, past a mailbox mounted on a slim stone pillar and on between two massive pillars like sentinels and which held the opened halves of a wrought-iron gate. I'd driven about half the distance to the house when there was Rye, jumping down the broad front stairs and running to meet me, looking wild and tousled even at that distance, the red hair blowing like a mane, waving one arm and looking all of 13 months pregnant instead of the 7½ she was supposed to be.

"Slow down!" I cried, though she was still too far to hear me. "You'll fall and break yourself! Oh, Rye!" I speeded the car to intercept the running figure. But now Rye had stopped to hold her side, grimacing, waiting beside the drive.

When I rolled to a stop she yanked the door open and tried to smother me with kisses.

"Pock! Pock! I knew you'd come! I knew it, knew it!"

I held her close, trying to smooth the wild hair, knowing in that moment how she had waited for me, dreading that I wouldn't come, and it was with a pang that I remembered that little while of indecision back there beside the road.

"Let me get in!" She gave me a last squeeze and ran around the car, opened the other door, and climbed into the seat. "I'll ride up to the house with you. Oh, Pock, you look wonderful! Too thin, but wonderful!" She slammed the door and then we sat, caught in a sudden silence, measuring each other. I noted a look of strain in Rye's face, a tautness around the eyes that betrayed the nervous tension and fear. "I hate to admit how scared I've been. So alone and scared. I just felt sometimes that I . . . I couldn't go on—" She put her hands over her face to hide the tears.

I pulled a hand away and laid it against my cheek. I was angry, but tried not to show it. "What's the matter with Aunt Wanda? Why hasn't she protected you?"

Rye choked over what she wanted to say, stopped to rub the tears from her eyes, and began again. "She does all she can, I guess. But she doesn't see any urgency. It's not happening to her and she has such awful responsibilities, it's all tied up with the will, what she has to do, and there's this Mr. Sutton who watches her every move. He keeps track of everything—"

"Don't try to explain it all now. We can talk about it later when we're alone at the house." I put the car into gear, and it crept forward. I was worried about Rye. I didn't want her to break down completely now that I was here; there was too much I had to know.

"We might not even *be* alone! There are the servants, slipping around. Some of them must be spies. Aunt Wanda seems afraid of them. And you just never know when they'll suddenly appear. It's spooky." Her voice died to a whisper and she sat dejected, hands in her lap. There was no sound except that of the tires crunching gravel. Then she sighed as if with resignation. "You're right. I can't tell it all now. We'll wait. But I'm so glad you're here! That's the main thing, that you've come."

"I'm glad too," I said. And I very much meant it.

Aunt Wanda met us at the porte-cochere, and I had to give her credit, she was trying quite successfully to live up to the house. Her hair was snowy now, and piled in spun-sugar rolls and puffs on top of her head; she had slimmed from that coarse weight she had carried in her forties, her dress was a subdued soft violet, almost gray, and her only jewelry was a single strand of small pearls. Her makeup was the biggest surprise of all, for Aunt Wanda had always, from the first I could remember of her, worn masses of powder, paint, eyeshadow and false eyelashes, lipstick, mascara; and this was all gone. There was a faint dusting of powder to soften the fifty-five-year-old face, and a trace of pale pink lipstick. Aunt Wanda looked the perfect lady.

I got out of the car and walked toward my aunt.

Just before she put out her hand I saw the flicker of dislike she couldn't quite conceal. "Esther!" The voice was the same, too, she hadn't been able to change that, it was the hoarse bass, the barroom contralto, that I remembered. "So wonderful to see you again after so long . . ." She pulled me against her in a brief hug. She smelled of sachet, a faint flowery odor, and this was the biggest change of all, because she had always in the past been given to passionate fragrances that made your nose wrinkle.

"It's nice to see you again, too."

She surveyed me frankly from arm's length. "Almost six years, isn't it?" She laughed shortly. "My, but we've grown up. How long have you taught school?"

"Three years."

"On an Indian reservation, isn't it? I'm glad you decided you could get away. We want you here for a nice long visit." This seemed to be said for Rye's benefit. "Barbara has been dying for your arrival."

In the old days Aunt Wanda would have said, "Barbara has been wetting her pants waiting." Some changes had gone deeper than I had supposed.

"I stayed last night in Dallas." I was making conversation to cover the awkward beginning of the visit rather than to try to outline my trip east. "I wanted to get here in the freshness of morning. I must say, you have a beautiful big place. Rye wrote me a lot about it, but even so, I was surprised."

She didn't react with the pride nor pleasure I had expected. Was there a shadow of regret, of weariness, in her eyes just before she smiled at me? If so, it vanished quickly. "You'll want to come in, now. No, don't bother with your things. Perkins will see to them." She held out a hand to Rye, gave one to me, and so led us up the stairs to the side door.

Inside, a long hall lay ahead of us, carpeted down the center, with polished floor on either side. There were occasional shallow tables against the walls on which sat fresh arrangements of flowers, tastefully done, sometimes reflected by a mirror on the wall above the table. It seemed to me in this first glimpse that the house shone with care.

Aunt Wanda dropped our hands and led the way, and as I followed I thought about the greeting she had given me. She hadn't commented on my appearance except to say that after six years I was quite grown up. But I knew that in her eyes I was drab and colorless. Aunt Wanda in any of her roles, given the money, had known how to dress. My clothes were schoolworn and plain. Any style sense I might have developed during the brief time of modeling in New York had long ago been submerged in my spinster personality. I was, too, a contrast to Rye, who even in late pregnancy and under the stress of what had happened here, kept her color and brightness. I was simply, after all, the ugly duckling who had grown up to be a very dull duck.

The vast parlor, softly lit by windows on three sides, was as Rye had described it to me in her letters, a great formal room with groups of graceful furniture, most of it upholstered in muted rose colors, plush and brocades. There was a grand piano at the far end of the room, rather alone against the French windows, and above the enormous mantel stood General Lee, his horse beside him, life-sized in oils. I was staring at the portrait and Aunt Wanda said, "The original owner of this place, the man who had the house built in the 1850s, was an officer under Lee's command in the War Between the States. After the war, the general posed for this portrait at his officer's request. And here it is, just as it was first painted and hung." For the first time there was a definite note of pride in her tone, a glimmer of possessiveness.

"It seems a good portrait. I had the idea from something Rye wrote that the general was *on* the horse."

We sat down where Aunt Wanda wanted us. She rang a small bell from a table beside her chair, and though it made such a tiny sound and could not have carried far, almost immediately a uniformed colored maid, young and slim and proudly neat, came into the room. Aunt Wanda asked her to bring coffee for the three of us.

"With his horse," Rye defended herself. "I'm sure I wrote, *with* his horse, Pocket."

Aunt Wanda blinked, and seemed confused for a moment. "I had forgotten," she said slowly. "You two have always had those names for each other—"

"I think of myself as Pocket," I said without emphasis.

"And I'm Rye."

We looked at each other, memories stirring, and then we turned to our aunt, two pairs of eyes defying her to ask us to change.

So long. So long ago, I thought. And I was remembering the dark, discouraged day, the bad day at school followed by the fading empty afternoon, wandering all alone in the house because our father and mother had gone out somewhere and had taken Barbara with them and had left no note, nothing to tell me where they'd gone or when they were coming back. Or *if* they were coming back—there had always been that irrational fear deep inside, unspoken. Loneliness had finally driven me out of the echoing house to the little garden shed, with its store of tools and sprays and the summer garden furniture, where I had curled up on a lounge to worry, to brood. Unloved, though I didn't put it into words, and the trouble seemed twined with my name, my name a badge of the unloved identity; and I had decided that I hated my name. When Rye had come searching at last I had said, "I hate my name. I won't be Esther any more. I won't," with the unexpressed hope that someone named not Esther would be loved again.

The little one, curling beside me on the lounge, had agreed. "I won't be Barbara, either!" (Though Barbara was loved.) Then, after thinking about it, "But who can we be? We have to be somebody new." It was not until the next afternoon, when I came home from school, that Rye had met me glowing. "Pocket full of Rye!" she had chanted over and over. "Pocket full of Rye!"

I had tried to smooth the red tousle, stop the jumping and skipping. "You sound silly. What is Pocket full of Rye supposed to mean?"

"Our names. Our new names. You're Pocket. I'm Rye. Our very own new names. Different names. We won't be Esther and Barbara any more. They can go to hell."

"Mama will wash your mouth with soap."

"I heard Aunt Wanda say it. Say, 'Go to hell,' I mean."

"Shhh!" At first I'd thought that having a name like Pocket would be the craziest thing in the world, but then I'd turned it over in my mind and had somehow come to like it. Nobody else, I'd thought, perhaps no one in the whole world was named *Pocket.* And now it was offered me, a new name and a new place in life. I had felt, with sudden excitement, rebaptized, reidentified, restored.

After that we tormented our parents by refusing to answer to any but our new names, and finally, taking the path of least resistance, our mother and father had begun calling us Pocket and Rye, and thus we had grown up. Two oddballs, I thought now, watching the neat little maid wheel in a small cart with a shining coffee urn, fragile china, silver, and napkins.

"Thank you, Martha," Aunt Wanda said, and set about filling a cup.

I couldn't be sure, but I thought that the maid gave me a swift, sure examination from under lowered eyelids.

Aunt Wanda knew why I was here, knew all about the ugliness that had driven Rye to beg me to come, but by no hint of voice or expression did she betray that knowledge, or show that she understood anything of my real errand. So we sat and sipped coffee and exchanged small talk, until I could read such impatience and despair in Rye's face that I—trying to sound like a polite guest, but looking Aunt Wanda straight in the eyes—told her that I needed to go upstairs to freshen up and to unpack.

And so Rye and I finally got away.

Two

As WE WALKED SLOWLY up the great front stairs of Larchwood to the upper floor, I was beset with a feeling of unreality. Of twistedness, strangeness. You might have said, I told myself, that we were three women in the grip of the past. For myself, it seemed that I existed in a limbo of spinsterish withdrawal and isolation, a curtain of shyness between me and the world and the people in it. And surely this must be an outgrowth of the life that had gone before, though I couldn't understand how nor why. Aunt Wanda, after a footloose and happy-go-lucky life, had married the elderly owner of Larchwood out of the blue—out of a bar in Tucson, actually—and had unexpectedly inherited the place on his death less than a year later.

Rye too had been married briefly, tragically.

I tried to throw off the sense of the past and bring myself into the present moment as we entered the room that had been given me for my stay here. It was a beautiful, big, airy room, with French doors opening upon a balcony. Rugs had been taken up for the summer, so that the rich grain of the floor shone under its wax. There was a huge white bed with a lace-ruffled counterpane, and at the windows long, lacy drifts of gauzy web through which the sun came, golden. Against the wall were a large antique-white wardrobe and chest of drawers. The French doors were open, and outdoors the birds were singing. The smell of the surrounding forest filled the air.

My luggage, two battered suitcases and the zipper bag that didn't zip any more, made a shabby show on racks across the room. They had been brought up and the fastenings unlatched, but tactfully left unopened until I should ask for help to unpack. Something I had no intention of doing. Rye seated herself in a low rocker, a little antique chair with pink velvet cushions, and I sat down on the pale-green satin lounge.

I looked around at the room and said, "This is too lavish for me. I've never lived in a room like this. I don't feel that I belong in it."

What I really meant was that the room belonged to a frivolous and lighthearted person, someone quite different from me.

"Oh, nonsense. You'll be fine. It's just a room. And you didn't come here to criticize furniture and such. You came because I need you." She put her hands together on top of her so-pregnant belly, almost in an attitude of begging. "You will stay and see what it's all about, won't you? And you won't let Aunt Wanda annoy you too much? I know the two of you never got along."

"I won't let her run me off," I promised. "But the thing is, you've never written me once, what Aunt Wanda thinks and says about what has happened. You've written as if you were living here alone, in a void, with no one else to help or advise you."

Her hands twisted together with an air of desperation. "I can't seem to get through to her. She kind of consoles me when I go to her, as if there's nothing to be done, really, and I ought to think only of the baby and not let odds and ends upset me. I told her what I'd found in the cemetery, I even made her look at the things I brought home, and she seemed thoughtful for a little while." Rye shook her red head in bitter perplexity. "She's so changed now. In thc old days—you remember—she would have come out swinging, and God help anybody who'd been pulling such tricks. But now there is this house. It has to be kept perfectly. There are the servants to look after, and then there is the land where the house is, the park, as it's called. And besides all this there are hundreds and hundreds of acres of forest all over this part of Louisiana. Plus land cleared for stock. The trees have to be harvested and sold for pulpwood, paper. And there are even gas wells on some of the land."

"Aunt Wanda inherited a great fortune," I said slowly.

"She inherited a pain in the rear end," Rye said inelegantly. "It keeps her wits whirling. And Mr. Sutton . . . well, you'll meet him. He's the watchdog, wretched man."

"Watchdog?"

"Yes. She says that when her husband's will was read, it turned out that Mr. Sutton was co-executor, or something. Anyway, he has lots of power. And her husband—another wretch, to leave her under the thumb of Mr. Sutton. She can't even draw a deep breath for fear of making a mistake, something that will bring everything crashing down around her."

I frowned. "Surely not that desperate."

"She has to watch her step like crazy. She just hasn't time for anything. Me, for instance."

I couldn't believe it. In spite of the surface changes, Aunt Wanda must surely have been impressed, if not disturbed and angry, over what had happened at the cemetery. "When you made her listen, what did she actually say?"

"She said it was just a prank. A couple of pranks, when the next thing happened. I said only somebody sick in the head did things to a grave, and she said perhaps it was a kid. Imagine—" Rye's eyes flashed with anger and despair. "A *kid!*"

I could see that Rye was worked up, terribly upset by the memory of what had happened and at the same time helpless and frustrated; and that this couldn't be good for her or for the baby to be born in little more than a month. I got up and walked over to her and touched the red curls gently. "Try to be calm, to keep a relaxed attitude. I know it will be hard to do. Meanness is hard to take, and anonymous meanness, directed against the dead, is hardest to take of all. But Aunt Wanda is right in one thing. You can't be tearing yourself apart over this while you're carrying the baby. If it means ignoring what goes on, not going near Jim's grave for the time being—"

"I won't be driven from Jim! I won't!" Rye began to cry, bent over as much as she could manage, the tumble of red hair falling across her face. Her hands twisted and shook. "We had each other for such a little while! I won't let some rotten f . . . freak separate us now!"

I knelt beside the chair. I felt awkward, at a loss, with nothing to say, no comfort to give in this terrible grief. There was no way to change the tragic past, perhaps no way to make Rye look toward the future—but I had to try. "Please, Rye. Please listen. If you love Jim, if you honor his memory, think of him. Think of his child still to be born. Would Jim want you to destroy yourself over some ugly trick played at his grave? Would he expect you, carrying his child, to make yourself a guard for his resting place? Day and night? You wrote me that you've gone there at night—" Even as I spoke, my angry thoughts turned to our aunt. How could she have ignored and dismissed Rye's agony, and passed over the appeals for help?

I promised myself that I would talk to our aunt, and soon, and that I would not be turned aside nor ignored.

As I knelt there beside Rye I heard a whisper of sound behind me, and turned to look. A young maid, almost a duplicate of Martha, had come into the room. She was Martha's height and wore the same neat dark uniform with bibbed organdy apron, with an organdy bow atop her semi-Afro hairdo. When she saw me kneeling, Rye crouched over weeping, she made a voiceless apology and hurried from the room.

Rye had not known that anyone had come in. She cried, letting me hold and comfort her, and then after a while the sobs lessened, she raised herself erect on the chair, pulling down the maternity blouse over her plumpness, and rubbed away the tears. "If you're going to say the same tired things Aunt Wanda has been saying, you may as well not have come."

I wanted to say, don't discard me yet; but instead, trying to keep any impatience out of my voice, I said, "What do you want me to do?"

She looked at me uncertainly. "Well . . . what do you want to do? What comes first?"

"Suppose you begin by showing me the things you found at the grave."

Her eyes fixed on mine with a look of distress.

"Have you kept them? Ugly as they are, they're evidence."

"Evidence of nothing, according to anyone I've talked to," Rye said bitterly.

"Have you talked to any police officers?"

"Yes."

Rye hesitated there, and I was annoyed. "Don't tell me the law here takes an indifferent view of the desecration of a grave. They brushed you off?"

"There was just the one. A young officer named Warne. He was very polite. I met him at the cemetery; he came along in a parish patrol car. He seemed to want to help. I guess it's hard for him to figure out what he can do. I explained what was going on at the grave, and how the caretaker is there only once a week to tidy up, to mow and rake. The old caretaker—they call him Deacon—has a couple of church janitor jobs during the week, and anyway, he isn't supposed to guard the cemetery. And this young officer only passes on that road a few times a week. I guess he has miles and miles of road to patrol. When I got through telling him about it, he . . . he touched my hand in a nice way, gently and sympathetically, and he said he'd check the law on the matter and so forth. I haven't seen him since."

"Was this part of the patrol, checking the cemetery? I mean, why did he stop?"

Rye looked huddled and forlorn, as if her burden of worry and stress were almost more than she could bear. "I guess he'd seen me there before, when he went by. And he must have been curious, why I should be there so often. I can't think of any other reason why he should have parked the patrol car and walked all the way to where I was."

"How long ago did this happen?"

"Six or seven days ago."

I thought to myself, the young officer must have been suspicious of a lurking woman in the cemetery, an oddity that had caught his attention, and then when he had found out the unsavory and probably unsolvable difficulty, had avoided the place since.

"Let's see the things you found on Jim's grave," I said, and Rye got to her feet slowly and went out of the room. She came back quickly, carrying what looked to be a roll of white shelf paper. I had reseated myself on the lounge, and she brought the roll there and spread it between us.

"This was first." She took out what seemed at first to be a plain sheet of plastic wrap, the kind of thing used to keep foods fresh. But as she uncurled it, a piece of newsprint could be seen in the center of the sheet, between the double plastic. "This was nailed to the grave, a nail in each corner, right in front of the plaque with Jim's name on it." She showed me the holes in the corners of the plastic where the nails had been.

I took the thing from her, aware of a feeling of aversion and fear. This thing, innocuous as it seemed on first glance, represented something sick and venomous. To have to touch it was rather like having to handle a snake.

Though Rye had written me about it, to see it was still a shock. The news item between the two sheets of plastic was brief; it simply announced the funeral to be held on a coming date of Lt. James Parrish, who had died in action in Vietnam. He was mentioned as being survived by his widow, Barbara Parrish, and by two aunts in Virginia. Services would be conducted by Reverend So-and-So. Burial would be in Countryside Cemetery. The stinger wasn't in the news item; it was written on a small scrap of white paper attached to the bottom of the printed item. The script was neat, plain, anonymous.

> Are you sure this is Jim Parrish
> buried here?
> I heard different.
> Too bad.

The last two words, I thought, were the sickest of all. The pretense at sympathy—

"You never explained one thing, Rye. Is there any possibility that Jim really isn't buried there?"

Rye was shaking her head fiercely. "No. His commanding officer wrote. There was no mistake. I know you read about such things once in a while in the newspapers, someone burying a body and then later finding their son or husband still alive. But it *is* Jim."

I laid the plastic with its enclosed clipping back upon the sheet in which it had been rolled. "That's the doll?"

She picked up a roly-poly little doll. Its feet were fixed to a short wooden stake by means of a twisted wire. In its arms was tied a tiny bouquet of faded blossoms with a piece of ribbon hanging free. On the ribbon was lettered:

Tell it in a house unknown

I frowned. "What does this mean?"

"I don't know. I've spent hours thinking about it, ever since I found the doll standing there on Jim's grave."

I reread the phrase slowly to myself. The ribbon had once been white but had been stained by damp and mold. "It seems as if the doll and the news item don't even go together," I said finally. "The thing written with the clipping is just meanness, or it seems that way, something to upset you and start you wondering and hoping. I mean, the purpose seems obvious. But this, with the doll . . . I can't figure out what the intention was."

"I can't either." Rye's greenish eyes had darkened with anguish. "Perhaps I'm supposed to think of the man I buried as someone unknown. Unknown to me, that is. Perhaps that's what I'm supposed to wonder about."

I laid the doll back upon the sheet of white paper, and Rye rolled it into a cylinder. She got up and took it away, and while she was gone, I brushed at a crumb of something on the lounge, then picked it up between my fingers to look at it closely. I found that I was holding a tiny crumb of earth, and I realized that it had fallen off the small wooden stake wired to the doll's feet. I was holding a bit of earth from Jim Parrish's grave.

The bittersweet memory swept through me of that spring day when Rye and Jim had been married, the view of the sea through the chapel windows, all glittering light and blue horizon and the promise of years to come, of love to endure forever; and now the years would not come, and the love had had to end.

I can't cry now, I told myself fiercely. I won't let Rye come back and find me crying. We'll go to pieces together.

I stood up and carried the crumb of earth carefully to the open French windows, to the balcony, and opened my palm and let the tiny dark bit drift down into a bed of flowers below. Rye came into the room behind me, and as I stepped back through the French windows I said, trying to sound casual, "There was a bird, singing so close I thought I might see it." And then I realized that Rye was staring at me, afraid that I'd already put her problem out of mind, and I added, "How long since Jim had lived at Moss Corner?"

Rye sat down again on the small rocker. "Jim never actually lived there. He went to college there. It's a good-sized school and it's . . . well, like other colleges, it's sort of self-contained. There's the town and—there's the school."

"Did Jim ever speak of anyone he'd known in Moss Corner?"

"No. Sometimes he'd mentioned someone he'd known in college. Remember that he graduated almost six years ago. There wouldn't be anyone left at the college who had been there when Jim had, except perhaps some of the professors. None of his fellow students would still be there."

I saw that Rye had explored this angle and was satisfied that Jim hadn't left any enemies in the town. "There has to be some connection somewhere. No one knows *you* here. You came here to bury Jim and to stay on with Aunt Wanda, and that was the beginning for you as far as this country goes. A bare four months ago."

"I know. It seems that there has to be a connection to Jim. But I can't find it."

Was there a sound of a footstep in the hall? Was someone out there beyond the door that Rye had left ajar?

Three

I SAT STILL, listening, but the sound—if there had been a sound—was not repeated. The mockingbirds squawked and trilled outdoors, and the breeze whispered in the magnolias, and that was all. I said to Rye, "Is this cemetery where Jim is buried the *town* cemetery?"

"No. It's too far from Moss Corner for that. It's just for the country people hereabouts. Some of the graves are very old. Pioneers are buried there, people who first came to this part of Louisiana. Bart's people, for instance. You haven't met Bart. He lives in one of Aunt Wanda's houses. There are two houses down the road."

I was surprised. "Big like this?"

"No, no. Nothing like this. They're small and ordinary. They must have been built for overseers, or someone like that. Years ago before he met Aunt Wanda, her husband raised a lot of stock. Cattle and horses. That was before oil and gas became so important. Well, the houses were built to house men who had charge of the stock. They're a long way from new."

"And so who is Bart?"

"He teaches at the college in town. He grew up near here and went through school, and finally came back here to teach. I guess he's forty or so. He's friendly, really nice, and I'm sure that when you meet him you'll like him."

I was reminded of that old habit of Rye's, finding people I was bound to like. "What's he doing in an overseer's house?"

"There aren't any overseers now. Aunt Wanda doesn't try to raise a lot of livestock. She has enough running this house and selling trees for woodpulp."

"You said there were two houses."

"They're both rented. They bring in an income. Aunt Wanda seems to have to manage carefully to make it all come out."

"With Mr. Sutton's help."

"He doesn't help. He criticizes and heckles. The people in the second house are the Stryfes. Mrs. Stryfe and her daughter. Angela is a little older than we are, and she's pretty."

"A good match for Bart," I offered, hoping for a smile from Rye.

"Well, you'll meet everybody," Rye said, not smiling, "and you'll see what they're like."

Perhaps not, I thought to myself, wondering how much persuading it would take to get Rye to leave. The simplest solution, after all, would be to go, Rye and I. I could take Rye back with me to New Mexico and let her study the simple dignity of an Indian woman with her baby. And how the sun could look coming up out of the bare hills without any trees to get in the way, and how friendly people could *really* be.

Was I being selfish? Was there a secret hope in me that having Rye to look after would break the mold of that enclosing shyness and isolation?

I put the thought aside. I was thinking of Rye, I told myself.

"Rye, could you rest for a while? If I asked you to? So that I could talk to Aunt Wanda?"

"I know what you've got to say to Aunt Wanda, and she isn't going to listen. And I wouldn't go anyway. I wouldn't go if she ordered me to leave." Rye's voice was shaking. "Don't you think that idea hasn't occurred to me over and over again? The easiest thing of all, just to walk away? I could have done that the day of the funeral, gone home with Jim's aunts to Virginia. They're wonderful people. But I didn't, and I'm glad I didn't, and now I won't. Whatever indignity comes next, I'm going to be here. If there's no one to watch over Jim's grave but me, then there's me. If nobody cares, I care." Her chin came up in the old stubborn way; and this was the child, the sister I remembered from when I was a child. But my resolve was frozen.

I had to see Aunt Wanda, I had to put it up to her.

"Please do take a rest right now, anyway. All that running on the drive, jumping in and out of the car—"

"I'm not a cotton-batting freak!"

Facing Rye at that moment, I wished that I had never come. I wished that I had turned around there where I had stopped beside the road. Every mental antenna warned of failure, of estrangement and bad feelings. I had come to help, but help wasn't needed. A lot of hard common sense was needed.

The drive from New Mexico had taken two days and had involved car trouble, plus roadside meals and a motel and glare and tiredness. I shut my eyes for a moment and rubbed my temples. Then I realized that Rye was looking at me anxiously, trying to measure my change of mood. "We could drive to the cemetery after lunch." Her tone was quieter and conciliatory.

I had the urge to say, let's just forget the cemetery, but Rye was trying to mend the moment of anger, and I couldn't get it out. In the old days Rye would have carried the argument to its bitter end, giving no quarter. It must be an indication of how badly she wanted me here, that she had so quickly dropped the dispute.

"Please?" she added softly.

Well, that did it. Rye could always get around me, one way or another. "Yes, I'll go with you to Jim's grave. We'll drive over right after lunch."

"We could walk."

I was surprised. "It's within walking distance?" For some reason I had imagined the cemetery as being miles from here.

"Well, it's a *long* walk."

"In which direction?"

"East."

"Is that the direction of those other houses of Aunt Wanda's?" I was remembering that I had passed no cemetery coming as I had from the west, and no houses for quite a few miles.

"Yes, but Aunt Wanda's houses are down a side road. You wouldn't see them from the main road. We could drive by if you wanted to. You could meet Mrs. Stryfe and Angela."

"Not Bart?"

"He's on a vacation trip. School just let out. He's gone to New Orleans for a few days."

Big loss, not meeting Bart, I thought. "If I agree to go on this jaunt, will you agree to rest now until lunch? And let me clean up? And unpack?"

"And see Aunt Wanda. I know." But Rye spoke without anger. She got up from the chair and came to me and put her face down against my hair. Her big bulge pressed my shoulder. "I'm not going to fight with you and I'm not going to start making you wish you hadn't come, the way you were doing a minute ago. And in the end if you say I have to leave, I guess I'll go. But not right away. And not until I've fought back a little."

I was deeply touched. This was like Rye, too; she tried to give in gracefully when she saw there was no other way. "Good girl," I said. "Take yourself a nap for Junior. And cotton-batting yourself a little is no sin, either."

"How would you know? You've never had a baby."

"I'd be in quite a fix if I had," I pointed out, "since it happens I've never been married."

In the upstairs hall the young dark maid was buffing the floors, which didn't seem to need buffing. "I would like to see my aunt," I told her.

"Miss Wanda will be in her office about now." Her voice was quiet, pretty with its southern softness. "You go downstairs and turn right, toward the back of the house, and it's the second door on the right."

"Thank you."

I rapped at the second door and Aunt Wanda's voice said, "Come," in an absent-minded way, and I opened the door. Only it seemed that I must not have been the one Aunt Wanda expected. She looked over her shoulder at me as I came in, and blankness filled her eyes, and then she turned swiftly to the desk and there was some kind of instant change or switch there, something I didn't quite catch. The desk was small and antique-white, graceful, touched with gilt along its curved front, gilt pulls on the bulge-front little drawers, legs long and slim, a beautiful piece of furniture—and Aunt Wanda had done something to it in the twinkling of an eye, and I couldn't figure out what she had done. So far as I could see now it had an unbroken top panel covered with white leather edged with gold-embossed leather strapping, and on this lay an open account book. In Aunt Wanda's hand was a slim ballpoint pen. Some pink color had come into her face, a trace of embarrassment to her eyes, and I wanted to say, "What on earth did you just do to the desk?" Instead, I told her, "I'd like to talk to you about my sister."

"Sit down." Aunt Wanda indicated a white chair not far from hers. The room was well lit from a bank of gauze-draped sunny windows, and my aunt's snowy curls shone in the light. The room wasn't big, but it was prettily furnished. It was a play office, I thought. The frail antique-white furnishings had no look of heavy financial matters. "I know you must be worried about Barbara. I knew that she was writing to you—" She laid the pen down upon the open account book.

"—but I just don't seem to be able to help her. She gets quite excited, and it seems to me to be a time to keep your head."

Well, well, I thought—Aunt Wanda, the two-fisted drinker and bar-hopper, former strip artist, blackjack dealer (Reno), and boarding house owner (Seattle), had come to this, had fallen so far from her former estate that all she could think of was keeping her head. If I hadn't known her from old, hadn't remembered every feature from my earliest childhood, I would have sworn now that the woman facing me was a ringer, an impostor.

The old Aunt Wanda would no more have thought of keeping her head in the face of insult, threat, or indignity than she would have turned down a drink.

Something of what I thought must have been revealed on my face, for Aunt Wanda went on, "I'm in a very difficult situation here. There are accounts to be kept—" She motioned toward the big book on the desk. "—and balanced, and I've always been so stupid in arithmetic, or in anything that has to do with keeping track of money."

"You don't seem to have time for Rye," I said bluntly, "which makes me wonder why you asked her to come here. When you learned of Jim's death in Vietnam, you urged Rye to come here to live with you. And to bury Jim here."

The look of embarrassment, of being caught in something she could not explain, hardened my aunt's eyes. "As I've just said, I thought the influence that was needed was calming, was to try to smooth over the resentment and . . . anger."

"Why, Aunt Wanda?"

"But I've just explained why—"

"Why did you want Rye here?"

She created a momentary distraction by reaching across the book for a pack of cigarettes. She offered me one, and I shook my head. She lit her cigarette from a small gold lighter. A white enamel monogram shone on the golden finish. Very pretty, I thought. "I was lonely." Her tone was hoarse, a little tired, and seemed genuine. "I was so lonely I could die."

I wanted to say, but you've got so many people here. The servants are people. But again she got in ahead of me. "Of course you'll say, there are the people who work for me. But I can't be myself around them. I am the mistress here. If anything, they make me feel more alone than ever. Set apart. They share a certain companionship."

I didn't know anything about servants; I'd never had any. "There's also a Mr. Sutton, isn't there?"

Aunt Wanda assumed a look that was offended and full of hurt disappointment. She crushed out the newly lit cigarette as though performing mayhem on Mr. Sutton himself. "I wanted someone of my own family. It seemed also that Barbara might need me. And at least I had something to offer." Her eyes implied that I hadn't. "Your mother and father are gone. You have your teaching job. Barbara was alone, except for those aunts of Jim's, and she scarcely knew them. And they're so much older than she—" Aunt Wanda saw where this was leading and added: "Of course I'm older too, an old woman, in fact. I don't mean that I could offer Barbara the companionship she needs. But there was another consideration. This property I inherited from my husband—the land, the houses, the income. After me, there is no heir."

"Rye wrote me of your idea that the baby should be the heir."

Aunt Wanda's gaze was guarded, intent, as if searching for some sign of disapproval. "And you thought—?"

"If the baby's becoming your heir means that Rye and the baby have to stay here, with the other things that are going on, I'd have to say that it isn't worth it."

She flinched. "That's much too drastic. You're talking now about the . . . the silly things that happened—"

"They didn't just happen. They were done. They were meant to inflict pain. Or to raise new hopes that hadn't a chance. And since Rye is the one concerned, and since she doesn't consider these things silly nor nonsensical, we won't either. We can't."

"But if you're going to *encourage* her! She'll just grow more and more upset and depressed—"

"Aunt Wanda, you are the one I don't understand. How could you just shrug off what was happening at Jim's grave? Did you expect Rye to shrug it off too if you told her that was what she should do? Did you think that Rye, carrying Jim's baby, and with Jim buried such a short while, would pass over a desecration of his grave?"

Aunt Wanda made an impatient, baffled motion. "That word. Desecration. Rye uses it. But what happened is just—"

"What?"

"Don't get angry . . . a prank. A silly and tasteless prank. But not desecration, defiling a grave—"

"Who do you think might have done this prank?" I was trying to hang onto my temper, guide what she was saying, think.

"A . . . a kid."

"What age kid? Five? Ten? Twelve?"

Her gaze was bitter, her mouth pinched. She looked as if I had backed her into an unpleasant corner. "How could I know? Kids do awful things now. Worse and worse as the years pass. Someone gets to fooling around the cemetery. They notice Barbara there in her grief. They make up jokes, hide, wait for her to come—"

She was talking to cover something. Her own mistakes, perhaps. I couldn't believe in any such kids. I disengaged my thoughts from ghoulish pranksters and looked around at the room. Blue walls. Pale blue carpet, tufted with pink threads here and there, a shadow-plaid that covered the entire floor. In one corner stood a tall display case, antique-white with gold touches, and inside, behind the polished glass, were collections of miniature animals, ceramic bells, and a whole shelf of china bouquets in little vases.

What had Aunt Wanda done to her desk in the moment I had come into the room? Had the whole top of the desk been up? Slipped back? What?

I realized that Aunt Wanda had quit talking and was waiting for a reply. The soft violet color of my aunt's dress made her skin look very white. Her hands were slim, cared for; they were not the hands of a woman who had scrabbled for a living for all those forgotten years.

Aunt Wanda spoke again. She said, "Esther, why don't you do Barbara a big favor?"

"Yes?"

"Why don't you just go back where you came from?"

Four

I BIT MY TONGUE to keep from answering her in the same vein. There were many bitter things I could have said. In those moments, I remembered the slights of my childhood. But instead I told her, as politely as I could, that of course it was her house and that if she was telling me to leave I would make my departure quickly. Then Aunt Wanda seemed to recover herself and to have other thoughts, and she said, No, she'd been hasty and tactless and hadn't meant that I should leave. It wasn't exactly an apology, though I was expected to think so.

She went on to say that we three, as the remaining members of our family, should stick together for comfort and support.

There didn't seem to be any argument to that.

Having thus gotten nowhere, I left Aunt Wanda to her accounting and returned to my room. I unpacked my clothes, laid out my sparse array of toilet articles and cosmetics, and freshened up in the bathroom.

Lunch was served on the veranda. It was a beautiful, fresh-smelling day. We were sheltered from the light breeze. The table was all silky linen and gleaming china, the glow of silver and the sparkle of crystal, with magnolia blossoms in a bowl. I met Perkins, a tall dark-skinned man with an inscrutable face, who was in charge of the serving, and who crushed the small maid with a glance when she showed some awkwardness in handling a platter of seafood. This was not Martha, who had brought us coffee that morning, but a smaller and younger girl.

I thought that the setting, and the skill with which the meal was served, must owe much to Perkins. He wore a quiet air of efficiency and assurance, and I concluded that he had learned his trade long ago and in a superior school, and I wondered how he had come to Larchwood. The little maid would not soon forget her moment of clumsiness. Under Perkins' guidance, except for that one small incident, everything went as smooth as cream.

It must be Perkins, too, who saw to all the details of running the house, overseeing the work of the others, and this was why the place shone with such beautiful care.

Right after lunch, Rye and I set off in my car for the cemetery. I couldn't help but be uneasy over the purpose of our trip. Rye must think that I might stumble on an instant solution to the ugly mystery. And on my part, I was just hoping we wouldn't run into something hideous. To distract myself I asked her who had done the cooking for the meal, such a display that it seemed we had not eaten half.

"Mrs. Mim is the cook. A widow with a little girl, a very nice person. Cindy is cute. Mrs. Mim's the only one who lives in. She has rooms on the lower floor, across from the pantries. The little girl takes the bus to first grade every day—or did, before school ended. Look—here's the road to the other houses, the ones where Bart and the Stryfes live."

I glanced to the right. There was a narrow road with the usual encroaching trees. "They must really like living in the woods. Are they side-by-side neighbors?"

"Not too close."

"Aunt Wanda inherited them along with the rest of it?"

"I guess so."

"And how much farther to the cemetery?"

I was picturing it: desolate, shadowed, silent. And so I was all that much more surprised to find that it wasn't like that at all.

If a cemetery can be considered cheerful, this one was. It was warm and bright with sunlight. The woods were in the distance, a surrounding bank of dark green, but this particular spot, this top of a slight knoll, was open to wind and sun. Besides that, it was a very neatly kept place. The older headstones and monuments were straight, the grass was trimmed close, the occasional tree neatly raked around, roses and ivy pruned. I parked near the entrance, and Rye and I got out. A low stone wall surrounded the cemetery on three sides. The fourth side was open toward the woods in the distance, as if in time some expansion would be permitted there.

Rye looked at the sunlit greenness. "The day we buried Jim here was like this. It was warm for the time of year, almost like spring, and I watched them bury him and I had to think that this was the spring of a year he wouldn't know anything about. His life was in *its* spring—"

I stood waiting, listening; I knew how Rye must need to speak of Jim, to express her grief and loss.

"There was sunlight that day, but he was being put where there isn't any sun. He would never see sunshine again. Never—and all at once I couldn't stay there watching, and I turned and ran, I ran like a crazy thing, and then I fell over some ivy or something. I tripped and went headlong. I made the most unholy disgrace of myself, Pock. When I think of it now—"

"You shouldn't. You should quit punishing yourself," I told her. My impulse was to put my arms around her and to comfort her the way I used to when we were children together; but if I did this now, I knew that she would go to pieces.

"Then, later, at home, I kept remembering that I hadn't seen Jim since that little while we'd had together in Hawaii, the little time he'd had off from war, and that now I would never see him again, and why hadn't I demanded that they open the casket? I read in the papers that a father of a soldier did that. He didn't believe his son was dead and he made them let him look."

I felt helpless in the face of her angry torment.

"And I went kind of crazy. Jim was down there in the ground—"

"Rye, let's get one thing straight. The body isn't Jim. Jim is somewhere else. He's not in the ground."

"What do you mean?" Sudden fear came into her face. "This isn't Jim's body? Those crazy messages—"

"I'm not talking about your anonymous freak and his miserable messages. I'm talking about something that anyone with good sense can see with half an eye. The body is buried, the body that for a while—for too short a while—held the mind and the personality of Jim Parrish. The mind and the personality are gone. The body does as . . . forgive the words . . . as the Bible says, it goes to dust. No, don't brush me off and turn away. The body goes to earth. But the personality, the things that made Jim Parrish a person, someone unique among all other persons, have to be somewhere else. Isn't it logical?"

Rye stood in the sunlight with her head bent, tears on her cheeks. Across the road a mockingbird began a long trill of song, and I glanced that way. Fifty feet off the road stood the wreck of an old house, covered with wild vines, empty windows showing the broken interior splotched with light. Another hundred feet toward the encroaching forest was another building, a big barn once, almost completely collapsed against an ancient tree. Someone's farm home of long ago was being retaken by the forest, I thought, before I turned back to Rye.

I touched Rye's hand gently, and Rye grasped back. "Come," she said, "we'll go to see the grave."

"Let me go alone. Just show me where."

"No." She tugged at my hand, and we started. The path was sanded, neatly raked, the borders set with wooden strips. The mockingbird behind us began to scold, cutting off the drift of song, as if he saw something that we could not see.

I was looking ahead, some uneasiness warning me, straining to see. "Rye, wait here. Wait for me, will you?"

Rye stopped abruptly. "What is it?"

"I don't know. I just—" I was trying to see what had seemed wrong, what I had glimpsed, without staring at it directly. There were marks, some kind of scorched track, on the grass ahead. But it might have nothing to do with Jim's grave—

"What did you see? Aren't you going to tell me?"

I was breaking out into a sweat, and not knowing what to do. "I'll go look and come back." I tried to keep an even tone, but my face must have given something away. Rye shivered as though some frosty blight had touched her; then she began to walk resolutely on. I begged her to wait, but Rye didn't even hear me.

She walked directly to the scorched marks on the green grass. She stood looking at them, her face dazed; she had covered her mouth with her hand as if to choke back a cry. I gripped her shoulders and tried to turn her around, but she refused to turn. There was the sound of the wind and the harsh cries of the angry bird, but no sound at all from Rye.

The grass had been burned somehow, letters burned into it.

NOT
HERE

I felt sick and buffeted, knowing how Rye must feel at this moment. "Rye, go and sit in the car."

She tried to twist away from me, but I held her. "Listen to me. The . . . the *thing* that made those marks on Jim's grave might be watching you right now, and if he is, he's getting his jollies out of how you react. His purpose is to frighten you, destroy you. Are you going to give him his fun? Or are you going to the car, and wait, while I see what I can do here?"

"Let me just touch—"

"No." Deliberately I tightened my grip. Rye gasped and looked dazedly into my face. "Can you walk without staggering?"

She made an effort to rouse herself. Her eyes swept the cemetery, the green woods beyond. "Where is he?"

I ignored it. "Can you walk? Slowly?"

"Yes. I guess so."

"Will you go to the car?"

"Yes."

I knew that one touch of comfort, of sympathy, would have had Rye clinging and crying. One touch of love—I wouldn't give it. Not now. Not out here. "Promise me you won't show any sign of breaking down. You won't walk with your hands over your face, or anything like that."

"All right."

I released her. This was the moment of testing, this told whether Rye would make it, or whether the unseen watcher—if there was one—would have the pleasure of seeing her collapse. Rye hesitated, her gaze on me, and there was a moment when I thought it was all going to come apart. And the knowledge that we had to behave like this because of the freak that might be peering at us brought a suffocating anger. I could kill him, I thought, as Rye turned to go. I found that my hands were twisted together, tight, with such force that my knuckles ached. And tears stung behind my eyes.

Rye walked off steadily toward the car, and I knelt and ran my fingers through the scorched marks. A few shreds of burned fabric sprang up, and I thought, they soaked strips of cloth in gasoline or kerosene, they laid out the letters and touched a match. The fire killed the grass, left the black scorch forming the letters. I set to work, pulling out what was burned and dead, ripping the scorched stuff out until there were only narrow slots left. I heaped all of the shredded trash to one side and then began to coax the living grass together to hide what had been done.

When I was finished, it didn't look too bad. If you came close you could make out dimly the hateful words. If you knew what to look for. I took the scorched stuff and tossed it over the wall.

I went back to the grave. I was breathless, sweaty with effort, my hair hanging across my eyes. But I had to try to figure this thing out.

What was happening here? What was really being done? What was the aim, the motive? I forced away the sense of outrage and anger and compelled my mind to function.

Rye was being hurt. Rye, in her present vulnerable position, helpless, dependent upon Aunt Wanda's generosity, anxious about her coming baby, was being destroyed. That was what was being done. That seemed the only result—and it also seemed senseless.

It seemed that there could be no enemy of Rye's here. She was a newcomer in this place who knew no one. No ancient grudge nor cherished hatred could be behind this torment. It was dimly possible that Jim might have an enemy here, someone left from the days he had spent at college in Moss Corner. Possible, but so improbable that the chance of it seemed out of sight. And Jim wasn't being hurt.

You can't hurt the dead.

There *was* coincidence. And an odd one. Aunt Wanda had married and had come here where Jim had gone to college all those years past. Was this coincidence the mainspring of the ugliness? I frowned over it, tried to tease something out of it, but it seemed merely happenstance.

The motive must be something else. Not to hurt Rye because of an old grudge, but to send her running. If the meanness kept up long enough, she would surely leave.

Again, what was the reason? She was a threat to no one. She offered no complication that I could see. She was living quietly with our aunt; Wanda was arranging for the baby to become her heir—but outside of the coming baby, Aunt Wanda had no other heirs anyway.

I wanted to leave the place, get into the car with Rye, drive away. There was nothing to be gained by waiting here. But when I turned, another car was parked out beside the road, and a tall young man in patrol officer's uniform was striding toward me across the lawn.

When he came close he lifted his trooper's cap. "Chris Warne, miss. I was just speaking to your sister. I understand there's been another depredation."

Even my anger could not release me from my wretched shyness. I was struck dumb. In reply I gestured toward the lawn above Jim's grave.

He knelt, brushed angrily at the grass, opening the slots I had so carefully worked shut. He was husky, a big young man, dark-haired and brown-eyed; he wasn't exactly handsome, but his face held intelligence and authority, and I thought, gentleness too.

Finally I managed to speak, hating the embarrassment and awkwardness that made my voice almost a croak. "I took out the burned grass and threw it over behind the wall. I tried to make it look good again."

He nodded and began to carefully pull the tough grasses together as I had done. "I've been doing some thinking," he said as he worked. Finally he rose, brushed at the knees of his uniform. "I believe that Mrs. Parrish should make out a complaint. Get something on the record, and then I'll have cause to keep this place under more of a surveillance. I can't give it all my time, I still have the patrol. But I could come by more often than I'm doing now."

He was staring at me, standing not too far away. I had a childish desire to shut out the sight of him by covering my eyes. But I forced myself to say, as calmly as I could, "We'll go and file the complaint now. Where do we do it?"

"Moss Corner. I'll follow you in."

Five

THE PROCEDURE for filing a complaint was a simple one. Rye signed the papers at a desk and Chris Warne promised his vigilant best at catching the depredator. He parted from us on the steps of the parish courthouse, in one wing of which was the office of the Highway Patrol. He shook hands with Rye, looking down at her bent head. "Try not to dwell on what's happening, Mrs. Parrish. We'll put a stop to the business. I know it must be hard for you to keep your mind off it, right now—"

"Thank you," Rye murmured. She was thanking him for his effort to console and encourage her, rather than with any hope he might catch the freak who was playing tricks.

He looked over at me. "Your sister didn't mention that you were staying with her."

I went down two steps. "I just came today."

"I'll stop by from time to time."

"Fine," Rye told him.

In the car I glanced at Rye. "Since we're in town, is there anything you need?"

"No."

"Do you want to go back to the house?"

"Not yet. Could we drive for a while?"

We drove down one forest-crowded road after another turning east, south, then west, passing through little towns of a half-dozen houses, a service station and store, a church. Occasionally there were acres of cleared land where cattle browsed on the lush grass of early summer. At last Rye spoke. "What does it mean, Pock?"

"I don't know. It's evil and frightening, but I can't make out a motive in it. I just can't."

"Does someone really want me to think Jim isn't buried there?"

"I can't see that at all. There have been cases where a mistake was made. You read about such things in the papers. But you heard from Jim's commanding officer, a man who knew him, who was there when the helicopter landed. And Jim's helicopter returned to base with all of its dead and wounded still inside; they weren't lost for any time to the enemy. It's not as if Jim had been out in the jungle and his body . . . destroyed, or anything like that. When they regain the scene of a battle, well—" I stammered to a halt. She knew what I meant.

Rye was shaking her head. There were tears on her face.

"It was Jim's body you buried," I finished. "I wouldn't give any more thought to that."

"Then—what?"

"I don't know. Someone wants to torment you. That's all I know right now."

"I could have Jim's body exhumed and buried in a military cemetery."

"You sure could," I agreed. "I thought of that, too."

"But I don't want to do it. Jim is at rest. I'm not a fool, I know that the man I loved isn't down in that grave, I know he isn't being bothered by the . . . the creep who's pulling his little stunts in the cemetery. But Jim is buried, his body is buried, and it should remain so."

"That's for you to decide."

I turned the car north at the next road intersection, where there was a service station, two houses, and a cornfield. We came after a while to an expanse of rolling country where the trees had been cut some time before. Under the bright sun it looked wild, rough, and ragged, with stumps, broken branches, young trees, and burgeoning undergrowth crowding the scarred earth. "Where are Aunt Wanda's forest lands?" I asked, wanting to change the subject of our conversation.

"All over. I mean, she doesn't own just a continuous great chunk of land. There are pieces of it here and there. This could even be a part of what she owns. Each year some of the trees are harvested for woodpulp."

"Never for lumber?"

"No, for some reason. The trees are terribly thick and crowded, but if you notice, not many of them are big. Well, they look big enough for me, but to a lumberman I guess they're too skinny."

"Do you suppose Aunt Wanda takes in a lot of money?"

"I guess she must." Rye was frowning at the sunny dazzle on the windshield. "She seems worried all the time, though, and she spends a lot of time on her account books."

I remembered the scene, Aunt Wanda at her little antique-white desk. "I saw the account book, or one of them, when I went to talk to her."

"I don't know exactly what her husband's will said, but I believe she has to keep the house up, you know, the way it was when he died. And the servants have to be organized. And Mr. Sutton has something to say about how it all gets managed."

I was looking at the green distances, the blue sky; and I told myself that beautiful as the country was, Rye and I had no business in it. I should go back to New Mexico and take Rye with me. I could return to my teaching job, and our lives would be quiet and safe there. Rye's baby would be born before too long, and Rye could plan for her future, then, hers and her child's. She could return to the college work she had dropped when she had married Jim, or she could study for some other kind of job. I would be there to help. I would be in a place to which I was accustomed. I was not tongue-tied nor shy around my children, nor would I be with her baby, and my life could continue in its quiet and narrow way.

It was in thinking of New Mexico that I realized a strange fact. I had come here with a hope of change. I had come with the unexpressed wish to break out of that cold shell of shyness and withdrawal.

This knowledge came in a flash of insight, and in the next moment I wanted to laugh at my own naïve hopes.

I turned my thoughts back to our conversation. "How does Aunt Wanda feel about Mr. Sutton?"

"I think he's the only fly in the ointment. I think she loves being what she is now, a real lady, with a beautiful big home, and lots of land, and an estate to take care of. She's changed so much. You must remember what she used to be like."

"I remember."

"I'll never forget how fat she was, and how her breath smelled of liquor when she kissed you, and how tatty her hair would look. She's slimmed down and she wears pretty things, and she looks nice."

"And she would be perfectly happy," I offered, "except for the watchdog."

"Yes, except for Mr. Sutton."

For the first time I felt a stirring of curiosity about the terrible Mr. Sutton.

When we got back to the house Martha met us in the hall and told us that our aunt would like to see us in her upstairs parlor. Rye thanked the maid, and I murmured to myself, upstairs parlor, and knowing what I did now about the house, I pictured what the room would look like—more antique-white and gauzy draperies; but no, when we went in, the upstairs parlor turned out to be early American, maple and chintz. I sat down in a maple rocker, and Rye took a place on a cushioned settee. Aunt Wanda had turned from her small maple desk to face us. On the desk was a pen set and a mounted calendar and a book. To my eyes it seemed the identical book I had seen on the white desk downstairs before lunch.

I thought that Aunt Wanda must carry her books around with her, like the Ancient Mariner with his albatross. Or were there downstairs books and upstairs books—separate sets? I'd heard of duplicate books being kept for nefarious purposes. I wondered which set she showed to Mr. Sutton.

And most of all, with her hopscotch background, where had our aunt learned to keep books at all?

She greeted us with determined cheerfulness, but after one look at Rye she skipped hastily over any questions as to where we'd been. Rye showed the depth of the wound she had had. Aunt Wanda wanted to know from me if my room was adequate. I assured her that it was perfect.

"If you need anything pressed, Esther, please give it to Martha and she'll look after it."

"Thank you, but I'm well able to press anything I'll need. I don't have much in the way of clothes."

An ironic glance from my aunt implied that Yes, she'd noticed.

"There is another maid," I added. "Isn't she your upstairs maid?"

"Oh, you've met Lydia? She's fairly new and I don't know how good she is with clothes. Barbara, you look as if you could use a nice hot soak and a rest. I have to get down to the kitchen and see what Mrs. Mim is planning for dinner." Aunt Wanda seemed to be dismissing us, but when we rose to go—Rye gratefully, her pale face full of dejection—Aunt Wanda said, "Esther, why don't you come with me? There might be a thing or two that you could take care of."

This was just an excuse, I saw; with all of the help here there weren't any jobs left over. Aunt Wanda had something to say and wanted to say it away from Rye.

Rye hesitated at the door, looking back at me. She wanted me to go with her, to reassure her, to tell her that everything was going to be all right, the way I'd been able to long ago when the troubles had been a lost kitten or a broken doll. But Aunt Wanda shooed her off, telling her to have Lydia draw her bath.

"All right, Esther. Let's go." Aunt Wanda opened a drawer of the maple desk and put the account book inside, turned the key in the lock, put the key under the base of the small leather-mounted calendar, and all of the time smiling at me as if to say, See how I trust you?

It made me uneasy. In spite of the clothes, the topped-up frosty hair, the complete look of the lady, there was something kind of off-center and pitiful about Aunt Wanda. I couldn't really pin down what it was; but it was there. On an impulse I went to her and took her hand and held it for a moment; and this was a mistake, because for an instant, out of Aunt Wanda's eyes there seemed to flicker the most awful fear, a kind of despair, regret, and a need for comforting far deeper and more anguished than Rye's.

Then Aunt Wanda pulled her hand free. She must have regretted that unguarded moment of revelation. "Let's go down and see Mrs. Mim. She's just wonderful in some ways and so monotonous in others. I have to keep an eye on her." She gave me a blank, almost antagonistic stare, as if defying me to comment on the emotion revealed a minute ago. Then she led the way from the room.

I felt as if I had made a fool of myself.

Aunt Wanda wanted nothing from me. And never had.

So I told myself, but surprisingly, I was wrong.

Both floors of this huge house had the same general plan, being divided into quarters by halls running, in one instance, east–west, and in the other, north–south. The house faced north, so that the lower-floor hall widened into the main entry in that direction. As we left her little parlor Aunt Wanda turned toward the rear of the house. We went down the back stairs to the kitchen.

Following her, I thought: There's something wrong here. There's something unexplained. Why should she want Rye here, and what was that terrified look all about, the look I'd glimpsed for one second or so?

The kitchen was an immense sunny room, well scrubbed and waxed, with yellow organdy curtains at the windows, with long tiled counters gleaming. But here for the first time I saw the anachronistic inconvenience of the old house. The refrigerator, large but far from new, was far too removed from the range; and the range, also large, older than the refrigerator, showing signs of long use though scrubbed and shining, was in its turn a long, long way from the sink and the storage cabinets. "It needs modernizing," Aunt Wanda said. "The equipment should all be closer together. For fewer steps. But Mrs. Mim doesn't seem to mind."

Mrs. Mim did have a placid, easygoing look about her. She was at the counter whipping something in an electric mixer. She was light-skinned, rather pretty, and turned toward us with a smile.

"Mrs. Mim, Esther. This is Esther Myles, my niece."

Mrs. Mim brushed her hand on her blue cotton uniform and offered it to me. "We all heard you were coming." She was looking at me with frank interest. "You don't resemble Mrs. Barrod, though, I mean, not like your sister does."

I didn't know what to say to this. I felt like answering, This is an old sore point with me and you've hit it dead center.

I got so tired, down through the years, being told that I didn't look like anyone else in the family.

There was that dream I had every once in a while, too. The miserable dream with the woman behind the desk in the office, the woman with the pale biscuit of hair on top of her head, myself being held on someone's lap facing the desk, and very small in a stiff white dress—that dream whose unknown dark menace always woke me and left me shaking. . . .

Aunt Wanda was poking into cabinets. "Did they bring the fresh yeast?"

"Yes, ma'am, and it's in the refrigerator."

"Dinner will be at eight," Aunt Wanda reminded.

Mrs. Mim didn't answer, just nodded, as though she already knew the time for dinner and hadn't needed to be reminded. I couldn't see that my aunt was accomplishing anything here; Mrs. Mim obviously had everything planned and going along fine.

I didn't resemble my sister nor my aunt, but this had been remarked upon before.

"You are going to have a baby sister soon."

"A baby sister? How big?"

"All babies are very tiny."

"Big enough to talk?"

"No."

"But I talked to you, Mama!"

"Not when you were tiny."

"But I did—"

Then, later: *"Mama, what's being born? Is it like coming here to live?"* I could never remember the answer to that one, though the half-formed memory held an aura of dread and suspense.

Aunt Wanda said, "Esther, let me show you the grounds at the rear of the house. We have a nice garden. It's too early for much in the way of produce, but things are coming up, and there are flowers. We grow most of our own flowers, plenty for the house almost the year around. Starting with early spring, hyacinths and early daffodils. Come along—"

I didn't really want to come to see the gardens. I wanted some time alone to think of that strange instant of self-knowledge that had occurred while I was driving along with Rye. I wanted to re-examine that buried hope that a change in surroundings might work a change in me, that the grip of lonely aloofness and reserve might be broken.

And then, too, there was the strange evil that seemed directed at my sister. Rye expected me to come up with an answer, a solution, which would end the cruel tricks at Jim's grave. I had that to think about, too.

But Aunt Wanda led me back to the hall, passing the open doors of pantries and storerooms, and on out into the yard. The afternoon was quiet and golden, and out beyond a couple of magnolias were the gardens, a broad and meticulously tidy expanse of earth, the ground reddish in color, with the growing spikes of onions and chard, the buds of lettuce, the young towers of corn all strikingly green against the soil. Aunt Wanda began self-consciously to tick off the names of all she had growing here.

The unnaturalness of her attitude drew my suspicious attention at last. I had never been my aunt's favorite; she was not spending time with me out of pleasure. I decided that she had some motive, an aim in view that would presently be revealed.

Six

MY STEADY REGARD and my silence seemed finally to ruffle my aunt. She asked abruptly, "Is there anything else you want especially to see?"

She wasn't ready, then, to tell me what she really had in mind. "As long as we're looking, I'd like to walk on the belvedere and see the view."

She hesitated for a moment, as if my request might involve more time and trouble than she wanted to spend. Or whether she might fit a trip to the belvedere into what was already planned. But then she said, "All right. We'll go up there and you can take in the view."

She led the way back through the house to the front, then up the broad stairs. The upper floor was quiet, shadowed in afternoon light, clean-smelling. Aunt Wanda turned east and walked to the very end of the hall. She paused here to explain that the stairs to the belvedere went up next to the entry to the tower. The tower was unsafe and needed repairs that had been neglected, and hence was kept locked at all times. At the end of the hall she opened a door in the wall to show a narrow stairs. We climbed in gloom, Aunt Wanda leading, and half-way up was a small landing, lighted by a tiny round window in the outer wall, a bull's-eye of rippled golden glass. "This way to the top. It's quite steep here."

At the top of the stairs above us I could see sunlight and hear the humming of the wind. We came up to a railed landing and then stepped out upon the floor of the belvedere, a square area of fifteen feet or so on each side, roofed over so that we stood in shade. We were so high that it seemed like being in the prow of a ship. The moving wind swept past, and all around us were the slopes of the enormous roof, with ranks of chimneys to the west.

I could see a river toward the southeast, water shimmering behind a veil of trees. More, from here I could see how the forest, which seemed to enclose the park, was actually only a strip of woodland, with other strips beyond, along with cleared fields, barns, ponds, cut-over woods, and what seemed to be groves of fruit trees.

The height, and the freshness of the wind, the view, the feeling of freedom, took me to the edge of the platform. I had a brief thought as I pressed against the railing that it was not quite as high as it might be. I touched my fingers down to the top of the railing, and at the same moment I heard some scratch of sound, or felt some movement behind me. Or perhaps some sixth sense, some intuition, warned me of danger. I half turned, swiftly, and stepped aside. My aunt was standing just behind the spot where I had stood, unaware, and one hand was up as if ready to . . . *to do what?*

I will never forget the sensation of fear that jarred me. The next moment I looked from her blank eyes to the great sloping roof below us. I could have rolled all the way to the edge, over and over, too tumbled to think of flattening myself to gain a handhold, and then on past the eaves, to drop to whatever lay below.

I might have survived such a fall. The house was, after all, only two stories in height. I could have lived, I thought. Or perhaps not—

My aunt had recovered herself. "Why are you looking at me like that? As if I might be a ghost—"

Inwardly I was shaking, but to my relief my voice came cool enough. "I was wondering what you meant to do . . . with your hand out like that."

"I was going to touch your sleeve and ask you to move away from the railing. God only knows how old that wood is."

For a moment we faced each other in silence there at the top of the great house, and I thought: Give her credit, she missed being a famous actress, because Aunt Wanda's face seemed filled only with hurt, now. She seemed grieved and mystified by my suspicious attitude. On my part, I saw that nothing was to be gained by a hasty accusation, by blurting out what I thought had been about to happen. In my mind's eye I was tumbling off the roof, screaming as I fell toward the hard earth below, and my instinct was to run headlong down those stairs we had just ascended. And to demand of Rye that she leave the place with me at once. But I put all this aside. There was, after all, the possibility that Aunt Wanda had been about to warn me, not to push me. And so I gathered my wits and pretended to be taken again by the view.

"Just think," I said, trying to sound calm, "you are monarch of all you survey here."

Apparently she decided also to ignore the past few moments. "Not quite. But a lot of it." She looked indifferently at the landscape. I thought that instead of examining the fields and forest, though, that she searched the sky as if with a thirst for freedom. "I should be grateful, I guess. Jess Barrod left me everything. Of course he had almost no one, except me. Almost no one at all. But he could have tied it up in a trust, or left a chunk to charity. . . ."

I should be grateful . . .

Did that mean she wasn't?

"It's very beautiful country."

She nodded. "At times it seems I've lived here always, almost that I never knew any other place." She let a moment of silence go by, and then in a changed tone: "Esther—"

I felt an involuntary tightening. Was she going to get back on the track of: Why don't you just go back where you came from? I might answer her much more rudely this time. I would not let myself feel as though I were a child again and that Aunt Wanda had the old power to embarrass and affront.

But my aunt's new tack caught me off guard. "I want to ask your forgiveness, yours and Barbara's, for seeming so unconscious of your . . . your distress when you came back from your trip today. I know that something unpleasant must have happened." Her voice was contrite enough, though she didn't meet my eyes. "I should have asked. Do you want to tell me about it now?"

"No," I said. "I guess I don't. I guess you'll have to talk to Rye." And you won't want to do that, I added to myself, after all these days of brushing her off with remarks about pranks.

"I thought you might act as a go-between. You could tell Barbara how sorry I am, how I wish I'd acted differently when she tried to talk to me before, and that I promise to take seriously anything she tells me in the future."

And why this sudden turnabout? I stared at her for any sign of hypocrisy. "If you feel that way, I think she'd rather hear it from you. I think it would make a tremendous difference to Rye to know that you cared."

She looked stricken, bewildered. "But of course I *care!* I've always cared! I did think, up until now—from the best of motives—that the thing to do was to smooth things over, to downgrade any unpleasantness, to try to get her to see these . . . these—"

"Tricks."

"Yes, tricks. Silly, tasteless jokes. Anyway, to see them as something beneath notice. Now I see I've made you angry." She paused as if helpless to cope with the resentment I couldn't hide. "Esther, this is what I did in the past, not what I'm going to do in the future."

"I'm glad to know it."

But I thought: Why doesn't she send Rye away? Why doesn't she want her to go where she can be happy?

I said, "Why not go now and ask her what happened today?"

She had no intention of doing this. Every signal of tension, repugnance, and exasperation showed that. The lady of Larchwood wasn't quite stitched together sturdily enough, the mask not quite so fixed in place, to hide these signs. The whiskey rasp in her voice came on in full force. "Well, then, yes. I might do that. Thank you for suggesting it."

This wasn't what the trip up here was all about anyway, I thought. And it wasn't Rye she wanted to soothe; it was me.

Provided I couldn't be disposed of otherwise—

"Please make allowances," she said with sudden humility. "The effort and responsibility of managing this house—" She motioned toward the green distances. "—is such a burden. I can't make one false move. I have to be thinking—thinking *hard*—every minute."

"Aunt Wanda, everything has its price. You live here in luxury and beauty, with servants to wait on you—"

She chopped me off with an abrupt movement. "I'm *paying* the price! I'm up to my neck in payments! What I have to say is . . . uh . . . well, I'll be brief and to the point. If you feel at any time that you're being watched, spied on, listened to—please don't do anything about it. Pretend you don't notice. Please." She was watching me narrowly now. "Have you felt that . . . since you've come—"

"Once or twice. But it may simply have been trying to be quiet, tactful." I tried to hide my surprise at the turn our talk had taken. It seemed unreal that Aunt Wanda should ask me to ignore prying and spying in her own home. I remembered her well enough in her old days. A clout with a skillet—I broke off the line of thought to listen to what she was saying.

"The second thing is—and it's kind of important. I feel foolish asking it of you. But it is a favor for me. I thought we might have guests tomorrow night for dinner. Enable you to meet our neighbors."

Did she know how the thought of meeting a mixed bag of strangers made me cringe? Had she remembered my prickly shyness of the old days, guessed about me now? Did she sense that I looked out at the world and the people in it as if through bars of steel? I turned my eyes from her, refusing to let her see my fear.

"This favor I'm going to ask . . . it concerns Mr. Sutton."

I couldn't answer her. I stared at the green sunny distances, wishing for a way out of my predicament. I could see myself at a dinner. Tongue-tied, shrinking, finally alone in a corner. The spinster whose world is made of ice.

"I'm asking in as humble a way as I can," Aunt Wanda said, "that you will make an effort to be nice to him."

I was baffled, mystified. Did she have some crackpot notion that my cold reserve was voluntary? Cultivated? An act of choice? I almost wanted to laugh. Finally I got out, in echo, "Be nice to Mr. Sutton? You're asking that?" And I hated it because I sounded like a puzzled child, asking reassurance from an adult. But at the same time I saw another truth: that in spite of what Rye had told me about Mr. Sutton's power over Aunt Wanda, I had pictured him as being barely tolerated here; and that should he appear as a guest he would be neglected and ignored. And none of this was true—

"Yes. Please be pleasant to him. He's not an offensive person. You won't have to make such an effort."

I threw a frowning glance at her. "You expected me to be rude to him." And this, too, was incredible.

She drew in a deep, perhaps exasperated breath. "Let's face it. You are not the most sociable and outgoing person in the world. You are especially short and standoffish with men. I've seen your behavior when you were young, and I haven't forgotten." She laid a placating hand on my sleeve. "So, for the one evening, just for the few hours when we shall have drinks and dinner—"

I supposed that I seemed to step on many a toe in my curt withdrawal. This idea had occurred to me vaguely before this, but when you yourself are deep in involuntary misery you have scant time to worry over the grievances of others. The male ego had seemed to me, too, to be especially vulnerable where rebuffs were concerned, sometimes tiresomely so. An ad executive in New York who had tried to rouse some interest in me about himself, had said, "What's with you, kitten? You've got the world's biggest chip. Who bounced you around?" And I hadn't been able to explain that there was no chip, nor to tell him that no one had bounced me around that I knew of. And I'd wanted to say, too, that some of us are huntresses and go after what we want. But not all.

"I have a feeling he'll like you," Aunt Wanda said grudgingly, a remark that I found completely ridiculous. The suspicion came over me that she was making fun, she was having a little joke at my expense. The thought of the coming dinner became more distasteful than ever.

"I might even like him." I wanted to say something she wouldn't expect, couldn't reply to.

She pursed her lips. "That'll be the day."

The impulse was strong to tell her that I was not a frozen icicle, that I had met more than one man that I thought I could have liked, had not my shyness stood in the way. But a grown woman would sound a fool to say such a thing.

She was looking into the distance, and the melancholy expression had returned to her eyes. After a moment she said, "Let's go down, if you've seen all that you wish."

Our little interview was over. The message had been given.

First, don't object to any noticeable spying and snooping. Snooping by whom? By the servants? But among them—who? All of them? Martha alone? Perkins, the perfect man-about-house? Mrs. Mim? The little maid, name unknown, who had served at lunch? Lydia, the upstairs mystery?

And spying for whom?

For Mr. Sutton?

I followed my aunt down out of the belvedere, into the narrow stairs, past the bull's-eye window, and out into the upper hall. Someone vanished, I thought, as Aunt Wanda opened the door, or it seemed there was a flick of disappearing shadow where the other, broader hall crossed from north to south. My aunt did not notice—if indeed the impression were not a product of my imagination. She paused to frown at some flowers in a bowl, sitting on a table to our left. I had not noticed them in passing to go up to the belvedere, but now I saw that about a half-dozen big purple blooms lay broken-stemmed across the rim of the white china bowl. "I arranged them just this morning," my aunt said, as if speaking to herself. "Careless. Someone passed too close and brushed them." She pulled out the broken bowers and rearranged the remaining ones.

It seemed to me that the flowers were too far out of the way of traffic to have been crushed by accident. I wished that I had looked at them on the way to the belvedere.

My aunt excused herself with a murmured apology and hurried for the stairs.

I stood and watched her go.

I wondered how much I had seen and heard had been the truth, and how much had been performed for my benefit.

Seven

AT A LITTLE PAST SEVEN O'CLOCK on the following evening I was being introduced to Mr. Sutton.

To me, the great parlor of Larchwood looked much different under lights. Under the sparkle of chandeliers, the gleam from wall sconces, one felt a grandeur and beauty come alive from out of the past, one appreciated the richness of the furnishings, of velvet and brocade, and the lights shone in the polished mahogany and turned the mirrors into lakes of frosty light. Past the piano that dominated the far end of the room, the French windows had been thrown open to the veranda, the heavy draperies of white-and-gold plush had been drawn back, and the twilit scene outdoors was visible, like a backdrop painted in mauve and gray. Rye sat at the piano, fingering the keys. She wore her red hair pinned high, topped with curls, and her maternity dress of navy blue fitted neatly and allowed for the belly, in fact almost made her condition unnoticeable.

I was trying to be unobtrusive amid the luxury and grandeur, keeping to a niche behind the jut-out of the mantel. My clothes were in sorry contrast to the surroundings. I was the spinster, ugly, plain, who should have been dressed in a sack. I tried not to think of myself, but to keep my attention on the things around me, Rye's apparent cheerfulness, and how Perkins managed to be almost invisible and omnipresent at the same time; I wanted to keep my inner panic under control. I didn't want to think of my clammy hands, my knees that threatened to shake, and the utter blank that filled my mind when I tried to conjure up any sort of conversational gambit to make myself sound easy and friendly to Mr. Sutton.

Perkins vanished and then came back with Mr. Sutton, and Aunt Wanda rose gracefully from a velvet couch to greet him at the doorway. She looked very much the *grande dame* tonight, and seeing her walk toward the young man—why had I thought this taskmaster had to be gray and hawkeyed?—I had an astonished moment of feeling an intense pride in her, in my aunt who had lived such a hard and rough life and who was now mistress of Larchwood and looked every inch of it.

Rye waved a hand to Mr. Sutton without interrupting the tune she was picking out on the piano. She didn't hurry over to make light conversation to cover her sister's gawky flounderings. Aunt Wanda would be no help either. Her gaze on me was grim with warning, I had better not make a botch of this; I had no choice but to behave as she had requested yesterday in the belvedere. And so as if to bear out her worst expectations, I yanked my hand out in his direction without a word, and much too soon; she hadn't even introduced us. It was as if I were saying, Let's get it over with. Shake and be done.

I knew I was white with mortification.

"Esther, this is Mr. Sutton." To him she said graciously, "My niece, John." She had forced a smile, she was trying to imply that of course we would like each other instantly.

"I'm very glad to meet you." He had my hand in his now. My first confused impression of John Sutton was that he was bigger and younger than I had expected, somehow, and that his clothes, though neat, didn't hang too well because he was kind of rangy and big-boned. His face was tanned, his hair a quite ordinary brown in color, and the only things that made him seem the terror that Rye had said he was were his heavy, rather glowering eyebrows and his chin, which looked stubborn.

I had expected someone with an overpowering air of mastery and meanness, a man who had Aunt Wanda scared to death; and instead I had been presented with a mystery.

He must be a mule of a man, discourteous and obdurate in ways that didn't show at the moment. I stammered some stupidity about being pleased to meet him, too, and withdrew my perspiring hand. I wanted to run.

Martha came in at that moment with a tray of cocktails, with Perkins at the door to make sure she didn't drop any. Aunt Wanda walked over to Perkins with some word for him, Rye went tinkling on at the piano, and I was all alone, struck dumb, here with Mr. Sutton. He accepted a cocktail after I'd taken one, and then asked me something about my trip from New Mexico. "I got very tired of driving," I heard myself get out in a hoarse voice. Well, my voice is kind of husky all of the time anyway, so perhaps I didn't sound too bad. I've even had fools tell me my voice is sexy.

I gulped half of the drink out of nervousness.

He lifted his glass toward me a little. "May you have a nice long visit, Miss Myles. And may we get to know each other."

Fool that I was, pale with embarrassment, I did manage to mumble, "Thank you." My chances of knowing Mr. Sutton any better were absolutely nil. He should sense that much.

"What have you seen of the country hereabouts so far?"

What could I say? That I'd seen a cemetery and what lay between it and Larchwood? That would certainly get the conversation off to a cheerful start. "Not very much. A good many trees." How wretched I was, trapped here facing John Sutton. Struck dumb again, I could only stare into his face. His eyes were the same color as his hair, very ordinary, very brown. "Do you live in Moss Corner?" I blurted.

"No. I'm just a country hick at heart. I have some land down the road, an old house on it that I'm trying to restore. Piece by piece. I found the original plans by some miracle. The place was built around 1860 and hadn't been lived in for about twenty years, nor kept up that I could see for a long time before that. So my work is cut out for me. The house itself is interesting. There are cypress beams in the first floor. Must have hauled them up from around New Orleans. Plus handmade bricks."

What on earth could I offer in return for the fascinations of Mr. Sutton's house? I could tell him about New Mexico and what it felt like to teach on an Indian reservation and a few odds and ends like that, but the words were locked up somewhere. I suddenly realized that he wouldn't care, anyway. He was, as I was, trapped here to make conversation with a plain, dowdy woman who happened to be the niece of the owner of Larchwood and who therefore had to be shown some kind of courtesy. Lamely I got out, "Your house sounds so interesting. I'd like to see it sometime." There, that was certainly brilliant, I mocked myself.

But for some queer reason his eyes did seem to light up. It must be that he was so fascinated by his house that any impressionable visitor would be welcomed.

"If your wife wouldn't mind," I added hurriedly.

For some reason he laughed. Aunt Wanda left Perkins and began to walk toward us, and Rye got up off the piano bench, carrying her drink, and also headed our way. What had I done? I'd made Mr. Sutton laugh out loud, but this should be no terribly strange thing.

"You know I'm not married."

"I really know very little about you." And if you keep on finding me so highly funny, I'll run upstairs, I told myself.

"I can fix that." His voice had softened. "I and my house can fix that," he repeated. "There isn't a woman alive who doesn't love to tell a man what to do with a house. And find out about him in the process."

He was going to play the game, then. And I couldn't, and wouldn't, play it. "If you're going to generalize about women, you'll find yourself up to *here* in exceptions."

"Let me find out if you're an exception. While you're finding out about me."

He was teasing me, and I was helpless to tease back. Rye would know how, and here she was, having overheard the last few remarks. "Come on, Pock. Tell him you'll make such a mess of his house he'll be overjoyed to see the last of you. Tell him you go for carpeted ceilings. And you want all the fireplaces done in pink bricks."

What happened next, in the brief moment before Perkins ushered in two strangers, I couldn't explain to myself. John Sutton gazed at me over the rim of his glass as if waiting for me to echo Rye's nonsense, to add some flippancies of my own, and as I remained silent I saw curiosity come into his eyes, and something more, a searching look that made me flinch. I fell back upon the only defense I knew, withdrawal. I turned aside from him and looked at the two women now entering the room, who could only be Aunt Wanda's tenants, the Stryfes.

The older of the two led the way. She was perhaps in her early fifties, a compact pocket-battleship kind of woman, aggressively plowing toward us, dull gray hair braided into two buns over her ears, dull gray suit too tight around the hips and uneven at the hem. "My dear!" she cried in the direction of Aunt Wanda, "it almost looks to be clouding up out there! And we left some of our house windows open!"

"Some of my roof is open," John Sutton said; I knew he meant the remark for me, though I was refusing to look at him.

"Have a drink," Aunt Wanda told Mrs. Stryfe, forgetting for the moment to be the perfect lady of Larchwood; to have a drink in the face of difficulties belonged to the old Aunt Wanda.

Angela Stryfe followed her mother. She was a pretty blond woman of about my own age; she was dressed of soft blue silk with ruffles at her throat, white pumps in the latest fashion, and her shining corn-colored hair framed her face with curls. If ever a woman belonged in a room, had the beauty and the style with which to set it off, this one did. Where Mother Stryfe was a battleship, this one was a graceful skiff, skimming the waves under the merriest of breezes.

And when she turned her gaze on Mr. Sutton there was no mistaking the expression in her eyes.

Eight

AUNT WANDA presented me to the Stryfes. Mrs. Stryfe was very businesslike about it—a grimly hearty grip, hands cold, the palms hard as if her principal job in life had been gripping a broom—while her eyes sized me up and then dismissed me. I was not unused to being summed up and dismissed so swiftly, but I always felt like saying, "I'm not wearing my flashiest attributes right now." But I sensed that Mrs. Stryfe used some complicated measuring stick of her own. And perhaps that measuring stick had to do with her graceful and pretty daughter; and a dishrag-drab spinster didn't halfway come up to it, and the judgment was: *Out.*

Angela was a different breed of cat. Or marshmallow. She flicked me over, an amused little adding-up, mentally seeing beneath the tired summer print dress to the split seams in the slip beneath, and noting the condition of my hair, on which I had lavished some five seconds of brushing. There was no dismissal here, but there was the cautious assurance that I was much too nondescript for Mr. Sutton to notice. For the entire time that Angela held my hand and looked at me, she had a third eye trained on John Sutton. I'd seen people hopelessly in love, or infatuated, before this; and maybe this was what Angela was feeling, or perhaps it was something else, possessiveness and monopoly, the feeling that John Sutton was her property by right of knowing him for as long as she had, and of looking the way she did.

I wanted to jeer at her, "Don't worry. He's yours—on a platter." But there was no necessity for any comeback; after the introductions Rye and I were somehow shunted aside, cut off from Mr. Sutton and less so from Aunt Wanda. The backs of Mrs. Stryfe and Angela, though occasionally they paused to glance back and to throw a few words to one of us, were like a wall. You shall not pass. I took Rye's hand and said, "This is going to be some dinner party. Let's get a fresh drink from Martha and go play a duet."

But by the time we got to the piano, Mr. Sutton was somehow with us. Rye sat down on the bench in front of the piano and smiled up at him, and I thought what a relief it was that she could rid herself even for the evening of her depression and grief; and then he said to me, "Did you mean it when you said you'd like to see my house?"

I moved past the bench to stand at the other side of the piano, but he followed me. I was absolutely frozen with embarrassment, mute with a feeling I couldn't explain even to myself. Aunt Wanda wanted me to be friendly to this man, but how could I be? In my desperate awkwardness I would have liked to slap his face.

He sounded a little angry now. "You're trying to make me play the fool. Is that it?"

"Where in the world did you get that idea?" I almost choked on my cocktail, getting it out, but at least it was said.

Rye sighed in the moment of silence. "Some day some dreadful man is going to teach poor Pock a lesson," she told John Sutton. "I don't want to be around when it happens. She's broken so many hearts already. What a shame to be treated in turn as she deserves."

This was an old joke of Rye's, that I led men on and then dropped them, and was a kind of witch, and ordinarily I could laugh along with her about it, if we were by ourselves. But Rye didn't know what Aunt Wanda had commanded of me, nor did John Sutton have any way of knowing about Rye's joke. I wasn't about to explain the miserable truth; I couldn't even look at him.

"Oh," he said, "so that's the way it is. I thought it was me, something wrong, I had some terrible flaw or something."

Rye assured him mockingly, "She's a man-eater."

"Good God! No sign of any change coming? Like right now?"

Well, they were playing the game. Rye had always been a flirt, with the typical redhead's capricious coquetry. Rye now pretended astonishment as she fingered out a tune with one hand. "You mean you want to try?"

"Why not?"

She took on a prim, severe manner in an instant. "It's so out of character. Here you've been Aunt Wanda's adviser, or moneyman, or whatever, counting profits all day long, and now suddenly you've become a reformer. And with such an unlikely subject. When I said that someday my sister might be taught to be nice to some man, I didn't really believe it. It would mean the end of the world, or something equally fantastic."

I was so miserable I could scarcely breathe. I was pinned like some bug while they made sarcastic comments on my squirmings; or so it seemed to me. The shy person—and believe me when I say I've studied all the psychiatrists' opinions on shyness—is one who has turned inward, retreated, in fear of rejection. But having absorbed the psychological mumbo jumbo doesn't change the person. How well I knew . . .

"I'm your aunt's estate manager through no wish of mine." His tanned face stiffened for a moment and his voice got huffy and hoarse, and I felt a rise of interest on my own part. Here was another vulnerable soul—not so vulnerable as I, of course. He quickly got over his momentary resentment. "I hate accounting. It's not the kind of work I should be doing. Why I went into it I'll never know. Someone should have warned me. I've got to make a change, get that land of mine producing—" He was frowning, he was seeing that land in his mind, and the old house that he wanted to restore; and though I was trying to stay as far from him as possible, I felt a surge of sympathy for his hopes and plans. "I wish I could tell your aunt and all of the other bank clients to do their own managing."

Rye wasn't interested in his desire to change his profession. She bent her red head over the keyboard and concentrated on her tune, leaving Mr. Sutton to turn in a brooding way to me.

"I do need someone's advice about the house. I don't mean an architect, I don't want big changes, professional remodeling. But I'm a man, and I don't know how on earth a house should be arranged so that it can be house-kept in."

"I don't either," I told him. "I don't keep house."

"What did you do while you were teaching in New Mexico?"

"I lived with an Indian," I stammered, which of course made me sound more of a fool than ever.

He brooded over this implausibility. "Do you know one end of a broom from another?"

It was too much. Even I could feel insulted. "I'm not really a witch, but I'm acquainted enough with a broom to know that one end has straws fixed to it, and you hold the broom by the other end to sweep."

He brightened up, as if I'd qualified as an expert on housekeeping. "Well, right now I've come to the problem of where to put the laundry. Electric washer, automatic, gas dryer. There's never been anything modern in the place. Where should the equipment be installed? On the first floor? Near the kitchen? Does that save on piping and plumbing? Or would a woman find it easier to keep the laundry setup at a distance?"

"Since you're not married," I told him, "why worry about what a woman would want? Why not put the laundry room where you want it? In the attic if you feel like it?"

And yet, I *was* interested in his house; I was interested in his dilemma, getting out of a kind of job he hated and into one he liked. There was no way I could show this; I could only beat a prickly retreat. And Rye, at the piano, was pretending not to listen.

But then he said quietly, kind of dignified, but not begging either, "Would you come tomorrow and look at it?"

I could only think: Why me? But this had turned into a crazy kind of evening, of course—look at beautiful Angela over there, for instance, with that aghast, shocked expression, as if someone had turned Mr. Sutton into a live toad before her eyes, and there was Mrs. Stryfe sipping at her cocktail and too dense to see that her child's world was shattering—and so, because it was becoming such a mixed-up affair anyway, so confusing that I'd almost forgotten to keep my guard up, I answered, "Yes. Tomorrow I'll come and see."

Why hadn't he asked Angela to look at his house?

Perhaps he already had.

Or perhaps Angela wasn't to see the house until it was finished. As a surprise. For her.

Something was terribly wrong with the wine. It looked pretty under the candlelight, a true ruby red, but as you brought it up to sip it, it gave off a nauseating odor. I didn't even attempt to taste it. I put it down casually and glanced at Aunt Wanda at the head of the table, and Aunt Wanda had just lifted her own glass and wore a thunderstruck expression. She recovered her composure quickly. She motioned the watchful Perkins to her side, whispered to him; the glasses were quickly whisked from everyone's place. A new bottle was brought. Perkins presented it to Aunt Wanda, and they examined the seal together.

Somebody . . . *who?* . . . had added a nasty concoction to the dinner wine. Who else had noticed besides Aunt Wanda and myself? No one, apparently. Mr. Sutton sat at the end of the table, the end opposite Aunt Wanda, the only male, isolated in lordliness, and he seemed only briefly puzzled when the little maid deftly removed his filled glass. Mrs. Stryfe, across from me, was sounding off on a political situation, something the governor was trying to cover up down in Baton Rouge, and didn't even see her wine removed. Angela was pouting. She was pouting at my left, keeping a shoulder up to cut off any accidental glimpse of me, concentrating on Aunt Wanda beyond, a kind of chill managing to flow over her shoulder toward me to indicate her displeasure. She thought I was trying to take away Mr. Sutton; I was laying little traps and snares, and in spite of my plain, spinsterish exterior he was being attracted to me. I had by now become convinced that my theory about Mr. Sutton's house was the true one; he wanted a practical and sensible woman to look at his house so that it would be nice for Angela. When the time came to ask her to please accept it, and him.

This small misunderstanding between them tonight could be used as a base for a lover's quarrel, a temporary estrangement which, when it ended, as I understood how the game must be played, would lead to even more intense involvement with each other. I yearned to touch Miss Stryfe's pink ruffled sleeve and assure her that I didn't want her Mr. Sutton. I didn't want him at all. He was truly hers.

But I didn't have time for ridiculous talk with Angela; I had to think about the wine.

The wine had been tampered with so that it stank. Not just my glass. The whole bottle had been infected, so badly that you wanted to retch if you'd smelled it very much; and it made you want to think, not drink. It made you think of big broken zinnias lying across the rim of a bowl. It made you think of Aunt Wanda's terrified, beseeching eyes, there in her little upstairs parlor, during that moment when you had held her hand. It also even might make you think of Jim Parrish's lonely grave and the ugly things that had been done upon it.

Between Rye and myself was a centerpiece, tall red gladiolus and baby's breath and ferns, and now through the mass of greenery and blossom I caught a glimpse of Rye. Rye knew all about that wine. She looked completely stunned and betrayed. She looked shut in upon herself, shut in with misery and fear. Rye had made an instant connection between the stench of the wine and the stench of what was being done to her. Perhaps she thought that the business with the wine was directed at her; she was already so tense with hurt that she might not see, right away, that this was Aunt Wanda's party and that whatever went wrong was directed at our aunt. In another instant Rye was going to jump from her chair and run out of the room, completing the disaster that was beginning to be smoothed over.

I put my napkin beside my plate. If Rye went, I went with her.

But after a moment she looked over in my direction. And I made a face at her, the kind of face we made at each other when we were children together, a kind of code, and the face told her what I thought of the wine, of Angela's ignoring me, and even of Mr. Sutton's laundry problems, all rolled into one. It was all there if Rye looked for it, and she must have, for the pallor lightened a little and she tried to smile.

If she can smile, she won't run.

Someone right here at the table might be very happy to see her run. Yes, very satisfied and smug.

Perkins' dark face hadn't changed a whit, hadn't betrayed his chagrin nor any discomposure. He was now at the buffet-sideboard, beginning to dish up something gorgeous-smelling, and Martha and the little maid whose name I didn't know, began to serve.

New wine, new glasses, sparkled all along the table.

Mr. Sutton kept trying to catch my eye all through dinner, and I didn't let him. Perhaps he was nervous now, seeing his mistake, seeing how Angela on my other side was making no secret of her sulks. I wished heartily that my nature had been bolder, that I could dare to look directly into Mr. Sutton's rather nice brown eyes and give him an outrageous wink. It would discomfort him no end, of course, but if Angela could somehow know about it, it might add fuel to that lover's tiff to be eventually so lovingly ended.

There was nothing wrong with the chicken we were being served. Nor with the sour cream and subtle herbs, the sherry and mushrooms, that went with it.

Never in my life, I told myself, have I sat at a private table such as this one, and been served so. I was like Cinderella, except that I was plain instead of smudged with ash, and no fairy godmother would have let me out of sight in my dowdy garb.

I was not the only one who'd been uprooted Cinderellawise. Aunt Wanda had certainly risen in the world. She had had her husband for a short time after their marriage. While they were here, had he shown her the routine and how it all should be managed? Or perhaps not, since he seemed to have left her securely in the hands of Perkins and Mr. Sutton, who in one way or another, between them, must know everything necessary.

There was no doubt about Perkins' ability. His skill and aplomb would have gotten him a place anywhere. I caught myself giving Mr. Sutton a quick, curious look. He seemed so young to be a curmudgeon, too open-faced to be an ogre. Well, there were those heavy eyebrows and the stubborn chin, of course. He must be terrifying with Aunt Wanda over those account books, adamant with every penny—and almost human everywhere else. He'd told Rye and me that he wasn't willingly managing estates, but this must be a way of defending himself against what we already knew, the ogre side of him. It was all very confusing.

For dessert there were guava shells with cream cheese, the candied guava shells warmed ever so slightly, the cream cheese very cold. I made up my mind that when I left the table I was going to slip back to the kitchen and compliment Mrs. Mim on the wonderful meal. Aunt Wanda had said Mrs. Mim could be monotonous if she wasn't watched, but all cooks should be monotonous like *this.*

The huge kitchen was warm and lighted, and smelled of food, but Mrs. Mim wasn't in it. In the dining room Martha and the other maid were loading dishes on a tea cart, I knew, while Perkins was in the parlor with liqueurs, brandy, demitasses, and probably a few items I'd never think of, while Aunt Wanda and her guests got seated comfortably.

This part of the house was silent.

I went out into the hall, looked in at the open door of a pantry, one part storage with shelves filled with canned goods and household supplies, one part a center for cleaning up. There were two big white sinks with long drainboards, the drainboards already stacked with rinsed china from the early part of the dinner. No dishwashing machine in here; the maids would do the dishes in the sinks. It was quite true, the place needed modernizing; and why wasn't Aunt Wanda spending the money to have it done?

I stole down the hall to the big back entry. The door itself stood open; the screen door was shut. I opened the screen door and went out. If there had been clouds earlier, there were none now: The moon was rising in splendor.

I found a pathway around the house to the veranda where the windows opened upon the lighted parlor. Aunt Wanda and her guests and Rye were in a group over near the mantel, with the portrait of General Lee looking down in dignity upon them. I had no wish to go inside. I had no small talk. I had no desire to make Angela any more jealous than she was, no wish to add to her mistaken conviction that I held some secret lure for Mr. Sutton. Nor had I any wish to sit in a corner and be ignored—which was what would happen in any case.

Out here was darkness, slits of moonlight gleaming at the top of the lower tower at the end of the veranda, cricket buzzings, the smell of magnolia blossoms, the whole feeling of night. I stood and let my imagination wander. Here I was not the narrow spinster caught in her cage of aloofness, the bungling, awkward misfit; I felt widened, freed, dispersed, as if I were somehow a part of the strangeness of the world, a piece of all of it, and that misfit or not I did in some way truly belong. I was a part of the night wind searching through the swamps, and I found the old barns smelling of hay, the ponds where ducks had left the water to sleep head-under-wing, the pines that narrowed to fingertip at the very top, and I knew how horses stirred and switched themselves with their tails in the blackness of their stalls, and I swept ghostlike over snapping turtles who lay at the rim of the swamp with jeweled eyes fixed on the moon.

Pocket, that mute and prickly old maid so filled with quirks and complexes, was made so big and free by the night that I felt quite released, a new being; and too bad, I told myself, that you can't carry this new feeling and this new person indoors with you now, since you have to go in eventually and make a proper appearance to say farewell to the guests Aunt Wanda asked here just for your sake.

Because Mr. Sutton might like you.

Now, that had been the craziest idea of all.

After a while I gave up the night and the feeling of being someone else, a nice someone, and I went in through the hall and so on into the parlor. Rye asked where I had been, but no one else cared, except that Mr. Sutton gave me that searching look I didn't like and couldn't understand; and it made me feel that the look was the kind of look you give someone when you know they're telling you a lie.

Nine

AUNT WANDA'S BEDROOM was at the front of the house, upstairs, and in contrast to so many of the rooms that were light, cheerful, graceful, this seemed a dark and heavy room. Perhaps it had been furnished by her husband, and so had this rugged, masculine taste displayed, and out of love and gratitude she had left it as he had wanted it.

At any rate, the whole room seemed massively outsized. The bed was huge, a four-poster in dark wood with a plain dark spread, no canopy; the dresser and wardrobe and nightstands were of waxed mahogany, rubbed and aged almost black. The rug was of a deep green-and-brown tufted wool and the draperies at the windows, drawn closed now, were almost a match for the rug. All that the room seemed to lack was the smell of pipe smoke and leather slippers and shaving lotion to make it completely a man's domain. I had knocked a moment before, and Aunt Wanda had told me to enter.

"I'll only take a minute."

She was at the dresser taking off her necklace and earrings. She glanced at me coldly. "I'm really very tired, Esther." In the old days she would have said, "Make it short and sweet, kid. I'm beat to the socks."

It was no easier for me to talk to this newly cultured Aunt Wanda than it would have been to talk to the old one. The slights and humiliations of childhood stay with you for a long time. Perhaps forever. . . . But I tried to sound firm and resolute. "Did your husband ever warn you of someone who might be holding a grudge? An old enemy? Someone he'd bested in a business deal, who refused to forget? Some old quarrel that had never been settled?"

In the soft lamplight she had taken on what seemed to be a look of real surprise. "Why on earth should he warn me of any such thing?"

"It might account for what happened at dinner tonight."

The surprise vanished and Aunt Wanda's face became passive, expressionless; I couldn't even find a trace of resentment. "What happened at dinner was just an accident. The wine had been decanted too long. Or something had happened to it in the cellar—even Perkins isn't perfect. The wine went bad, that was all. It happens."

"It went bad in the strangest way I've ever known. It smelled of skunk, or of something like skunk. If we had swallowed any of it, I think we would all have been sick."

Aunt Wanda's huge bed had been turned down neatly. She went over to it now and stood there as if to emphasize that she wanted to get into it, get rid of me, rest. "Let's talk tomorrow, if we must. Right now I'm in no mood for an argument."

I wanted to ask: "What is going on here, in the middle of all of this beauty and luxury? What ugly thing hides under the surface? Why do you lie and put me off?"

But she knew me so well; she had known the small prickly Esther, the left-out one, the unloved one, and she knew me now, the spinster so easily put aside and dismissed. "I know you mean well. Don't think I'm not grateful. You are my friend, and it is good to have a friend here. But for now—please go to bed."

There wasn't anything else I could say or do. There was a wall between us, but it belonged to me, my old familiar cage.

"Good night, Aunt Wanda."

"Good night, dear." There was no mistaking the gratitude in her voice as I gave up and turned toward the door.

Everyone who stayed at Larchwood was in bed, asleep, but me. Perkins had driven off with Martha and Lydia and the maid I thought of as the Small One, in his station wagon, headed for Moss Corner. The house was silent, with only night lights left on along the halls and in the bathrooms. The silence sang in your ears. But I was restless and sleepless, sitting up on the bed and staring out of the windows. I could see the balcony railing against the moonlight, the dark mass of trees beyond.

Things had happened this evening that I couldn't explain, and some of them had happened to me. I felt strangely that a part of me had been chipped away, or at least loosened, or prized up. A piece of the shell? I could almost feel that buried part that had been exposed; it was raw, unfamiliar. I'd gotten out of character, though I couldn't understand where or why. Had I been rude to Angela? No, though she tempted even me. Did I fail Rye? Had she expected some magic answer from me when she had taken me to see Jim's grave?

She hadn't wanted me to stay and talk tonight, when I went to her room after the dismissal by Aunt Wanda; she'd said frankly she wanted to sleep and to forget. I hadn't brought up the subject of the wine at dinner. Let her forget that, too, put it away with the rest of what had happened to disturb and grieve her.

But something tonight had changed things, had perhaps changed me. I poked puzzled into my own mind, afraid too of what I might come upon, and I told myself: Pocket, old girl, you cannot always be searching for bogeymen. Who had told me that? My father? The big man with the myopic eyes, thick black hair, and gentle hands who had tried to comfort me in some of my wilder storms?

I'm not your child.

Yes, I had screamed that at him once. When the clawing inside me had to have a way out. And he had only held me closer against his tobacco-smelling coat and stroked my hair and murmured, "Always, Pocket. Always. Always."

I had been a horrible child, and it was completely a case of justice that I should grow up into a mute, caged old maid.

After a while I put on my shoes again—I hadn't undressed as yet—and went downstairs through the silent house and outdoors at the back. No doors were locked. South of the house and past the gardens were the garages, and I got my old car out quietly and drove off, not through the porte-cochere but by a side driveway that went direct to the road across the lawns. I drove first to the turn down which the Stryfes and Bart—Bart *who?*—lived, and I found the houses down the road, all right, a half mile of woods between the two, white houses that looked much alike and rather lonely there under the moon. Not too big, but two-storied and set back fifty feet or so from the road, with gardens in front. Lights burned in both houses. In one of course Angela and Mama must be preparing for bed. Perhaps Mrs. Stryfe had tired of political matters, quieting down, and Angela might be brushing those golden locks and thinking dreamily of her loved one, and the scene jumped into my mind, incredibly clear, Angela before a mirror and looking very beautiful in something lace-ruffled and filmy, pink in color, her eyes full of dreamy desire, and then without warning I became aware of this awful wrench inside myself. And I found, unbelieving, dumfounded, that whatever had been chipped away or prized up inside me had something to do with John Sutton.

Impossible.

I said the words out loud, "It's impossible."

I'd promised to go to see his house, his house that had to have laundry equipment and a completed roof and who knew what else before he could present it to Angela.

The promise meant nothing. I'd tried to seem friendly to Mr. Sutton because my aunt had asked it of me. That didn't mean I was going to become a fool.

That last look he'd given me, though—that bothered me. For a moment there I'd felt like a liar, like one who wears a mask for the purpose of covering what must not be seen.

I wouldn't think about it any more. I'd wonder about the fact that both houses had lights on inside, though Bart was supposed to be away. Either Bart had returned home tonight or he had a servant who lived in or the Stryfes turned on his lights for him as a favor to scare away burglars. Since I had been given to understand that burglary and indeed almost all forms of crime were unknown out here in the northern Louisiana countryside, perhaps the lights being on meant that Bart was home again from his vacation in New Orleans.

I turned the car at a dead end of the road where a sign said, "No Trespassing, No Hunting." I drove back to the main road and turned right and went on to the cemetery. It was very lonely-looking by night. The lawns under the moonlight seemed almost black, and the marble monuments in the older part of the cemetery, the angels and pillars and shafts, seemed arrested for an instant in an order of march. I didn't get out of the car at once. I waited there, turning things over in my mind, seeking answers.

Were there two separate lines of meanness going on, or only one? Were Aunt Wanda's broken blooms and stench-filled wine a part and parcel of what was being done at Jim's grave?

There seemed no obvious link or connection.

As to the things happening at the house, it seemed that one of the servants had to be in on it. Only someone there tonight could have spiked the wine, Perkins being as vigilant as he was. If the Stryfes or John Sutton had detoured through the pantries on the way in, it must have been noticed and commented upon by those not in the plot.

Across the road, in the old broken house that faced the cemetery, an owl let forth a questioning hoot or two. The moonlight touched the mossy shingles, the slightly leaning walls, and made black rectangles where glass had long since vanished from the windows. The moonlight had almost the quality of water, shimmering in the air, and the old derelict house might have been sitting lonely at the bottom of the sea.

Question: Why had Rye pictured John Sutton as a critic and heckler, disparaged him, spoke of him as someone who made Aunt Wanda's life a frantic hell of bookkeeping? Tonight he had spoken with what seemed to be genuine feeling of a desire to get out of estate management. Was he simply overconscientious with my aunt? A tyrant only because he had the conviction that he must do his job perfectly? Somehow that didn't fit, either. John Sutton hadn't seemed the type to be a meticulous perfectionist. I'd met such people, and they were seldom perfectionists in only one direction. So, could the fault be Aunt Wanda's? Was she so inept, so poor with figures, so bumbling at managing money, that John Sutton was stricter with her than ordinarily, lest some blame attach to him?

But Aunt Wanda had once, not unsuccessfully, run a boarding house in Seattle. And you don't keep people and feed them without learning pretty well the difference between income and outgo, and what made a profit.

Aunt Wanda's attitude, when I examined it, seemed that of a woman with something to hide. She had tried to suppress Rye's complaints about the desecration of the grave by inane talk of pranks. Her outburst inviting me to go back where I came from had no doubt come from the heart, and sprang from a real wish I'd be gone. I represented a threat because I would not be put off like Rye, even though so far Aunt Wanda had managed to evade my questions. I was not handicapped by grief, by being pregnant and a widow.

Aunt Wanda knew that something was going on inside the house or she wouldn't have asked me to overlook anything that might seem like spying. She'd asked me to be nice to John Sutton. Two requests—there must be a connection between them, though I couldn't see it. There was a pattern to whatever was happening, and these two unlike requests had to fit into it.

Well, I've figured out that much, I told myself.

She has to have an enemy, a tormentor. She's protecting him, or her, for reasons that I know nothing about. Rye also has a tormentor but she wants to do something about him, and she wants me to help her do it.

There was movement in the cemetery, under the watery moonlight, and I came out of the thoughtful daze with a jerk. Something small was tumbling, or jumping, out across the lawns. In the distance it looked like a toy, something wound up, springing along. I got out of the car swiftly and stood with pulses thumping, and then forced myself to cross the dew-wet grass to where the thing was, and found myself being stared at by a large toad.

I squatted and put out a tentative hand. The dew sparkled like scattered diamonds and the toad looked almost black, though his big eyes gleamed with green lights. "You're a good-looking guy for a toad," I told him. He squeezed himself lower and smaller, warily ready to jump.

Behind me in the old house the owl hooted again, and I thought I heard the sweep of wings, and turned involuntarily to look, and something tall and black and faceless stood there just behind me, a thing out of nightmare. For a moment I simply didn't believe what I saw, the moonlight was playing tricks, this couldn't be.

I tried to get off my knees.

The black thing didn't move. It had vaguely the shape of the human form, but this was the last thing I thought.

I did what any fool would do, confronted by a black specter in the middle of the night in a graveyard.

I fainted.

Ten

FOOLS MUST COME TO THEIR SENSES in different ways. I became foggily aware that I was out somewhere in the chill of the night, stretched on my back, earth under me and wet grass, and having my hands folded over something that lay on my breast. After a few disoriented moments I propped myself up. The thing that had been lying on my bosom like a spray of lilies was the toad, dead now. Looking around me by moonlight I found that I was on Jim Parrish's grave.

This was no surprise, for some reason.

I was alone. No black figure stood tall and watching.

The toad was crushed and slimy and I dropped him quickly, but then the death of this harmless thing, this creature with whom I'd shared a solitary moment in the moonlight before the horror made his appearance—this senseless killing made me so mad that my pulses beat in my still-groggy head, and I forced myself to pick up the poor toad and carry him over to the wall. I found a depression there and buried him beneath the turf.

I lay against the wall and cried, knowing myself a ninny, a useless thing that had no business here pretending to help my sister.

After a while I dried my eyes and went to my car, half expecting some vandalism here, but the car started as it should, and I drove back to Larchwood without incident. The moon shone in the night sky, and everything was at peace.

If anyone was awake at the house, watching and gleeful at my broken and crestfallen return, I saw no sign. I put away the car, crept into the house, shed my clothes, put on my shabby nightgown, and got shivering into bed.

I knew that I would never forget that moment of looking over my shoulder at the shape that stood there, nor that other moment of waking upon the grave.

It was perhaps appropriate that the nightmare that was new and real should cause me to dream again the nightmare that was old.

The dream was never the same, though it always took up at the same point every time. It began in a hallway. The hallway was wide and had somehow an institutional look about it. A woman in a gray dress was fussing with me, smoothing my hair, reforming the pleats in the skirt of my white dress, and pulling up my socks. The impression I got, in the dream, was that I had recently become highly disarrayed, and that I was too young to tidy myself up properly.

Next seemed to come introductions, of looking up into big grown-up faces at the top of big bodies, and of putting my hand into another hand that was large. This did not happen in the hallway, and in some of the dreams it did not happen at all. In some of the dreams I found myself right away on the *Lap*. Sitting on this lap, I faced a desk. All of the dreams contained the woman behind the desk, the woman with the biscuit of pale hair on top of her head. This was not the woman in the gray dress, or uniform, who had straightened my hair and clothing in the hall. I had no memory of the face of the woman in the hall, only the bent head with a nurse's, or matron's, cap pinned to the back. The face of the woman across the desk, though, was always unforgettable and frightening.

Not that the face held menace or cruelty. It was a mild, decorous, compassionate face, the face of a woman about forty-five who had spent a long time looking into other people's troubles. It was the face of a woman who did social work or taught Sunday School, or perhaps did both. She did not wear a uniform, but a modest shirt-waist type of dress, blue and white with a black leather belt. You saw all of the dress, finally, when in the dream she came from behind the desk.

What made the woman frightening was not how she looked but what she was going to say.

In some of the dreams she said nothing. Her mouth moved, and I tried to catch the words, but didn't. I knew, though, what she meant. I knew she was trying to get across that part about the *unknown woman.*

In some of the dreams she came right out with it in her soft, regretful voice. Regretful, but businesslike. "This child was brought to us by an unknown woman."

An unknown woman . . .

I always tried to wake up at this point in the dream, because I'd learned long ago that it *was* a dream, and a horrible one, but in the dream I merely tried to squirm down off the lap in order to run away. I wiggled, the owner of the lap restrained me, and the woman with the biscuit of hair shuffled papers on the desk. "Ordinarily we wouldn't accept a child under these conditions, but there were circumstances that caused us to take her in."

Even in the dream I grew indignant because these were not the words a child could understand enough to remember; they were stored-away words, buried deep in hurt, and I tried to scream them down. The *me* of today, the grown woman, tried to scream them down, though the screaming went on in the voice of the child in the dream.

The woman smiled as if apologizing for my screaming, and then, the last thing she said was, "We think first, and always, of our children's welfare."

And there the dream ordinarily ended. Sometimes there was a kind of postscript to it, a brief scene of standing on some big steps, staring down at a busy street, each of my hands held in the hand of someone tall, and a waiting car below. And something else—in the distance a large white building with the bronze statue of a woman on the peak of its portico, a statue bigger than life, a woman with a shield propped at her knee, one arm uplifted and holding something aloft. In the dream, in this part where we stood at the top of the flight of big steps, I could feel that over my dress I wore a coat, and that there was a hood over my hair.

That was the final scene. It was the final scene tonight, my second night here in Aunt Wanda's house. I woke at last and lay gathering my senses, and then I beat the pillow savagely—this too was a part of the pattern—and I howled soundlessly, I howled out all of the words I had tried to scream during the dream.

I called the woman names, all of the names I'd ever used in the past, plus some new ones, and I demanded to know just where she got the gall, and the cold guts, to dispose of people like so much firewood or soap or knitted caps. I stopped pounding the pillow for a moment because it occurred to me all at once that these were *real things* of which the woman in the dream had had charge of distributing . . . and knowing this now seemed to threaten to lead off into other byways, things I knew about the woman without knowing that I knew. And this was the most frightening of all, the unexplored. I lay curled and tight, gripping the pillow, and turned my thoughts from the old nightmare to the new, from what must have happened long ago to what had happened tonight.

In the morning I would have to decide what I should tell Rye, and perhaps how much to tell Aunt Wanda.

When it was dawn I got out of bed and went out upon the balcony. The great green world looked innocent and fresh, newly alive, a world to be young in and happy in, not to be hagridden in.

This morning I am old, I told myself. In sleep I was tormented by the past, or by some dream that never happened though it seems to spring from truth. On top of that I have the memory of what occurred in the cemetery. Instead of leaping to my feet to drag the cover from that black-hooded face, I slumped in unconsciousness. He had his fun with me. Perhaps I'd been lucky it hadn't been something even grimmer.

How can I help Rye when I am weak and witless in the face of danger?

What's to do? Catch the creep in the act of desecration by hiding at the cemetery and keeping watch? But by now the enemy knows much more about all the approaches to that cemetery than I do, all the hidden spots, any possible traps. Hadn't he seemed to rise out of the ground behind me last night? How could I catch such as he unawares?

And anyway, I told myself, I'm getting the fiercest hunch that whatever is going on, the secret of it all doesn't lie at the cemetery at all. It doesn't even have anything directly to do with Rye. It's centered *here,* in Larchwood, and revolves around our dear aunt.

Rye hadn't written me about what was going on at the house because through misdirection and concealment Aunt Wanda hadn't let her know.

Our aunt is running so scared she pretends not to see the jumps. All she's going to do is break her neck.

She must have been horribly alone here before Rye came.

It was easy to understand why Aunt Wanda had begged Rye to come, to bury Jim here, to stay on with the promise of an inheritance for the baby. What a merciful relief it must have been at first to have a friend in the house—but only at first, before the ugly things began to happen at Jim's grave.

And then Aunt Wanda had tried to say to Rye, without really saying it: Look, dear, we have to pretend. We have to not see. I'm blind and blithe, and you must be likewise. This is the safe way to be. Worse things could happen. Keep your mouth shut. Don't make complaints. (But don't go away; for God's sake, don't leave me!) I'll take the heat off by complaints about my heavy duties and about Mr. Sutton's harassments. *He's* making me miserable; *he's* hounding me into fits.

Was this the true story of what was going on?

To add to it—what should I say about my miserable misadventure of last night?

How could I add to Rye's confusion and fear by letting her know that the evil had touched me, too? Then, too, there was that sense of shame at my own weakness and ineffectiveness, my collapse in the face of fright. Must I tell of that, too?

Worst of all, what had happened last night had the hallmarks of the phrase Aunt Wanda liked; it smacked of a prank. I hadn't been injured, raped, embarrassed seriously, had I? And so, strangely, I decided to keep quiet about what had happened to me. I told myself that it could be interesting perhaps, during the coming day, to see who seemed to look for signs of shock or fear, or showed a sly glint of satisfaction.

I wonder how differently things might have been if I'd simply told everyone the truth.

Rye came into the room as I finished dressing. She wore her maternity nightgown, a tentlike object embellished with ruffled embroidery, and I whistled teasingly at sight of her. "Straight out of the Follies. Where are the ostrich plumes? Where's the music?"

Rye tried to smile. She shrugged and sat down on the edge of my bed, drawing the voluminous gown tight about her knees. "It's a monster. I don't know why I bought it."

Her tone was morose and I felt a pang of worry. "Do you feel well?"

"Oh, I'm all right. I get these dragged-out, discouraged spells. Pregnancy is about five months too long."

"I don't think the nine-months arrangement will be changed

soon." At the same time I was thinking: Rye's baby is here with us now, a person, almost ready to be born, someone to be included in all of our plans for the future. And this baby must be given a safe and happy place in which to grow. "Who's your doctor here?"

"Dr. Potterby, in Moss Corner. He has a very good reputation. He's older, very kind, a mother hen kind of man."

"Go and tell him you have these dragged-out times. And speaking of mother hens, why hadn't you told me that Mother Stryfe had hatched herself a swan?"

Rye looked over at me curiously. I was giving my hair its usual five-second arranging. "Angela? You think she's pretty?"

"Very. And elegant. And dainty."

"Pock, you in front of that mirror, and you're talking about that . . . that marshmallowy doll. Honestly. . . ." She seemed suddenly disgusted with me. "Look at *yourself*."

I looked. "I know I'm too skinny, I ought to weigh what I weighed when I lived in New York. I made a fairly human appearance then. I have an ordinary face, two eyes, a nose, a mouth, and I've been lucky, no pimples or blotches. Otherwise, what?"

"You were a model in New York. You didn't beat down any doors. You were *asked* to be a model. A fashion photographer told you things about your face, your appearance. And now you pretend you've forgotten all of them."

"Whatever he thought I had, or whatever I seemed to have, is gone, Rye. I'm an . . . an old maid, I believe the saying is. A spinster. Dried like an old apple."

"Horseshit," Rye cried.

"That little word is not used in polite society."

"Well, so sorry, then. But since you're such an old spinster and dried up beyond belief, what are you going to do about Mr. Sutton?"

"Why should I do anything about him?"

"Well, because of the way he acted last night." She rolled over on her side, still hugging her knees. "I give up. I mean, absolutely—I give up. Nothing unfreezes you. Here's poor Mr. Sutton, practically on his knees. . . ."

"Don't be ridiculous. Besides, Angela's in love with him. You couldn't miss that."

"So, he turns her on. Does she have a ring in his nose? Or on her finger? Not that I noticed."

I didn't want to argue with Rye. "To set your mind at rest and to prove that Mr. Sutton isn't on his knees, so to speak, nor even slightly interested in me—" Somehow, there was again that sense of some of the shell having been pried up, a nerve-racking rawness. "—we'll go to see his house and advise him about his remodeling."

"We will? Promise? Today?"

"Yes."

After a short silence, Rye said, "About the other, Pock. About Jim's grave. Do you have a plan about catching the creep? Have you figured out a way to pin it on somebody?"

An icy shudder ran through me. I hoped that Rye hadn't seen my involuntary shiver. "I . . . I wish to God I did."

"No hunches at all? No ESP tinglings? Could it be one of those with us at the table last night? Mrs. Stryfe? Angela? Mr. Sutton?"

I remembered the black figure, the sense of roaring nightmare. For an instant I felt sick and giddy. Who had been inside that cape, or robe, or whatever it was, with a hood hiding the face? Wasn't Angela too short, too slender, to stand that tall against the moonlit sky? Could I absolutely cross out Angela? "No hunches as yet, Rye," I managed to say. I wanted to change the subject, too. "When is your famous Mr. Bart coming home?"

"He should be here at any time. You like Bart as a suspect? Oh, Pock, you won't when you meet him. I wish you'd marry someone like Bart. He's so nice and civilized and intelligent. You're going to like him immensely. You just have to."

I might like him; I would never marry him, or anyone. It wasn't even fatalism any more; it was rockbound conviction. No one marries a woman whose shyness turns her into an icicle.

Rye went on, "If we go out to see Mr. Sutton's place, we can stop at Bart's afterward and see if he's home."

"And someday soon we'll call on the Stryfes." Get Rye's mind on future plans, I told myself; get it off me and my shortcomings and off the past in any form. "I guess as far as etiquette goes they're supposed to call here, a kind of thank you for the dinner or something, but who cares? We'll visit hen and swan in their native lair." I rubbed some lipstick on my mouth, a final gesture toward makeup. "You said something about a way to get to the cemetery that wasn't by the road. A path, is it?"

"Through the woods. Very pretty."

"And does this path go anywhere near the house where Bart and the Stryfes live?"

"Yes. Almost right past them." She waited, lying there looking at me curiously. "Do you think *that* means something?"

"I don't know."

I stared into my own eyes in the mirror, and they seemed empty, the eyes of a coward who knows himself—herself—too well. I'd come all brave and storming, and now I had no ideas, no hunches, no inspirations; I had only the memory of a terrible fear and a degrading trick having been played upon me.

In my mind the foolish weakness I'd shown in the cemetery was becoming woven into that other, older nightmare, the one about the woman with the biscuit of hair who came toward me from behind her desk.

What could I do?

Run, of course.

Where the new idea came from I never knew, but suddenly I decided that what was needed was some minor prying and looking on *my* part, a semiburglarizing of Aunt Wanda's hidey-holes, including those pretty desks. I'll never go back to that cemetery by night, I thought. So let's see what kind of phantoms I could raise right here in Larchwood.

Eleven

Martha served us breakfast on the veranda. In the morning sunlight Aunt Wanda looked crisply turned out, wearing a blue seersucker dress that was cool and fresh, her hair not in curls on top of her head but becomingly drawn into a white puff at the back, and it was only around her eyes and in the unguarded set of her mouth that you sensed haggardness, a bitter disillusionment. Rye had put on a maternity frock, bright green piped with red; she made me think of a pregnant Christmas tree. I wore last summer's extravagance, a white pique shift, out of date now and which had been laundered too many times. So much for attracting Mr. Sutton, I told myself.

He won't even notice nor care that I haven't donned fine raiment for him. Why should he?

From the tea cart Martha brought strawberries under thick cream, an omelet dusted with fine herbs, bacon and popovers, country butter, fig preserves. Where did one begin? I felt stuffed just looking at it all.

Aunt Wanda pecked at her plate, spoke little, smoked, drank black coffee. Rye ate like a starving refugee, everything in sight, probably defying Dr. Potterby's rules. While I buttered popovers and nibbled at the omelet I decided to take a quick tour of the house, upstairs and downstairs, as soon as possible. See where everyone was and what went on in the mornings. I excused myself presently and left Rye still eating and Aunt Wanda lighting a fresh cigarette. I thought that my aunt gave me a studying glance as I left.

The lower halls were empty, echoing only my footsteps. Mrs. Mim was in the kitchen, her little girl there with her, the child small and straight on a stool, wearing a pink pinafore and pink ribbons, and having breakfast off the counter. I passed with only a smile and a nod for Mrs. Mim. I wanted to move fast and to locate everybody. But where was the inimitable Perkins?

Perkins' dark face turned toward me as I stepped from the back door. I had surprised a look of tension and of fear about him, I thought. He had been staring at the direction of the outer driveway, the one I had taken last night on that trip to the cemetery. Was there some trace of that late trip?

Or had something else caught his attention?

"Good morning, Perkins."

"Good morning, Miss Myles."

He was almost instantly himself again, the domestic overseer of impeccable manner, dignified deference, authority. He said smoothly, "Would you care to choose some flowers for your room, Miss Myles? You might look them over. Some of them are at their best now."

"That's a good idea."

Not sure of anything but that he wanted me to move on, I walked on out to the dewy plots of blossom and made a cursory inspection of the flowers there. When I heard the quiet closing of the rear door I headed for the outer driveway. Sure enough, there were deep marks in the damp grass that lined the graveled drive, and they looked as recent as the past midnight, and someone had driven here inexpertly, or—what it looked like—with a snootful; but I couldn't remember running off the gravel like this. Nor were the marks distinct enough to tell me that my tires had made them.

Well, verdict in doubt, I told myself.

At the same moment the thought came: Last night I'd been given a warning. Putting me on Jim Parrish's grave had been no prank. I was being told to keep my nose out of things, or much worse could happen. To me. To Rye.

The cold fear touched me to the bones.

For a moment the brightness of the morning took on the garish brilliance of nightmare, and the marks of tires in the wet lawn squirmed like snakes. There was a way out, though, an escape if I wanted to take it—I could run to my room and pack, and demand that Rye come with me, back to New Mexico.

For a moment the panic shook me, and then I remembered Perkins' expression as I had caught him unawares, and I knew that I was not the only one here who was afraid. For some reason this calmed me.

I went back into the house, passing the kitchen again—Perkins was there with Mrs. Mim, talking over the menus for the day, perhaps, and the child was playing with fork and knife, making them dance a minuet on the counter. I heard the rattle of the cart from the veranda as I turned up the stairway to the upper floor. Here was bustle, the subdued sounds of housekeeping, vacuum cleaner sounds from Aunt Wanda's room, water running somewhere in a sink—all of yesterday's flowers had been taken away, I noted, and probably the vases were being washed.

I intended to try to get up to the belvedere to see what those tire marks looked like from above, but Rye came out of her room carrying her purse. "I'm ready to go to Mr. Sutton's."

"So early?" I hadn't found out anything about the morning's routine, I thought; all I'd seen was Perkins staring at some marks in the grass verges.

"He wants us early."

"How do you know that?"

"I just know it." She gave me a smug, half-defiant look that was familiar. "He wants you to see his house. He really does, Pock, old dear. And you have to go and like it a little bit, to please him."

"Why should I?" Now that, according to Rye, the time had come, I found I'd had no intention of going near Mr. Sutton or his house.

"Don't pretend with me. I've known you all my life."

Not really, I thought. Rye had no knowledge of the cage, the walls that shut me in, the barrier that had grown up around me, built of something from the past. Shyness. A silly word; it gave no least implication of the crippling withdrawal into which I'd been forced.

She went on, "You're going to cut him down and cut down his house. He'll try and try to get you interested, and he won't believe that it can't happen, because your face doesn't show it, Pock, it's still that beautiful face your photographer friend fell in love with in New York. But then, after trying and trying, Mr. Sutton will start looking sick."

I didn't want to quarrel with my sister. "That's enough, Rye."

"I know you," Rye said, and stuck out her tongue.

What else could I say? "Wait till I get my purse. And keys." I hurried off to my room. Here were signs of tidying, of good housekeeping. The bed I had smoothed as best I could had been remade into a tautly tucked marvel. I ran a brush through my hair, rubbed my powder puff over my nose—Rye was blind, I told myself, she sees me as I never was—and grabbed my purse and went out.

In the car, passing between the stone gateposts, Rye said, "I want to get away from the house today. Aunt Wanda's got that funny faraway look, and pretty soon she starts giving everybody a bad time. It's as if there's something bitter and sour and all wrong inside her and she has to get it out."

"*Whom* does she give a bad time?"

"Everybody."

"You, too?"

"No. But she acts as if she wishes she could, only I'm preggie, and therefore holy or something."

"Perkins? Surely not him?"

"She just jumps all over the maids and Mrs. Mim. Picks everything they do to pieces, finds fault, brings up old mistakes. Looks at them as if she hates them all. I never saw this side of her until I came here. I think it must have developed after she took over this house, after her husband died and the responsibility fell on her. Mrs. Mim gets very dignified, very tense, and goes into her room and shuts the door. The maids take it for so long and then they just disappear, too. I don't know where they go. Perkins keeps in sight, but he's very quiet and morose; he must want to quit like everything. During the afternoon sometime Aunt Wanda withdraws into her bedroom. Locks the door, keeps to herself for the rest of the day. No dinner. No lunch either, for that matter. You saw her at breakfast. Maybe I shouldn't say it, but I think what she does in her room is *drink*."

"How is she then the next day?"

"Like somebody with a hangover. Sick, listless. Miserable."

"It couldn't be migraine?"

"Maybe it could be. I'm saying what I think."

"Does anything in particular seem to bring it on?"

"Not that I've noticed."

I drove in silence for a few minutes. The trees crowded to the fence line on either side of the road, thick among underbrush, a few tentative little trees out past the fence, like a cat putting forth a paw to test things. "How often does she have these spells?"

Rye shrugged. "I can't find any pattern to them."

"Perhaps it isn't any one thing happening. Maybe it's just the accumulation of small things. Did you hear anything late last night? Someone snooping, coming to the house? A car?"

"You mean, did someone come to see Aunt Wanda in the middle of the night and give her a reason for getting drunk? I don't know. It sounds highly improbable. I was tired and I didn't listen for anything, but I thought, when I got up this morning, that I'd heard you tippy-toeing in real late. But I know where you would have gone." Impulsively Rye took one of my gloved hands off the wheel and rubbed it against her cheek. "And thanks, Pock."

I could have told her then, all of it, the midnight visit and the silence of the moonlit cemetery and what I'd looked behind me to find. Perhaps this was the time to speak, but my throat closed in memory of fear; there was no way I could speak of that horror.

Surprisingly Rye went on, "There are ugly things happening at the house, too. Did you think I hadn't seen? They aren't as open, as cruel, as what's going on at Jim's grave."

I managed to get out, "I've seen a thing or two."

Aunt Wanda's shaking hands, plucking at the broken flowers—

Why had she called my attention to them?

"The wine last night, Pock."

"Yes."

"It makes you feel unclean. You're infected with the dirtiness, the filth."

"Yes."

Again there was silence. It was strange, I thought, to be talking about depravity in the middle of the most beautiful country I'd ever seen. The sky had its pure blue marked by the rim of tall white clouds, and in the distance the blue was reflected in a little lake. "Aunt Wanda warned me yesterday, during a talk we had up in the belvedere, to please not notice any eavesdropping or snooping I happened to run into. But I see now, she was really asking me not to notice these creepy little meannesses, either. Just as she tried to get you to pay no attention to what was happening at the cemetery." I saw a house on a cleared rise in the distance. It must be Mr. Sutton's place.

"You're lucky. I've never been allowed in the belvedere. Aunt Wanda seems to think I'd fall off, like a fool, and lose the baby."

The mailbox by the road had Mr. Sutton's name on it. I swung off into his meandering driveway. And Rye had been right; he'd been watching for us. He was out in the yard with a tool of some kind in his hand, a crowbar or some such, shading his eyes with his free hand to see who was coming. He wasn't dressed up for us, either, I noted, with a funny twinge that almost resembled disappointment. He wore a blue denim shirt that had endured even more laundering than my shift, and old khaki pants spotted with paint. I pulled to a stop and set the brake and he laid the crowbar carefully on some building supplies under a tarp and came walking toward us.

"You're just in time to see something interesting." He opened the car door on Rye's side, offered her a hand to help her out. I stepped out on my own, took off my gloves and stuffed them into my old handbag, threw the bag into the car, and slammed the door. He was saying, "You never really know what you're going to find until you dig in. Some of these old places were put together out of anything the builders could lay their hands on."

He was looking through the car at me.

Was he searching for signs of fear and shock left by the encounter of last night? Was he my phantom in black? Behind the honest look of the brown eyes, were there hidden sickness and cruelty?

"Well, you've got my curiosity sizzling," Rye was telling him. "I hope you've uncovered a pirate's chest full of doubloons at least." Once out upon the packed surface of the driveway, she was straightening the green-and-red maternity dress neatly.

I couldn't think of anything to say to him. I wished mightily that I hadn't promised to come here, and not having promised, hadn't come. John Sutton seemed very ordinary, very pleasant; he didn't look in the least ominous nor mysterious. But wouldn't the caped thing of last night, emerging into the light of day, take on just such ordinariness and innocence?

Besides this, there was that feeling that something about him had pried up part of a carapace, or shell—anyway, a piece of something that protected me, and this I didn't like. I decided to concentrate on Mr. Sutton's house.

As we walked toward it I noted that it was about half the size of Larchwood and had none of Larchwood's airy grace. It looked heavy, as if grown from the earth on which it stood. There were signs of the neglect John Sutton had mentioned, but in spite of this I found myself liking the place. It was a house that had endured much and had survived, had worn the years of neglect as best it could, a house that hadn't given up under adversity. There was a floor right at ground level, right on the earth with no steps leading up into it. This floor was fronted by a porch with pillars. The pillars were of wood, paint peeled off; and the porch floor had been ripped up in spots, as if John Sutton had been looking for dry rot or an infestation of bugs. The top of the porch made the floor of the veranda across the front of the house upstairs. The veranda railing was of ironwork, pitted with rust but of a graceful pattern of leaves and grapes, the kind of ironwork you associated with the Old Quarter of New Orleans. There seemed to be an attic in the hipped roof, since three dormers had been cut through. The middle dormer had broken panes. A stairway led from the ground to the second floor at the west end of the veranda.

"I'll show you my discovery later. It's not doubloons, I'm sorry to say. I want you to come upstairs first—that's where it looks best."

We went up, Rye first and I next, with John Sutton following. We had to avoid more building materials, two-by-fours in a neat block, sacks of cement under a plastic sheet, some bricks. The stairs showed signs of repair. The railing was new, had been sandpapered to a satin smoothness, now waited painting. The floor of the upper veranda was all new, fresh clean lumber, and the doors in the plastered wall were also new, also unpainted. John Sutton opened the first door and ushered us in. The room was spacious, almost square in shape. Here was new cream-colored plaster on walls and ceiling, a floor of beautiful old wood restored to gleaming warmth. The fireplace of native stone had fresh grout in the chinks. Windows of diamond-shaped panes let in the morning light.

I couldn't help myself; the room pleased and excited me, and I envied John Sutton heartily in that moment. He had something here that through his own planning and work was going to be magnificent.

But Rye said mockingly, "Don't hold it back, Pock. Tell him it's nice."

I don't know what I would have said to John Sutton in that moment of surprise and pleasure, if Rye had kept still. But her light mocking tone shut me into silence, as if she had turned a key in a lock. I didn't speak; I went over to one of the beautifully proportioned windows and looked through it at the view.

He was waiting for me to say *something,* though.

I wanted to say, "Angela's bound to love it, if she doesn't already," but this would have been presumptuous and crude, and he might have read something into it that I assured myself I didn't feel. Such as jealousy. I got out—finally— "I wish I'd found it first. And had the money to buy it."

"It didn't cost much." I could tell from his tone that he was pleased.

"Pock, you wouldn't have known what to do with it. And he does," Rye pointed out. To John Sutton she said, "How are you going to do the windows?"

"I don't know." He walked closer to me, frowning in perplexity. "I keep trying to see something there in the way of draperies— I don't want to turn this over to a professional. Sometimes, then, a room looks as if it had been worked out by a computer. I want . . . well, I just don't want it all of a piece. I want some discrepancies. I want it homelike."

I was puzzled, and for once spoke without thinking. "You have a bank job. And this is Friday. Do they just let you off whenever you wish?"

"They sure don't." His chin looked very obstinate. "But for today, I told them I had a personal appointment I couldn't miss. I didn't tell them it was important to me for you to see my house. I let them think whatever they wanted, just so they knew I wouldn't be in to work."

Rye looked heavenward as if to call angelic forces to the aid of poor John Sutton, who had at a single misfortunate stroke let me see how important I was to him, on such short acquaintance, a fatal mistake. Her lips even moved in mock-supplication, and I wanted to smack her as of old.

So of course, stumblingly, I had to give forth with some ideas about the draperies. I told John Sutton about some handwoven things I'd seen in New Mexico, made in an Indian village workshop. "You couldn't find them anywhere else, and they'd be perfect for this room. I can give you the address." Hateful Rye, prodding me into making a fool of myself.

He seemed grateful and interested, though, and after Rye had made a few more suggestions about the room, he took us back downstairs to the part of the house he lived in, a big room right beneath the refinished room upstairs. And here were to be found all of the wreckage and untidiness of bachelorhood. He gave us coffee, which was terrible, and we drank it sitting on rickety wooden chairs, and I could see that John Sutton used this room for everything. There was even a desk, old, full of papers, which I imagined to be estate-management materials. There was a wardrobe, its door open slightly to disclose John Sutton's supply of clothes, and a stove where he'd made the coffee, and a shelf from which apparently he ate, since there was a plate and fork abandoned there. There was a narrow bed in a corner, made up more crookedly than even I would have done, and I told myself in pity that here was the bachelor at his disorganized worst.

I remembered then, warily, what he said last night about our getting to know each other while I told him what to do about his house. Unfortunately, though my thoughts spun out many ideas, there was no way I could communicate them to Mr. Sutton. When he turned his brown-eyed, hopeful, and interested gaze on me, I froze, and my tongue stuck to the top of my mouth. So much for getting to know each other.

The uneasy idea occurred then that perhaps he was learning about me, even so, from my silences and my withdrawal.

This was the most disturbing thought of all.

Rye was arch and teasing with him, perhaps to make up for my spinsterish quiet. "Now you'll have to show us your doubloons. We promise not to tell anyone."

"I wish it could have been a secret cache." He took our cups and then led us down the broken porch (planks had been laid to make a path where he'd dug up the floor), and he held Rye's hand as if fearful she might tumble and present us with an emergency. He threw open the door of the last room, and we found ourselves in a long, narrow space that seemed to smell of stored potatoes, though it was completely empty now. Nothing had been done here except that some of the wall plaster, wet and fungus-spotted, had been torn off.

One of the braces in the wall, a short, mitered board, had painted lettering on it:

th Infantry *General Purcell*

A painted arrow pointed onward, actually upward from its position in the wall, from the end of the general's name.

"From a war," John Sutton told us. "A war that must have been right around here, like the one between the North and the South. All we ever had close were a few raiding skirmishes and burnings. Like Larchwood, it was burned then. But this piece of wood wouldn't have been brought too far. Perhaps from Vicksburg. They were all dug in there for a while."

"There's a story to it, all right," Rye agreed. And then, for my benefit, of course, she added, "Where are you from, originally?"

"Kansas." He looked wryly apologetic about Kansas.

"I knew you didn't speak with a local accent. Do you like Louisiana?"

"I like this particular part of Louisiana."

I had to say something, not stand like a graven image. "You said something last night about getting this place on its feet. What do you intend to raise here?"

"Oh, trees for woodpulp, of course. Like parts of your aunt's property. If I'm lucky someone will come along someday with a drilling rig and ask permission to drill for gas or oil, and find some. If I'm not lucky I'll try my hand at raising stock, I guess. Cattle or horses." He waited for me to say something in reply, something optimistic, hopeful, encouraging, no doubt.

But I pointed out—God knows why— "Meanwhile you have the bank. You dislike estate management, but it's paying for your house and it buys paint and lumber. It makes you lord of the castle, when you're home here."

"Pock," Rye said softly.

He glanced from her to me, and there was a brief, uncomfortable silence. I could have bitten my tongue. Pocket, the bristly child, had spoken in my stead. There was no way I could change what had been said.

"I'm not playing at anything," he said after a moment.

"Pock knows that." Rye wanted to make amends.

"And as for managing things," I rushed on, in the grip of the rising anger—or was it a kind of fear?—out of long ago, "what's so awful, so inept, about Aunt Wanda's account-keeping? Do you really have to make her miserable? Do you have to be so entirely critical?"

It caught him off guard. Rye, too; she turned a scolding glance on me. But this was really something I wanted to know, I wanted to have made clear, even though, being cornered in a situation I had no appetite for, I spoke out of tactlessness and bad temper.

John Sutton stood there for a moment as if he were running my words through his mind, a playback, not believing what he'd heard. "You've got the wrong idea. My job is just to help and advise. I have no permission to make a nuisance of myself."

"But Aunt Wanda's husband left a will, and you're in it."

He shook his head. "The bank is in it. The will specified that the bank should offer the services of someone to help manage things for a few years—in case she was left alone. If I were hard-nosed about anything, anything at all, she would only have to complain, and the affairs of Larchwood would be someone else's business, right away."

"But hasn't she—" The anger was gone; there was a strangeness here, an ambiguity, something that didn't ring true. "Doesn't she ever act toward you as if you were giving her a bad time?"

He hesitated. "The only thing—" Then he stopped. "I guess it isn't something I can talk about."

I wanted him to go on. "Aunt Wanda seems to carry her account books around with her, like the proverbial Ancient Mariner with his albatross. I think she's terribly afraid of doing something wrong, of making a mistake in the accounts, and that you'll disapprove."

He had taken on a puzzled, defensive look. "No, there's nothing like that. All she has to do is to keep a household budget, sort of. Balancing the allowance from the estate with what she spends on salaries, food, upkeep—" He looked at Rye as if seeking confirmation, as though she must know he was speaking the truth, but Rye had gone to the door as if ready to leave.

Her attitude, I knew, was in response to my tactless remarks to John Sutton.

"Do you have to countersign all of her checks?" I persisted.

"Of course not."

"I don't know what I'm trying to find out," I said, more to myself than to him.

"I'm afraid I can't help you." He was uneasy because I was prying into what was none of my business. And now he, in his own turn, changed the subject abruptly. "This is the room where I thought of putting the laundry equipment. What do you think of that?"

"You should draw a plan, to scale, of this lower part of the house," I told him, glad of the change to an impersonal subject. "Make measurements of what you mean to buy, and see where things would fit. And find out where pipes are, if there are any, or whether you have to put in all new plumbing."

He seemed thoughtful, looking at the wall he'd stripped. "Can't you come back again? After I get some of the furniture for upstairs? Or perhaps even sooner?"

Why did he persist in the face of my unbending indifference?

"Oh, sooner, of course," Rye assured him from the doorway. "Pock will have more ideas for you the second time around. She'll be over her strangeness."

Call it what you will, I thought—I'll never be over it. And for an instant an image flickered in my mind, the bronze woman from the portico in the dream, the bronze woman with the shield propped against her knee. Now where did that come from?

I hurried after Rye, and we left John Sutton looking after us as we drove away.

"There is a lie involved here," I told Rye when we were out of sight of John Sutton. "Aunt Wanda's trying to juggle things. Mr. Sutton against someone else. I can feel it."

"But it isn't our business," Rye pointed out. "And she won't want you poking and prying. Something has her on edge—but it's nothing to do with us."

"How do you know it has nothing to do with us?" I was remembering that moment when I'd turned, in the moonlit night, and found the unspeakable just behind me. Along with the shivers was a feeling of outrage.

Rye glanced at me uneasily, sensing the unspoken motive. "What are you going to do?"

"Commit burglary. Raid those desks."

"Pocket, she'll blow up. And I need you here. Please don't make it impossible for you to stay."

"You come in," I said doggedly, "when I do the burglar bit and I might need you to keep Aunt Wanda occupied for an hour or so. Like a trip to Moss Corner. No, that won't work—you'd have to go in the daytime, shopping or something, and that means the servants would be at home. It has to be in the evening. Where does Aunt Wanda go in the evenings?"

Rye shook her head. "Nowhere. Just absolutely nowhere."

"Civic affairs. Meetings. She's a taxpayer, a big landowner."

"Never."

"Mother and child Stryfe? Bart the Good?"

"Pock! But no, not there."

"They came and dined. Dined royally. Doesn't she dine back?"

"I haven't noticed. We went to tea once at the Stryfes'. I guess they just wouldn't attempt a full-scale dinner. Their place is small, and they have no help. The tea was nice, they made a nice spread for us. But there was just us four."

"Let's go sound them out," I insisted. "We meant to go there anyway. And maybe your dear Bart is home from New Orleans. There were lights in both houses last night."

Rye seemed thoughtful at this bit of knowledge. And then she said, "You've got to promise that you won't take any chances. We don't know much about this creepy creep who inhabits the cemetery. I don't want you poking around in the dark."

She couldn't see the icy feeling that seized me, nor the shudder I repressed. I pointed out, *"He* creeps in the dark."

"I don't want you meeting him there."

"I came to find out his identity. Or hers." And how successful were you last night, Miss Myles? There he was, and there you were. Alone together in the moonlit night. Why weren't you yanking off his mask?

What would have happened if I'd done so?

Something much worse might have happened to me than being stretched on Jim's grave with a poor dead toad on my bosom.

There will be a next time, I thought, with a flash of foresight. And how will I fare then?

"I'll be careful." And looking at the day, the blue Louisiana sky full of sun, a few little clouds as white as cotton, the green woods thick with birdsong, it was hard to hold to that memory of last night and the sense of fright that went with it.

"When I got here," I reminded Rye, "you were talking about Mr. Sutton as though he were a dragon. Do you feel any changes about anyone else?"

"When Mr. Sutton showed that he liked you, I discovered that I liked him."

"He doesn't like me, Rye. He wants help with his house."

She laughed, a brief yelp of scorn.

We turned into the road leading to the tenant houses, and then she said, "Pull up. Bart *is* home."

Bart was outside, working in his yard. He was using pruning shears on some shrubs. When he heard the car he turned, and I put on the brakes beside his gate. A smile lit up his face as he recognized Rye, and he hurried to greet us. "Miss Barbara! Good to see you!" He swung the gate wide. "You're looking swell. . . ." I was sizing him up all this while. He looked nothing at all like a college professor, as far as I was concerned. He had none of the bookish air, or touch of pedantic stuffiness, or absent-mindedness that make up the usual image. He could have passed for a farmer, a field hand, even a lumberjack; he was husky and had the quick movements, the elastic, hard-knit body you associate with men who work outdoors. Tanned, too. A well-shaped head set on a muscular neck. His graying hair, cut short, made me think of rusty-wheat stubble. His eyes were a direct, brilliant blue, and they gazed past Barbara at me with the impact of searchlights. His clothes were what you would wear to work in earth and roots, not as toilworn as those of John Sutton, but nearly.

Not a bumbling, peering professor at all.

Climbed trees and swam rivers with equal ease for exercise, probably. He looked perfectly capable of doing both. Rye had by now rolled down the car window, and he stood framed there with his tanned arms crossed on the edge of glass.

Rye said, "Bart, I want you to meet my sister. Pocket, this is Bart."

He reached in, across Rye's belly without embarrassment to shake my hand. "Glad to meet you at last. Rye told me all about you. Except what you looked like, and that's the surprise. She didn't do you justice."

I felt my face freeze, but at the same time I was noticing that there was something off-center about the intent gaze of those blue eyes; at first it seemed as if he were gazing directly at you; but then, after a moment, *not*. I sensed a wariness in him, in spite of the heartiness, the compliment. He was sizing me up as I had him. But he was doing it with tentacles of intuition. I felt that he was waiting for me to speak so that he could assess my voice, read something out of it.

"I'm very happy to meet you." I spoke without expression, I thought. If he expected to find emotion, some response to the male gusto, I hoped to disappoint him. But Rye caught the flat note too, naturally, and gave me a glance.

You're going to like Bart, the glance warned, and roused in me the proper response of guilt and regret.

Rye asked him, "How was New Orleans?"

"Good, as always. Hard to do everything you'd like to do, on a limited budget. Lucky for me, I have friends there and I could shack up with them. We went into town in the evenings and raised a little hell—as much as we could afford. Saw some shows and toured some bars in the French Quarter, and ate the kind of food you find only there. What's been going on here while I was gone, besides your sister's arriving?"

"A dinner. Last night. One of Aunt Wanda's productions." Rye made a mocking face at him.

"Come in and tell me about it." He opened the door beside her and helped her out, while I in turn let myself out on my side and tossed gloves and purse into the back seat.

Bart was saying, "You forget how good this part of the country smells until you get into a city. Fresh, free." He was leading the way toward his house. Though it was two-storied it wasn't really large. We had crossed the lawn and he had thrown open the front door, and there was displayed a front room that seemed comfortable but shabby. Nothing dramatic had been done in the way of furniture. I thought it seemed to be things he might have inherited from his parents. There were a lot of books across one wall, some bound magazines, a stereo outfit; and here at least one found the expected aura of study.

When we were seated, Bart offered cigarettes. I accepted; Rye turned him down. He asked if we cared for coffee or tea, and Rye decided that tea would be nice, perhaps to erase the memory of John Sutton's awful coffee. He went away and presently came back carrying a tray with a teapot, cups and saucers, napkins, spoons, cream and sugar—and even, for Rye, a tiny impromptu bouquet in a miniature vase. He moved lithely and easily, setting the tray before Rye so that she could pour for us, and for the first time I felt a sense of gratitude melting the icy withdrawal within me. He *was* nice. He had made a special effort to please my sister, making her feel special in the act of doing so. Rye admired the flowers before she began filling the cups.

In spite of the litheness and grace, he was completely masculine. He was a man who moved with an economy of effort, naturally without awkwardness. And surely this was nothing to be disparaged.

After Rye handed him his cup of tea he sat down and stretched his legs, crossed them at the ankles, and smiled at us. "Tell me about the dinner. Spare me no details. How were Mrs. Stryfe and Angela? I haven't seen them since I got back."

"If you were at home last night, you should have come to the house with them," Rye scolded.

"I was bushed. But thanks. You said it was a production. Did your aunt invite John? And did Angela—?"

Rye tried not to grin.

"If you think I don't know how Angela acts around John Sutton, you must think me blind. I take it she pounced, and kept him cornered? Which means that Mrs. Stryfe was on one of her political binges?"

"True," Rye admitted. "And Angela looked very pretty. She wants him. But I don't think he realizes it."

Bart laughed shortly. "John's no fool. He's got an innate courtesy, I'm afraid, and of course the bank wants all of its employees to give a good image. In the old days banks tried to look safe and stern, and now they want to be your bosom buddy. Time makes changes. But John won't be rude, which is what Angela damn well needs." He glanced surmisingly at me. "Are we disgusting you with our gossip? Are we being unkind? Tell us."

I decided that he was teasing me. "Angela had a hard time keeping Mr. Sutton under thumb last night. Or it seemed so, on the surface. Which puzzles me. They've known each other for a long time, haven't they? And how can he be so blind both to her appearance and her desire for him?"

Rye was pleased. I was actually making conversation with Bart. He was listening to me with a wry amusement.

"How do we know what John wants in a woman?" he asked. His eyes swept over me, and again I was aware of the intuitive appraisal. Bart searched below the surface; he listened for nuances, for hints of things unsaid. "As for the other question, yes, they've known each other for a long time. Perhaps that's part of the problem. Someone he's never seen before might make John sit up and take notice. Like you."

"Oh, he did," Rye put in, giving me a defiant flick of a glance. "We went to look at his house this morning. To give advice. He wanted Pocket to see what he was doing."

"As a surprise for Angela, no doubt," I corrected her stiffly. "The house, I mean. We were to advise, and she was to reap the . . . the results." I was stumbling, embarrassed; both Bart and Rye were enjoying my misery. But in Bart's eyes I thought I read sympathy, too, and inwardly I found myself responding with—Rye'd been right—liking and trust. "I have no right putting such an interpretation on things, of course."

"We see what we see," he said easily. He wasn't denying that the house might eventually be Angela's, by one way or another.

So why was I flinching over the thought?

"Has Angela ever held a job?" Rye asked, somewhat changing the subject.

"You think she's wasting her time here with her mother," Bart interpreted. "Well, Angela went to college for a while. Not in Louisiana. I don't know what she studied nor what she did with what she learned. She came home again, and that was it. Mrs. Stryfe—Tracy—was born here, you know. Born at Larchwood."

"How did that happen?" I found myself asking.

"Well, her father and Mr. Barrod's were cousins. That makes her a second cousin by marriage to your aunt, doesn't it? Or is it first cousin once removed? Anyway, around fifty years ago some disaster had befallen Mrs. Stryfe's family, her particular branch of the Barrods, and the relatives at Larchwood had taken them in. And she was born there. And she and your aunt's husband grew up for a few years, I guess, more like brother and sister than second cousins."

Rye said, "But then, wasn't she . . . shouldn't she have been an heir, when he died?"

Bart shrugged. "Well, the blood relationship wasn't very close."

"Would she have been an heir, though, if Mr. Barrod hadn't married Aunt Wanda?"

He thought about it, smiling slightly. "I suppose so. In the lack of any other heir, I guess she would have gotten it all."

Twelve

"You didn't know of this?" I demanded of Rye.

"No. I'd never heard of it at all."

"Does Aunt Wanda know?" I asked Bart.

"I should think so." He put his empty cup back upon the tray and gave me a quizzical smile, as though we shared some understanding. "It isn't important. What difference can it make?"

I wanted to say, Yes, this might be very important. But I couldn't pin down all of my ideas, my theories, even to myself. Aunt Wanda's game, whatever it was, was one of desperation, and it went deep. I remembered the moment in the belvedere when I'd turned to find her right behind me, hand outstretched; and I remembered the moment in her small office when it had seemed that the most urgent appeal for help and understanding had shone in her eyes. So which was truth? And in which had I misinterpreted?

Rye was suddenly sitting a little slumped, her eyes cheerless. "Pock, I guess I'm feeling kind of . . . of tired. I hate to break up our visit, we're having fun, but—"

Bart was on his feet, solicitous, worried. "Would you like a brandy? Or to lie down?"

I could see how exhausted Rye seemed—and why hadn't I been alert for any change, since she had complained to me that morning?—and how a sudden pallor had swept across her. I stood up, trying to show no alarm. "I'm going to run you into town to see Dr. Potterby."

Rye tried to manage a reassuring grin, but she didn't protest.

Bart wanted to drive us; he thought that Rye should be in the rear seat, half lying down, bolstered with pillows and wrapped up and with me in there beside her. He seemed genuinely concerned, worried. But Rye was firm, she didn't need coddling, we'd be fine. I drove as fast as I dared on the country roads. The day was still brilliant with sunlight, but now there was a nervous air to it as if the brightness was overdone and artificial, and distances twitched in the glare, and the roadside monotonously repeated itself so that you felt you weren't getting anywhere.

And why didn't I own a better car with smoother shock absorbers and a steadier motor?

I cried from nervous fright, trying not to let Rye see. Rye was pale and thoughtful, her arms holding her belly, holding her baby really, in a way that was both maternal and frightening. By the time we got to Moss Corner I was wet with sweat and could feel my eyes puffing.

The clinic office was neat, modern, cheerful. The nurse took Rye away immediately, shutting the door on the rear areas and leaving me in the waiting room. She paused long enough to explain that Mr. Linton had called to tell them Rye was coming. She called Rye *Mrs. Parrish.*

Well, now I knew Bart's last name. Linton. And my respect for him had increased; he had had sense enough to telephone ahead for us.

I waited in the small lobby for a while. This waiting area served three doctors, so there were people coming and going. After about an hour I went outside and walked around the block and smoked a cigarette. I could see the college buildings in the distance, a great enclave of old soft-red brick. A lot of big trees, shadows on the lawns, young people coming in and out of the buildings, pausing to talk, a world removed from that of the town, a world of study and learning and youthful hopes. I told myself, I won't believe that anything bad can happen to Rye. If the baby is born now, earlier than it was supposed to be, it will be all right. Premature babies get born every day and turn out all right.

Please God, don't let anything happen to my sister.

The tears came then and obliterated the street. I turned aside and pretended to be looking into a store window. Someone passed behind me, and I shuddered with fear because through the mist of tears the figure looked black in the reflection from the glass, and I wanted nothing black standing behind me. Every time the memory returned it was more frightening, more ominous, as though my subconscious recognized some new menace in it.

Inside the window were displayed rakes and shovels, and bags of lawn seed, an electric lawnmower, the means of looking after land if you owned any, and then suddenly I wished I could call John Sutton. But I couldn't. I could call Aunt Wanda, but from what

Rye had told me this was a day Aunt Wanda wouldn't be available; she was raging at the maids and presently she would lock herself into her room. Perhaps to drink . . .

Whatever had seized her, it seemed, must run its course. I wouldn't call my aunt unless things got very desperate here.

I returned to the doctor's office, and the nurse noticed me through the window to her inner office and came out to tell me that Rye would be a little while longer, the doctor wanted to have some tests made, and I was not to worry.

So I worried.

I got to feeling hollow and realized that it was past noon. I had no desire to eat anything, though. The smell in the office took away my appetite. It smelled of antiseptic and made you think of operations and of being sick. It made you think of when you were fifteen years old and had to have your appendix out, a thoroughly scary affair.

One of the doctors was a pediatrician, and a little boy came in with his mother; she had him sucking a lollipop to keep him distracted, and he came out ten minutes later howling with rage and hurt, his mother rubbing his behind where he'd had his shot. A small blond girl who was waiting with her mother—the mother was reading a magazine—walked over to me and leaned on my chair and informed me that she was going to have her tonsils out. It would be fun and when she was through, if she had been good, her mother was going to give her a party. It wasn't even going to be her birthday, either.

"Eat a chunk of cake for me," I told her.

"There won't be a cake. It's not my birthday. We're going to have hot dogs and soup."

"Good luck."

Rye came out at last, speaking to the nurse in passing. She was still pale, but intact, and the look of fear was gone. "Oh, Pock, I'm sorry you had this long wait. It must have been boring for you."

"I'm so glad to see you in one piece—and I mean that literally—that I don't regret one minute of it."

Rye smiled gratefully and touched my hand. "Dr. Potterby says I have to rest. Lie in bed. Flake out. Meals brought, all that stupidity. He consented to let me go to the bathroom on my own, but only on condition of perfect behavior otherwise. And no excitement. Or he'll put me in the hospital. Oh, damn."

"It won't be too bad." At least it might take Rye's mind off the things that had been done to Jim's grave. She'd be thinking about her baby. I hoped.

I left the car in the porte-cochere and we walked in at the side of the house and down the hall to the spot where the two halls intersected. Down the hall toward the kitchen entrance I could see the three maids and Mrs. Mim, silhouetted there in a knot, and something spoke strongly of trouble. "Rye, go upstairs and get into bed. I'm going to rustle up a sandwich and some tea for you, and a tray with ice water and such for beside your bed, so you'll look properly taken care of."

Rye took a long look at the four women in the distance. She must have sensed the air of indecision and worry. "I wonder if Aunt Wanda's all right. Or if—"

"You are not to fret about our dear aunt. And if she is drunk and for any reason decides to roam, I'll see that she doesn't annoy you."

"It's not like that, Pock. She might need help."

"Not your business. Go."

I decided to go with her upstairs and make sure that her room was not occupied by an out-of-sorts Aunt Wanda. We found everything vacant, orderly, and peaceful. I left Rye getting ready for bed and hurried back downstairs. For once I felt my shyness, my reluctance to contact others, disappearing— I knew that something was seriously awry.

They were still there at the end of the hall. They watched me guardedly as I approached, caution in their dark faces. But Mrs. Mim took it upon herself to be spokeswoman. "It's Perkins, Miss Myles. He's disappeared. We've looked all over. The girls want to go home, and it's his job to take them."

"They're leaving so early?"

"Because of Mrs. Barrod, miss. She told them to leave. Sometimes she does this, when she's . . . when she's not feeling well. Sometimes not. We never know."

I couldn't see any reason for beating around the bush. "Has it been bad today?"

After a moment's hesitation, Mrs. Mim answered, "Yes, very bad. About the worst we've had. To be frank, we've been standing here talking about quitting. The things Mrs. Barrod said to us today—" She shook her head and seemed embarrassed, not looking at the others.

"Things she said ain't true." The small one, the one I had no name for, had spoken. "I can work in town if I got to do maid's work. And no bad names. Jes' because we're black . . ."

But Mrs. Mim objected to this angle. "No, Pearl, don't think that. Mrs. Barrod never laid anything on us because of color. It's just that she has these bad days. And not very often." She seemed to be apologizing to me for my aunt's behavior, excusing it to Pearl. "It must be nerves. A kind of strain. She's not used to the burden of running the big house and the lands, all that she had to take over when Mr. Barrod died."

"Still and all," Martha said, "we're doing her no favor when we let her talk to us like that. I want to see Perkins. Let him tell her we won't take it any more."

"None of us has seen Perkins for over an hour," Mrs. Mim said to me, "and it's not like him to hide out. The rest of us do, when things get too rough. But he never did. Until today."

"Did she say something particularly bad to him?"

"No, not that I heard. Mostly she takes it all out on us, on me and Martha and Lydia and Pearl. Perkins never got upset with her. It seemed he might have understood some reason for the way she acted. I mean, a deeper reason."

"Where is my aunt now?"

"In her bedroom. After a while she goes there and locks herself in, and we won't see any sign of her until tomorrow. Tomorrow afternoon."

"Perhaps she sent Perkins on an errand. I'll go up and speak to her."

"I don't think she'll answer your knock." Mrs. Mim's tone was more than ever conciliatory. "I made the mistake once—it wasn't too long after Mr. Barrod had died, I think it must have been the first time that she acted . . . uh . . . cross with us all. And she made me wish I hadn't disturbed her."

"I'm going to try, anyway. Meanwhile, I wonder if you'd get some lunch ready for my sister. She's had nothing since breakfast, and the doctor has ordered her to stay in bed." I outlined briefly to Mrs. Mim what had happened and what Dr. Potterby had laid down as law. Then I went back upstairs.

There is no use pretending that before Aunt Wanda's door I didn't hesitate, my courage wilting. The memories of childhood are long ones, the humiliations and rebuffs still full of hurt beneath the scars. More than that, some of what she had done had been inexplicable—perhaps these things had left the deepest scars of all. But I forced myself to lift a hand and to knock.

Nothing happened.

Unreasonably and suddenly angry, I pounded. How dare she hide herself away to drink after offending those people downstairs?

I even shook the doorknob.

"Who is it?" Muffled and slurred, the voice was close to the door, and then there was a bump on the panel as if Aunt Wanda had tottered against it.

"I want to talk to you."

"C . . . can't. Can't ri' now. Please go 'way—"

"Open the door."

There was silence. I wanted to kick the door, batter it, but this would make a racket that could rouse Rye, alarm her, worry her. "Come back and open up!" I demanded, my mouth against the doorframe.

Finally there was the reluctant sound of a turning key and the door drew inward—an inch. Aunt Wanda peered at me, a single eye obscured by falling hair.

Rye had been right. The smell of liquor stole out.

"Perkins has disappeared. He hasn't taken the maids home."

The eye blinked. A hand, out of sight, pulled back the hair. "I don't know . . ." Aunt Wanda drew in a deep breath, and weaved for an instant so that her face passed across the narrow opening and I saw the flushed skin, the unsteady mouth, a trickle of what might have been tears. "So, let them stay. Stay here."

"We want to know where Perkins is. Did you send him on an errand?"

"No."

"Aunt Wanda—" I started to touch her hand, where it held the door, but her hand slipped away. "Will you listen to me? Rye is ill. She could have a miscarriage if she doesn't rest, if she doesn't have absolute quiet. Please don't get yourself into such a state that you might disturb her. Please try to remember—"

Aunt Wanda straightened, her eye narrowing. There was a definite pulling together of self, a putting on of composure and angry dignity, almost an effect of sudden sobriety. She wiped the tears, if that's what they were, from her face. Her eyes bored into mine. "I would never do anything to hurt Barbara. Not at any time. No matter how dr—" She adjusted the opening to its former narrow width. "—how disturbed I might be. Of all the people on this earth—" The single eye seemed to burn with scorn. "You might not see that. You might not understand. Orphan that you are."

Orphan . . .

The door shut; I had no desire to see it open again.

Thirteen

FAMILY, I said to myself. *Family* . . .

Why had they pretended to give me a *family?*

I was the oddball, the unloved and unlovable one. I didn't even look like the rest of them, the way Rye did.

I was forever outside, the one they'd taken in who didn't really belong. The stray. Rescued from the orphanage. Where I'd been dropped off by that unknown woman.

I stood at the head of the stairs, the beautiful stairs of Larchwood, and thought: Unknown Woman, my mother, why didn't you want me and keep me? Was I such a burden, an embarrassment, that I had to be gotten rid of right away? Small as I was? Couldn't you have kept me for even a day longer?

I had to have been somewhere else for a while, before that day when I'd sat in the office facing the woman with the biscuit of hair on her head. I had to have lived somewhere else, up until then.

Had I lived in the orphanage?

If there, why aren't there memories of the life in the place, the day-to-day doings, the routine? The other children? Why does time seem to begin in the hallway with the woman in the uniform and the matron's cap, kneeling to tuck up my socks and to straighten my dress, and whose face I cannot remember? What came before that?

Where was I until then?

There's a whole lot missing, there's something crooked and obscure and cockeyed about my nightmare memories. I can sense it without pinning it down.

I went back downstairs to Mrs. Mim and the maids, trying not to show any signs of upset. Mrs. Mim was preparing a tray. I told her that if Martha and Lydia and Pearl wanted me to, I could run them into town.

But Mrs. Mim said, "His car is out there. What about that?"

"I don't know what we can do about it. The car will have to sit there until Perkins comes back for it." I looked at the maids. "Do you want to wait for him? Is that it?"

They were unanimous in not wanting to wait.

We went out to my car, and from the porte-cochere I could see Perkins' station wagon out beside the garages. And I remembered then how engrossed he had been early that day with the marks on the verge of the drive. I told the maids to wait a minute, and walked off. When I got to the car it was empty, and when I looked into the garages by way of a small side door, there was nothing in there but Aunt Wanda's big sedan. I walked around briefly and examined the terrain—there were several big magnolia trees, some well-trimmed shrubs, and the lawns, and in the close distance the massed forest, but of Perkins no sign at all. I returned to my car.

I drove back to Moss Corner and delivered the maids to their various homes. Martha was the last, and I thought to ask her, "Is there a trail or path leading from anywhere near the garages?"

She had one foot on the ground. She turned her dark face back to look at me. "Yes, miss."

"Where does it go?"

"Off into the woods. I've never explored it, but that's what I've heard."

"And comes out where?"

"Those other houses, I think. The tenant houses. In the old days it must have been a track the overseers used, coming to the house in the morning to see about the work to be done that day; least, that's what somebody told me once. But I don't remember who."

"Have you been at Larchwood longer than the others, Martha?"

"No, miss."

I made a guess. "Perkins has been there the longest?"

"Longer'n anybody. Sometimes he acts like—" She gave a short laugh. "—like he kind of owns the place, like he's responsible for it. Thanks for bringing me home."

"You're welcome."

Mrs. Mim was in the kitchen. The tray was gone, so presumably it had been carried up to Rye.

"Would Perkins have taken the track that leads off into the woods?"

Mrs. Mim frowned. She was polishing the tiles of the long sink counter, a keeping-busy job, I decided, feeling she ought to be in evidence when I came home since my sister was ill. "No, I hardly think so. Why would he? Unless Mrs. Barrod sent him—"

"She says she sent him on no errand."

"We looked all over. He's not in the house."

"He's not at the garages."

"Then there's nothing we can do."

"I want to go into the woods, just in case. Will you show me where the trail starts?"

She paused with the cloth in her hand and for a moment her eyes seemed worried, and I thought she was going to advise me not to go. But then she said, "I'll send Cindy with you. I'll make it very plain, and perhaps you will too, that's she's never to go in the woods alone. Just this once, she'll guide you."

"No, all she has to do is to show me the beginning of the path."

"I want her to go with you, as far as you want to go."

Cindy was solemn as we set out, her hand in mine, small mouth pursed in thought, perhaps over Mrs. Mim's strict warning. After we had passed the garages, she tugged free and ran to pick a flower, a yellow daisy that had grown up through the grass. "I think you'd better stay with me on the path," I told her, trying not to sound stiff and disapproving.

"I know." She held out the flower. "I picked it for you."

"Thank you." The stem was narrow and prickly between my fingers.

"If we meet a wolf in there, I'll scream and you hit him with something. Then the good woodcutter will come."

I remembered that I'd left my purse in my car. Well, there was little to tempt anyone, a comfort there at least. "Is there a good woodcutter around?"

"*Always* is. Wears green clothes, a pointy hat. I saw his picture. He has whiskers. Carries an ax. He chopped the wolf all *up!*"

Cindy looked into the forest with confidence. Once into the trees the afternoon light was dimmed, shaded green and gray, and the sounds of birds became hushed, almost secretive. The path was easy to follow; it looked as though it had been used for so many years that all seedlings, all possible new growth, had been pounded away. Or perhaps someone used it still. . . .

"There's a witch's house in the woods, too," Cindy told me. "We have to be careful not to find *that*. She puts you in an oven."

"I wouldn't like that."

"With your clothes on. She'd have a hard time with you." Cindy appraised me frankly. "But me, I'd fit in fine. Are you really Miss Barbara's sister?"

"Yes."

"You don't look a bit like her."

From a child it didn't sound so bad. Or I'm used to it, I told myself. I've come around. I've adjusted.

"You're lots prettier," Cindy said shyly.

"I'm afraid not, but thank you anyway." I was watching the path ahead. It was more or less straight for about a hundred feet, and then there must be a turn because it seemed to disappear into a wall of trees and underbrush. A spangle of light seemed to lie on the path at the very end, speckled with dark. White *white,* spotted with red. I came to a full stop, holding Cindy's shoulder. "Wait here."

"What do you see? Is it the wolf?"

"No. But it's something I want to look at." I turned Cindy so that she faced the way we had come. "Will you stay right here?"

"Shall I get ready to scream?"

"If you want. But don't scream until I tell you." I bent to look into the mischievous, dancing eyes. "Cindy, this is very serious. Do you know what *serious* means?"

"Yes. It's when you get spanked, sometimes."

"You must wait right here until I get back."

"All right."

The thing I had glimpsed far ahead at the end of the path, or rather where the path turned, was a man's handkerchief. The stains on it looked like blood, and the handkerchief was spread to cover Perkins' face. He lay on his back, oddly crumpled. The front of his coat was dusty as though he might have fallen face down, then turned over.

I was aware of a roaring sense of fear. The fear dried my mouth and plucked at my pulse. My heart gave a great painful thud. I wanted to run, to run out of the woods into the safety of the sunlight and the sight of Larchwood. Instead I leaned against a tree, and the other trees appeared to twist and shake, and something overhead, a mingle of branches and sky, revolved briefly. Then I got hold of myself.

No more flutters, I commanded myself. No silliness.

I forced myself to kneel and to pull aside the handkerchief and to put the back of my hand gently against Perkins' bloody face.

Almost more of a shock than finding him here was the feeling of warmth from his flesh, when I'd expected the cooling of death. I reached for his wrist. Inside the neat white cuff there beat a slow and almost indistinguishable thread of life.

I got up quickly and went back to Cindy.

"You must hurry back to your mother. You will tell her that we found Perkins and that he must have a doctor. A doctor and an ambulance."

Cindy wanted to turn around, to look, but I held her firmly by the shoulders.

"Can you remember all that?"

Cindy nodded. "We found Perkins. He needs a doctor and a . . . a . . ."

"Ambulance."

"Am . . . Ambl— What's that?"

"A big car to take Perkins to the hospital."

"Is he hurt? Did the wolf get him?"

"He's hurt. But don't tell your mother a wolf got him. Just say that he needs the doctor, and to call for an ambulance. A big car that—"

"I know," she promised, "I'll remember." She touched my hand in a gentle way of reassurance, and skipped off through the trees.

I went back to stand guard beside Perkins. I thought I ought to do something useful, loosen his tie if nothing more; but the shirt collar, when I looked closely, was not tight around his throat. Whatever I did might be the wrong thing, might injure him further. I was wearing no coat and so couldn't take it off to roll for a pillow, and perhaps this too was for the best. All I could do was to wait.

After a while I was aware of a prickling sensation of being watched, that a third person stood looking at us. Was it the same feeling I had experienced just before turning to look behind me in the cemetery? Or not? Or was it just imagination now? The "touch" of eyes was a myth; your eyes received light rays, they didn't *reach*. No more than a radio reached to touch the transmitter of the station it was tuned to. So I told myself, and rubbed away a shiver that started up my arms. But the ugly feeling remained. It was hard not to look around, not to wear a listening expression.

If that black-hooded thing comes out of the trees, I thought, I won't do any better than last time. My legs won't take me far. I'm such a coward.

Was my shyness, my inability to meet anyone new on an easy basis, a part of that same cowardice?

This idea was so disturbing that I tried to distract myself by making a visual examination of Perkins' injuries. His face was terribly bloodied but didn't, as far as I could see, bear any open wounds. The wounds seemed to be in the head, in the hair and at the back. A large bloodstain had dried in the earth at the base of his skull. His graying hair was thickly clotted. It occurred to me that the blood on his face had run from the head wounds and that he must at first have lain face-downward.

It would seem then that he had been struck viciously from behind, had fallen to bleed while lying on his face, had been turned over after a while, dusted off a bit, and his face covered with his handkerchief. The handkerchief had been first used to mop off some of the fresh blood. It seemed a sick thing to do, and didn't make sense.

To start with, what could have brought Perkins *here?*

His place and his job had been strictly at the house. He kept Larchwood going, and if there were no longer overseers for the field hands, Perkins was still an overseer in the house. He performed the function of seeing that everything meshed, ran smoothly and graciously. So what had he been doing so far into the woods?

He was no longer young, but he was far too able and husky a man to have been dragged here. He had come into the woods for some reason—if not on an errand for Aunt Wanda, then on one of his own—and had been struck down. Curiosity might have brought him, and the only thing I had seen him being curious about were those marks on the verge of the driveway. Those marks in the grass had seemed to puzzle and anger him. But on the surface they'd seem to have nothing to do with this old path in the woods.

Shivering, I moved closer to Perkins, and kneeling, I picked up his hand to search again for the pulse. The pulse was still there, but barely. "Hurry, hurry," I whispered, in my mind speaking to Mrs. Mim, the doctor, the driver of the ambulance. Perkins' half-shut eyes looked at nothing, there was no visible sign of breathing, though he clung to life. I knew that he slept a sleep that could easily lapse into death.

And still, as I knelt, I sensed that someone watched.

Time went by.

Had I done the right thing, sending Cindy? Was the child reliable enough to go straight to her mother and not to garble what I had told her to say, not to bring in the witch's house and the good woodcutter, and to make Mrs. Mim think she might have been sent back because of her chatter?

What else could I have done? Someone had had to stay with Perkins. Hadn't they?

Did the handkerchief spread on his face mean that his attacker presumed him dead? And so wouldn't come back?

I couldn't be sure of that, I told myself.

And then, in one strange moment, it seemed that the watcher left, that the unseen one removed himself. It was as if something clammy evaporated from the air. I was alone with Perkins, truly alone there in the forest with the unconscious man. Then, in the next instant, I heard running steps from the direction I had come.

Mrs. Mim burst into view.

I stifled a cry of disappointment. Mrs. Mim hadn't believed Cindy's story. She'd come to see for herself. And meanwhile—*not* calling the doctor, nor the ambulance.

Mrs. Mim ran toward me and now I could see how the woods had filled with twilight, because no speckle of light fell on her. I could see her eyes, gleaming with fear, and then her voice, choked, crying, "Miss Myles, you must go back to the house and let me wait here. Your sister must have heard Cindy crying out, calling from the edge of the woods—"

"Have you sent for help?"

"Yes. The doctor, an ambulance. I was going to wait at the house to show them the way here, but then Miss Barbara came down, and she's going to worry—please go to her! I'll stay with him." She rushed past me to fall beside Perkins, to reach a shaking hand to touch his face.

Was this the right thing, going now, I wondered in sudden suspicion. Should I leave Perkins with Mrs. Mim? Was she being honest and considerate in relieving me here, and was Rye really wandering the house, upset, and most of all—would Perkins be safe here with Mrs. Mim?

I hated the suspicion that filled my mind. But one thing must be true. There was someone in the house who worked with the creep. Someone had to ruin the wine, someone who had access, if only briefly, to the decanter—I remembered with strange clarity the sight of Perkins bending toward Aunt Wanda with the new bottle, and now I realized how outraged he had been. He had been furious at the tasteless desecration, the threat to the smooth progress of the meal.

To Perkins, I thought, somehow those tire marks on the verge of the drive had been of a piece with what had been done to the wine. This morning when I'd come upon him outdoors he had been angry again, and in the same way.

As if wondering at my hesitation, Mrs. Mim turned to look up at me. There were tears on her face; she looked sick. "Please tell Cindy to stay in our rooms. She isn't to come out at all. And when the doctor and the ambulance get here, you don't have to leave Miss Barbara. Just point out to them where the path begins."

I bent worriedly toward Perkins. "How do you think he is?"

She brushed at the tears and shook her head. The grief seemed genuine enough, and so I hurried away, leaving Perkins with her.

Cindy came at my knock on Mrs. Mim's door, carrying a doll, and promised to stay put until her mother came back. I ran on upstairs. Utter quiet lay here, though I listened for some sound from Aunt Wanda. Rye was in bed, propped up with four or five fat pillows, a magazine on the bed with its pages tossed. She hunched her knees higher when I came in and demanded, "What's the rumpus all about?"

"Perkins has been hurt. In the woods. Cindy and I found him; I sent Cindy for help." There was no way I could keep this from Rye. The doctor and ambulance were on their way, she'd hear something of their arrival.

"Is he hurt badly?"

"I couldn't tell. He's not conscious."

She was looking very frightened now. "How was he hurt?"

"I think someone struck him down from behind." I eased out a pillow, then another. Rye was frowning up at me. "But it's just a guess."

"Who would do a thing like that?"

I met her eyes, I wanted to say, *Who would desecrate Jim's grave as they have? Who's terribly sick in the head around here? And what's wrong with our dear aunt?* But what I had to do was to smooth things over—Aunt Wanda's technique, I thought—and so I said, "Perhaps the police will find out."

"What made you go looking for him?"

"The maids told me he was missing. His car was still here. I took them all home to Moss Corner—Aunt Wanda had dismissed them for the day after what must have been a very ugly chewing-out. When

I got back and Perkins was still not around I thought someone should look for him, and the only place I could think of was the woods. Rye, I'm sure your doctor meant for you to lie flat and not all propped up like this. You might as well be in a chair." I got out all the rest of the pillows, though she hung on desperately to the last of them. "If you won't behave, if you go running around the house as Mrs. Mim said you were, I'm going to call him. I mean it."

"But, Pock—"

"There's someone pretty important depending on you," I reminded sternly.

"Yes, Great Earth Mother," Rye said rebelliously.

"I'm not trying to be mean or bossy. I am your sister and I want you to do what your doctor told you to do. I don't crave any more hours of waiting in Dr. Potterby's office, the kind of hours I spent today." I straightened the bedcovers somewhat and checked the bedside array: The luncheon tray had been removed and there was an insulated jug of ice water, a clean glass and a spoon, several small immaculate linen napkins, and even a tiny bouquet in a silver holder.

Rye tried to sound repentant. "I know, you're trying to be the patient big sister. But I have the feeling this is going to be as boring as hell, lying here."

I tried to think of something to say about the boredom, and could only admit the truth of what she said, and went out with a promise to be back soon.

A car had pulled up beyond the side entry, and a short, gray-haired man with a ruddy face was getting out, carrying what must be a doctor's bag. He looked well-seasoned and experienced, and when I approached him he introduced himself as Dr. Gilbert. I led him out toward the woods, showed him where the path began, and let him go on alone. I had to wait for the ambulance.

The wait seemed long, but at last it came, a long blue-and-white machine with two uniformed attendants in the cab. The driver, once he understood where Perkins was located, maneuvered his car backward as close as he could get to the trees, and then, working together in an efficient, businesslike way, the two men opened the rear doors and took out a wheeled stretcher, checked supplies, and were off in the direction I had indicated.

The afternoon had taken on a misty quality, the sky darkening as the sun sank lower, and the bank of woods looked almost black and as if indeed it could hold the creatures of Cindy's fantasies, the wolves and the woodcutter, the witch with her oven; my mind seemed wrapped with cobwebs. I didn't want to believe that what had happened here could be the truth.

But now came a third car headed my way, a sheriff's cruiser, and it braked and a tall young officer got out. I recognized him at once. Our friend of the cemetery.

"The ambulance passed me, and I thought of Mrs. Parrish."

"The ambulance didn't come for my sister. It's Perkins. Do you know him?"

"I know who he is."

I rubbed my head tiredly, aware of a mistake. "I should have called the police before now. I just didn't think. Not until I saw you. But perhaps you'd better go to see what happened to Perkins in there." I gave him a quick sketch of my search, and what I had found. Chris Warne thanked me and started off at once.

Fourteen

LYING ON HER SIDE, watching the door, Rye cried, "What's been happening?"

"The doctor came, a Dr. Gilbert. And the ambulance. And our friend Chris Warne of the parish sheriff's office."

"I'm glad he's here. He'll know what to do."

"He came because he saw the ambulance, and thought of you."

She was obviously pleased. "Nice of him. But aren't you going to stay down there and find out how Perkins is? And what they think about how he got hurt?"

I sat down on the side of the bed. "I'll go back in a minute."

"You think I'm prowling when you're not here."

I shrugged, trying to seem unconcerned. "Mrs. Mim did say you'd gotten out of bed."

"Just once. I heard Cindy yelling. I'm not made of stone. I thought she might have been scared, or hurt. Look, Pock, if you'll go back and garner the news, I promise to behave. I'll be the perfect little old invalid. Only come back and tell me what's going on. It's awful to be stranded like this."

"Can I trust you?"

"Cross my heart!"

"I don't make the rules." I stood and retucked the bed, checked the bedside water supply, and turned on a couple of lamps to dispel the grayness of twilight.

"Nurse Pock on duty," Rye jeered, but her eyes were not mocking, and I knew that she was glad to have me here. It was a warm, comforting knowledge after Aunt Wanda's bitter thrust.

I picked up Rye's hand. "Be good."

"Pock, I'll have to have dinner up here on a tray. Please eat with me."

"I was going to." I suddenly remembered I'd had no lunch.

"Do I sound terribly spoiled little-sisterly?"

"You sound fine."

I went downstairs and outside at the rear of the house. The ambulance was pulling away, turning gingerly at the edge of the gravel, its lights on though daylight was not quite gone, one man driving and the other in the stretcher compartment, bent over Perkins, of whom nothing was visible but a long wrapped shape.

Dr. Gilbert, Mrs. Mim, and the young trooper were at the doctor's car. Dr. Gilbert had his car door open and was obviously going to follow the ambulance into town. Chris Warne was making notes in a small book. Before I reached them the doctor got into his car, shut the door, and started away; the other two turned toward me, and I could see that Mrs. Mim was crying.

When they came close Chris Warne said, "He's been badly hurt. I need to ask a few questions about your finding him. I wanted to look around there in the woods, but it's getting dark and I could run right over something important and not even see it."

"We can talk inside, if you'd like."

We waited, unspoken between us our unwillingness to go on in and leave Mrs. Mim alone with her grief. After a few moments she dried her eyes with a handkerchief from her pocket and began to walk slowly toward the rear door. I wished I could have taken her hand, touched her, given her a sense of my own sympathy, but the tormenting shyness was back, the fear of rebuff. I felt awkward, too, with Chris Warne walking beside me down the hall to the parlor. I fussed there, turning on lamps and closing the French doors to the veranda. He took a chair and waited quietly for me to join him.

At last, unwillingly, I sat down to face him. Now that the shock of discovering Perkins was over, the feeling that I had to rise to an emergency was gone, I was my old self again. The self I hated. When Chris Warne asked about Rye I stumbled around, explaining the rules Dr. Potterby had laid down for her.

He nodded. "Well, she'll be getting rest and quiet, and in a way it's a good thing, she can't be running to the cemetery to see if some new depredation has been done there. It's a hateful situation, and one that we don't have the manpower to cope with, providing the sheriff was willing to put anyone to stand guard."

"No, we couldn't expect that."

I wanted to tell him of my own experience there, but my throat closed at the thought. I'd looked behind me at a . . . a what? A phantom? Something made of shadows and fright? Later I had awakened on Jim's grave. The ghostly sense of menace almost opened my mouth then, but not quite. Chris Warne, seated there in the parlor of Larchwood, was too solid and too normal a being for me to start spinning a tale of a tall black thing in the moonlight.

"Well," he said, "I keep as much watch as I can. I haven't found any new signs of tampering. Before we start talking about Perkins—is your aunt at home? Perhaps she could join us."

He'd noticed Aunt Wanda's absence during the excitement, then.

"My aunt is . . . uh . . . not feeling well." I avoided his eyes. "She doesn't know anything of what's happened. She's been in her room all afternoon." He was looking more and more mystified, and so I added in desperation, "It's a kind of . . . of migraine. Very painful and disabling." Liar.

"Oh. I see." His expression indicated that he didn't see at all. The mainstay of this establishment had been struck down in a mysterious attack, and the owner didn't even know it. "Well, perhaps you can tell me about finding Perkins."

I tried to collect my thoughts, make a coherent statement. I managed to tell him about coming home from town with Rye, finding the maids waiting for Perkins—carefully avoiding the subject of their being dismissed early—and my own feeling of being at a loss over his disappearance. "As short a time as I've been here, I could see how dependable he was, how he assumed the responsibility for running this house, and how much my aunt left in his hands. So, his being gone didn't make sense—"

The young officer was nodding in agreement. "He's been here for years, must know the place inside out. Mr. Barrod coaxed him to come here from New Orleans. As I understand it, Perkins was working at a big hotel there. Then Mr. Barrod inherited Larchwood from his father, and found the house and grounds kind of rundown. This is what I hear from the old-timers, you understand. Mr. Barrod went looking for someone to take over and get the place into shape, and Perkins was the one he picked."

"A good choice," I managed to get out.

"Mrs. Mim told me that you took the maids to town and then came back and went looking for Perkins. Why did you decide to go into the woods?"

"There didn't seem to be any other place to look for him. I knew there was a path through the woods toward the rented houses and on to the cemetery, because Rye told me she went that way sometimes."

"You had Mrs. Mim's little girl along, I understand."

There was no way out; I had to sit still and get through the explanations as best I could. I hoped that he could not sense my foolish cringing and desire to withdraw, that he would not misinterpret my stammering, my hesitations, as something guilty. "It was Mrs. Mim's idea. She must have thought that without Cindy I might get lost in the woods."

"When you found Perkins—"

"There is something I'd better explain. When I saw him lying in the path, he had a handkerchief covering his face. It was badly stained with blood, as though it might have been used to try to wipe away or stanch the bleeding. Anyway, his face was covered by this handkerchief as if . . . as if he were dead."

"You removed it?"

"Oh, yes. I had to know if he were still alive. I know one is not supposed to touch anything, change anything—"

"Well, what became of the handkerchief?"

I gazed at him blankly. "I don't know. Mrs. Mim came. She thought I should come back to the house, to reassure Rye, to show the doctor and the ambulance where to go, while she stayed with Perkins. As far as I know the handkerchief was pulled down from Perkins' face, was folded or crumpled there on his chest—"

"I'll check with Mrs. Mim about it."

"Perkins didn't speak, didn't move, while I waited there with him. There really isn't anything else I can tell you."

Chris Warne must have sensed at last my desire to get away. He rose politely. "I'll go and talk to Mrs. Mim now. If anything occurs to you, anything you remember that you think I might want to know, I'll be around for a while."

"Thank you."

He left, and for some moments I sat there in the midst of silence, with only the presence of General Lee in his great portrait above the mantel to keep me company. The kind of company, I told myself, in which I found comfort—a painted figure without life, without speech. Without the power to hurt . . .

I went back upstairs to Rye, who demanded to know all of the news. In telling her what I knew, I tried to sound commonplace and noncommittal, calm, disinterested. She gave me suspicious looks, as if I were guilty of hiding things from her.

"When you're hungry, I'll fix a dinner for us and bring it up," I finished, getting off on something new.

"I'm hungry now. Mrs. Mim made me a very dainty lunch, but she must have been afraid I'd overeat and get indigestion or something. Please don't fix a silly invalid's tray with teensy portions and linen doodads and a bouquet. I need *food.*"

"I'll bring something enormous," I promised, half exasperated.

"Has that officer been to Jim's grave?"

"Yes. And you are not to worry about that."

Rye looked thoughtful. "He's a nice guy, isn't he?"

"Yes." And thank you, I added to myself, for not trying your matchmaking powers on the cop and me. I tidied up the room a bit, to the tune of more remarks from Rye, and went back downstairs. Chris Warne was in the hall, as if he might have been looking for me.

"Mrs. Mim can't remember what happened to the handkerchief, nor whether she even saw it on Perkins at all. I'll look for it in the woods tomorrow. Of course, if Perkins regains consciousness, no search will have to be made. He may have seen whoever it was who attacked him. Or I hope so." He smiled at me; his big fingers tapped the cap he held. "There's not much we can do until daylight. On my way out of here I'll stop at Linton's house, and at Mrs. Stryfe's, and ask if they noticed anything, anyone running out of the woods, or acting suspiciously."

I had to manage somehow to say what I had seen. "It seemed to me that Perkins had been struck from behind, that he had fallen forward, that blood had run down his face in that position, before he was turned over as I found him."

He gazed at me for a long minute, thinking about what I had said, perhaps wondering why I hadn't told him everything during our previous talk. Then he said, "The doctor will settle all of that. Don't bother seeing me to the door, I'll let myself out. And give my best wishes to your sister."

"Thank you."

In the kitchen, Mrs. Mim was peering into the oven, and Cindy was cracking pecans at the counter. I said, "Is there any use trying to take something to my aunt?"

Mrs. Mim looked over her shoulder at me and shook her head. "I'm afraid there isn't. I tried it once."

"Very well. I can fix something for Rye and me."

"That's what I'm here for," she said firmly. "Please let me make a nice meal for Miss Barbara."

"I'm going to eat with her in her room. I can manage a big tray."

"There's no need for you to wrestle a big tray up those stairs. In one of the pantries there's a dumb-waiter to the upstairs, and I'll put the trays on that, and there's a tea cart in the upstairs closet. You can send things down again the same way. This old house has a lot of things they don't think of any more."

"But not many conveniences for you here."

She smiled a little. "That's all right. I'm used to it now, and I've gotten to like having all the space, even if it means a lot of walking."

I said thoughtfully, "You're too young to have been here as long as Perkins has."

"Except for Lydia, I'm the last to come. When Mr. Barrod brought your aunt here as his bride, the cook he'd had for years quit on him. Really, just used her coming as an excuse, I figure. Martha said he was an old man, a good cook but crippled up with arthritis, and cranky. Wouldn't stay with a woman to boss him, was the way he put it, and took off to live with his son in Baton Rouge. It was Mrs. Barrod who hired me. I've been very grateful." She gazed at me for a long moment as if to be sure that I understood. "Not many people want to hire a woman with a child, a woman who intends to keep her child with her and to raise the child herself. They seem to think that the child might interfere with the woman's doing her job. But your aunt chose me, and I won't forget that."

"I see." What I saw was that Mrs. Mim would take a lot from Aunt Wanda in the way of abuse, out of gratitude.

"Now, as to dinner, everything's about ready. A nice salad and a small roast. Sweet potatoes. Biscuits. You understand, last night was special. Usually dinner is plainer than that."

"I would imagine."

"There's wine if you'd like it."

"I think that some wine might make my sister feel more cheerful."

"There's another thing." She hesitated as if wondering how to venture farther. "Would you rather I called you and Miss Barbara by these names you use for each other? I can't help noticing—"

"It doesn't matter. Aunt Wanda has never given in, never called us by the names we chose. Our parents did, but she wouldn't." A reason lay there, I told myself, but *what* reason? Why should Aunt Wanda care if Barbara wanted to be *Rye?* Was it because Pocket and Rye, those silly names, made a pair? And orphans mustn't have a pair and mustn't be a part of belonging? "Suit yourself as to what to call us."

"Yes, then, Miss Pocket."

"And you can drop the *Miss.*"

"Don't *you* drop it," Mrs. Mim said distinctly to Cindy.

Cindy looked at me and giggled, and I found myself laughing with her.

At midnight I opened my door and looked out. The hall was long, dim, and empty, lit only by the night lights in their miniature brackets. I had a flashlight that I'd brought from my car, and I was barefooted, though I was fully dressed otherwise.

The dinner with Rye had been fun. At first there had been a somber mood, both of us oppressed by what had happened to Perkins, no word as yet from the doctor or the hospital, and knowing that his attacker was running around loose. But then we'd gotten halfway high on the wine, had eaten Mrs. Mim's delicious dinner, and had begun to talk of old times. I had told some of my funnier teaching-in-New-Mexico stories, and Rye had countered with tales of her brief time as a service wife. The trays had gone down again on the dumb-waiter, that wonderful invention. I had called down, offering to help clean up—I knew Mrs. Mim had the maids to help with that, usually—but Mrs. Mim's hollow-sounding voice had come up the shaft and assured me that she could handle everything, thank you.

In the midst of assuring me she wouldn't be able to sleep, Rye had drowsed off. I'd done a final compulsive tucking and straightening, turned out the lights, and had gone to my own room. I remembered the flashlight after a while, and went down to the car for it.

There was a coachlight on the wall under the porte-cochere. The night was dark and still, with a mist rising. It hadn't felt friendly out there.

Now, stepping out into the silent hallway, it struck me that what I was about to do was sneaky and underhanded, a despicable kind of spying. I was going to do it anyway.

My position at Larchwood wasn't on a very good footing to start with. I was the guest of an unwilling aunt, invited here by a sister who was pregnant and confined to bed. I'd had a repulsive trick played on me. . . .

There I was, I told myself disgustedly, using Aunt Wanda's term: *trick.*

I decided to check on Aunt Wanda's door first, to see if light showed around it, indicating she might be up. No light showed. Either the door had been installed when work was so good that light couldn't escape from behind it, or my dear aunt had passed out. And let us hope by now was deeply and peacefully sleeping it off.

I went to the room that Martha had called the upstairs parlor. The door opened under my touch. The small room was warm and smelled of clean draperies and upholstery, of woodwax and polish. I snapped on the flashlight. I found the key where Aunt Wanda had placed it while I watched—trusting woman—and I opened the locked drawer without any trouble, took out the account book, and put it on the desk. I relocked the drawer and put the key in its place and carried the account book back to my room.

My windows faced west, so that hopefully any light shed on the misty patches outside could not be seen from Aunt Wanda's room nor from Rye's.

The book was heavy. It was almost square in its dimensions, perhaps eighteen inches on all sides and at least six or seven inches thick.

The cover was of plastic in a pebbled design, with a smooth framed rectangle embossed on the cover, presumably where a title might be applied. Nothing was lettered into this space. I laid the book on my bed, sat down by it, and understanding perfectly that I had no business peering inside, I opened its pages. Aunt Wanda's writing was surprisingly neat, all entries made in plain black ink.

I saw the various items listed: food, utilities, household supplies, laundry, repairs, florist, outside cleaning help, garden necessities. . . .

To start with, the food bills made me shake my head. The totals seemed incredible, even considering the number of people to be fed here. Liquor, too—not even Aunt Wanda, not even on a toot from one twenty-four hours to the next, without letup, could have put all that booze away.

There was waste here, or theft of some kind, or an incredibly sloppy way of keeping track of money.

Then I looked again at something I'd passed over. The florist bills. Over and over, bills had been paid for cut flowers. Into my head swam the image of Aunt Wanda fussing with the broken blossoms in the upper hallway—and her telling me that Larchwood's gardens supplied almost all of their needs for bouquets.

Here were items paid for flowers, to the tune of a hundred or so every few weeks.

No wonder poor John Sutton had seemed perplexed. No wonder he had cut off in the middle of what he'd wanted to say. Rye and I might think him a picky and cranky taskmaster were he to bring up his bewilderment—and he must have some—over Aunt Wanda's household accounts. Here we were, apparently, enjoying all those flowers.

Then I saw how perfect John was for Aunt Wanda's purposes. He was a bachelor, completely unfamiliar with running a home. Just getting his toes wet now, as it were. A year from now he would be a much more knowledgeable man regarding such things, but for now Aunt Wanda had him in perfect ignorance.

And, I thought grimly, if John Sutton were ever to decide to let someone else take over the accounts of Larchwood, someone who might be married, a family man who had a hand in financing household matters, how Aunt Wanda would fight like a tiger to keep her terrible Mr. Sutton!

John Sutton—with the wool over his eyes.

The food and liquor bills were without doubt highly padded. The whole florist business was a fake. The rakeoff must come to a nice sum every month, to be tucked away in Aunt Wanda's private poke. Aunt Wanda was salting away a personal bank account.

It had to be escape money, money squirreled away for the day when the life of the lady of Larchwood could no longer be endured, not even with the help of periodic drunks and oblivion. The beautiful and refined façade would come tumbling down, and Aunt Wanda would make her getaway and go back to what she'd come from. And for some reason, seeing what her future was going to be, I wanted to cry bitterly.

I forced my thoughts back to the book, the task I'd set myself. I noted that there were no personal expenses entered here for my aunt. Nothing for clothes, cosmetics, trips to the beauty shop—so there had to be another source, a small, private checking account—surely her husband had left some minor funds at her own disposal.

Not enough for flight, for disappearance.

I took the book back to the desk in the upstairs parlor, relocked it into its proper drawer, and carrying the flashlight, unlit, went down to the dimness of the long halls on the lower floor. Again, no door was locked. The whole house was open, in fact, front and rear, the door at the porte-cochere, and everything in between. Outdoors must be someone, a vicious someone, who had struck down Perkins and left him for dead. But at Larchwood it was still a case of enter as you pleased.

Of course, the one who might have given orders for locking up was out of touch, so to speak.

In this small lower-floor office I ran into trouble, though, for I had no idea where the desk key might be hidden. The drawers refused to budge. I remembered that the desk itself held some kind of trickery. Aunt Wanda had done something strange to it when she had caught sight of me entering the room, when she had expected someone else. It occurred to me now to wonder if the one she had expected had been Perkins. He seemed to have been the trusted one, the loyal one. At any rate, at the desk Aunt Wanda had swiftly slid something shut. The whole top of the desk had changed before I could see what was happening.

I knelt before the desk on the pink-and-blue tufted rug. The pale blue walls reflected the glow of my flashlight so that I could see all of the room's interior, even to the tall glass-fronted hobby case in the far corner. I let the beam of the flash shine up into the underparts of the desk. There was a kneehole opening with a fairly deep drawer on either side. Above these drawers and extending the whole width of the desk was a panel some eight inches deep. It was topped by the flat panel that made the writing surface, a smooth, level top inset with a rectangle of white leather with gold-embossed strapping to form the trim. The whole desk, in spite of the delicacy of the decorations, was quite substantial.

I moved the light about. The gold drawer-pulls gleamed in the light, the narrow legs made graceful shadows on the wall. But there were no keyholes, and I was getting nowhere.

The blank panel across the top, under the rim of the desk, had no decorations save three chastely carved flowerlike medallions that in no way resembled anything to be pulled. So I tried pushing them, gently, and when I pressed the rosette to the far right there was a metallic click, and the top of the desk slid a third of its length to the right.

"My, oh my," I whispered in the stillness. I felt a child's eagerness and fright when confronted by a mystery. I scrambled up and turned my light into the space the sliding desktop had revealed. It was a white-velvet-lined compartment, worthy of a queen's jewels at least, but all that seemed to be inside were some letter-sized legal Manila folders, tied with worn tape.

Experimenting, I found that the drawers could now be pulled open. I took out Aunt Wanda's other account book and laid it on the floor; I had decided against taking it back to my room but would simply give it a quick look here.

In appearance it was a twin to the one upstairs. Inside, the accounts were another matter. Here was listed the income of the estate: royalties from gas leases, payments for logging operations, money from the sale of grazing rights and the sale of cattle. Rents, too, though this item was very small. The Stryfes and Bart Linton had no doubt been here for years and had never suffered a rent increase. All amounts except for the rents were large. The estate brought in a high level of income. Balanced against these items were relatively small disbursals: purchases of farm equipment, repairs to equipment and farm structures, road construction, paint, cement, pipe, gravel, seed, veterinarian's bills, workmen's pay. My gaze slipped down page after page.

This is where John Sutton does his work, I told myself. No funny business here. There was no way Aunt Wanda could order imaginary pipe, build phantom roads, paint imaginary barns. She was getting her escape bankroll together from the only source Mr. Sutton could be bamboozled about, the house.

I closed the book. The pages rustled into silence.

I heard it then, the merest breath of sound.

Someone was in the hall.

Larchwood was old, settled into place long since, well built to begin with. There were no squeaking treads in its stairs. No boards groaned or popped when you walked. But still, there had been the faintest creak where a foot had been put down outside that door.

I clicked off the flashlight, rose in the dark, and waited. If this was the phantom of the cemetery I was going to give a good account of myself at last. I hefted the flashlight. I'd bought a big one in case I needed light on a lonely New Mexico road, and it had a sturdy metal, not plastic, case. It made a reassuring weight in my hand. I would not be a fool, a coward, again.

Of course, it might be Aunt Wanda out there, suspicious that someone might be prowling her desk.

But the place Aunt Wanda should be worried about was the room upstairs, with its account book full of nonsense. The account book down here was as clean as soap.

I drew back in the darkness, farther from the door. My hand touched the phone by accident, the antique-white phone on its small stand near the desk. If I were to dial, of course, the one in the hall would hear me. He's waiting. Or *she's* waiting. Not quite sure that anyone is in here. Listening closely, and prepared perhaps with whatever was used to strike down Perkins.

And if I dialed, whom could I call, who could get here in time to do me any good?

A scream would be more to the point.

Would anyone come? Would Mrs. Mim hear me and respond? She was at some distance down the hall, and she had her child's safety to think of.

I could just throw open the door, turn the light in his face. . . .

And get myself killed?

It was hard to stay quiet, tensed, waiting and expecting I knew not what. Nervous tension brought an ache between my shoulders, an inclination to wet my lips and to breathe in a shallow way—I felt that in drawing a deep breath I lost a moment of listening.

But another sound came, after all. A departing sound. A going-away footfall. And as if a light had gone out on the other side of the door, I felt the departure of the other presence. I was reminded of the moment in the forest, while I'd waited beside Perkins. Had this presence and the one in the forest been the same?

I put away the account book and shut the drawer. Experimenting, I found that pushing the desktop into place automatically locked the drawers. A very tricky little desk.

I was seized with another idea now. I used the flashlight to find the phone again, dialed information and got John Sutton's number, hung up, and dialed his house. The phone must be there in that rag-bag room where he lived. His everything room. Perhaps on the desk, buried under papers. When he finally answered he sounded tired and hoarse.

"This is Pocket. Miss Myles. I'm sorry if I got you out of bed."

"Oh, no, it's—" He must have tried to muffle a yawn. "It's okay. Early yet. How are you?"

"It's about one in the morning. I want to go to Jim's grave, but I'm scared. I'm afraid to go alone." After last time, I'd be crazy to go alone, I thought.

His silence told me he was having a hard time sorting this message out. "You want to go *where?*"

"You know that Rye's husband is buried here."

"Of course. I went to the funeral. But—"

"And you know that someone's been leaving ugly . . . uh . . . messages at the grave, hinting that Jim isn't buried there?"

"What?" The word exploded into the wire. "No, good God, I'd never heard anything like that. What do you mean?"

I explained briefly but carefully. "I thought that you must know.

And that you knew this was why I came here, to try to find out what's going on, and why."

He made a half-choked, exasperated sound. "I've never heard a word of it. What I can't understand is why your aunt never said anything to me, never asked my advice—"

"It hasn't anything to do with the estate."

"I never considered myself just an estate manager—I wanted to be a friend, too. Her friend. Your sister's friend. Yours, if you'll have me."

There was nothing I could say to this. What had possessed me to pick up the phone and call John Sutton? I had reacted to the fright given me by the silent listener in the hall, of course; I had defiantly chosen to rush off to the scene of his meanest and ugliest abuses. And there was no graceful way to backtrack.

He said, "You want to go to the grave *now?*"

I wanted to say "No," but couldn't get it out.

"You think these things must be left there at night?"

I forced myself to say, "No one would fool around there in daylight. The last time, rags were burned to leave lettering on the grass of the grave. No one would do that when he might be seen."

"It would be a million-to-one chance, catching him up to something."

He was giving me a way out. "You're right, of course. And it's too late, and we're both tired—"

"I'm coming over, of course. I'm putting on my pants with one hand and holding the phone with the other. Are you alone? Is anyone up besides you?"

"I . . . I thought I heard someone in the hall a while ago." I didn't want John Sutton here now, but he was coming anyway; I had a new inspiration. "Don't ring the bell when you come; I'll meet you at the side door of the house. You've heard what happened to Perkins, haven't you?"

He hadn't heard, and I sketched the events of that afternoon briefly.

"Keep the doors locked," he ordered.

"No door is ever locked at Larchwood."

My thoughts added: except Aunt Wanda's, when she has to get away from it all.

Fifteen

You're using him, a nag-type voice said inside my head. Suppose he takes you all the way to the cemetery, properly chivalrous and protective, and then becomes slightly naturally romantic, out there in the moonlight?

Asking for payment in return for a good deed didn't seem like John Sutton, I told myself. But then, in the misty dark, a lot of very chivalrous gentlemen would feel moved to . . .

My skin grew hot, and I knew that if there had been anyone there to see, I was blushing like an idiot. Of course, it was crazy, it was happening because I felt so alone here in the dark, making up my mind to go out into the hall; but for just a moment I had found myself wondering, my mind straying, my wits scattered—wondering what it would be like to be kissed by him.

For no reason I remembered the man I'd known in New York and his curiosity about me. "Who bounced you around?" In other words, why can't you show an interest in me, and what's shutting you off from the world other people find so enjoyable? And I hadn't answered because there was nothing to be said; the wall was there, and he was on the other side of it.

The old perplexity rose to plague me, even standing in the dark in Aunt Wanda's little office and just having rifled her desk.

If my attitude toward other people, people outside my family, and especially those of the opposite sex, had always been that of mistrust and rejection, there had to be a reason. It could be a fairly recent reason, easy to understand, like being treated badly by someone you wanted to think well of you. It could be an old and forgotten reason, like being neglected and ignored by your parents; it could be that since your parents loved someone else better than they did you, you felt yourself unworthy of love entirely.

You could feel this so deeply and instinctively that any approach showing tenderness and affection was instantly thrown back into the face of one offering it as being false, untrue, a lie.

I had read all of the books and I had learned all of the theories, and none of the effort I'd spent had done any good at all. Something had gone wrong back there when I was little, when I was first putting out the feelers of attachment, of belonging. There had been that woman behind the desk with the biscuit of hair on her head, the woman of my old and recurring dream. I wondered why I always ended up thinking of her.

But these thoughts had to be dismissed. I had to go for a coat, shoes, a scarf for my head, and meet John Sutton. But I would use the phone one last time to call the hospital to see how Perkins was doing.

A starched voice from the hospital told me that Mr. Perkins was doing as well as could be expected.

Wasn't that the phrase they used when people weren't doing well at all?

Feeling upset now, I went boldly to the door and threw it open and shone my flashlight in either direction down the hall. No movement, no furtive sign of life greeted me. I ran upstairs for shoes and coat and scarf. I listened at Rye's door and at Aunt Wanda's. Rye's room was silent, not even a whisper; from my aunt's room I thought I caught the clink of bottle on glass, but this could have been my imagination.

I took the flashlight with me and went down to wait beside the door that let out to the porte-cochere. The light on the wall out there must burn all night, I decided—a gesture of southern hospitality, and had burned so since Larchwood had been built, first a candlelight and then an oil lantern, and now electricity was here and the idea was the same, you welcomed whoever came in out of the night.

When I heard the sound of a car, I opened the door and stepped out. The fog was thicker and held a smothering, wet smell. In the distance were car lights, a bouncing, cottony glow. I stood under the lamp and waited for John Sutton, wondering what had possessed me to bring him out like this on a crazy errand. What I wanted to do was run.

He pulled up in a small sports car, foreign, not new and not one of the expensive kind. The windshield wipers whipped across the glass, and the paint of the car was frosted with damp. He opened the door and got out quickly. He had on a light-colored all-weather coat over his suit. For a moment he stood there with his hand still on the car and we looked at each other, a funny kind of moment, I thought, as if this might be some turning point and we'd both forgotten.

I felt defenses going up inside, the barriers rising. I looked behind me at the door.

He did the worst thing he could have done under the circumstances; he came around the car and took my hand in his. He wanted to do more than that, I sensed, cringing; he was excited because I'd called him here in the middle of the night. I had turned to him. And now we were alone.

I tried to think of something to say, something to remind him of Angela if possible, but I was dumb.

"You're cold," he said solicitously.

I shook my head, denying it.

"I feel awfully gallant and derring-do," he admitted with a grin. "You know—to the rescue. Here I am, saving you from something." His face sobered for an instant. "Well, you shouldn't go to that cemetery by yourself at night."

How well I know—

I managed to say, "I shouldn't have gotten you out of bed."

"But I'm glad you did."

I forced my wits into some kind of order. He *had* come because I'd asked him to, he was a decent and likable young man, there was nothing leering and suggestive whatever in his manner, I was perfectly safe with him—so why couldn't I rise to his effort at light humor and gentle self-mockery?

I heard myself saying in a stiff, serious tone: "I'm very grateful that you came when I asked you to."

He gave me a curious look, that look I didn't like, the look that seemed to pry at me, to suspect something hidden beneath the surface, another woman he was trying to find there. And inside, the barriers were turning to ice.

But he covered the moment quickly, putting me into his car with a manner that was solicitous, gentle. For a moment, there in the foggy night, I had a glimpse, or a kind of fugitive notion, of the kind of woman I might have been; it was almost as if John Sutton had conjured up another person who looked back at me as from a mirror. A woman who would have accepted, even liked, being handed protectively into a car, with the guarantee of masculine protection at her side.

My frozen thoughts told me: They must get a lot of fun out of this game. I can see where it would lend itself to a great many pleasant situations. Too bad I never learned how to play.

He started the motor, backed the car, and headed for the road.

"Tell me more about Perkins. Everything."

I forced my thoughts into coherent order and told him all that had happened from the time we had left his house, the visit to Bart, the trip to town, Rye's illness and Dr. Potterby's ironclad rules, my search for Perkins and its result.

"What was your aunt's reaction to all of this?"

That brought me to a full stop. He was watching the road through the fog, and his profile was lit by the glow of lights on the dash; it seemed a very ordinary question. "Aunt Wanda was ill in her room, laid up with a . . . a headache."

"But she does know about Perkins."

"Someone must have told her by now," I evaded.

"Why would Perkins go into the woods in the first place?"

"I don't know. But he had. I found him lying in the path. As far as I could see he was lying where he must have been struck down. I think he had lain for a while face-down, then turned over afterward, the handkerchief used to cover his face."

"That's an odd bit of business."

"Yes, it seemed so at the time."

"Whoever struck him came back, perhaps, to see how he was. And thought he'd found him dead."

"I don't know," I said. "At the time I thought of . . . of two different people."

"Which doctor came?"

"Dr. Gilbert."

"Well, that explains something. He's fairly new in town. One of the older doctors would have called the bank, knowing that we'd be interested, and the bank would have phoned me at home. Your aunt should have called me, though."

"She had this . . . this headache."

He glanced at me briefly, half frowning. "But surely she wasn't too disabled to do *something*. To use the phone, for instance. Didn't the police interview her?"

"No."

He put his foot on the brake, and the car slowed to a crawl. The fog had thinned here, and I could see the forest on either side of the road, blacker than black. "I guess I'm not getting the whole picture. Perkins was knocked down in the woods, hurt badly, taken away in an ambulance—"

I was pressing myself into the corner of the seat against the door.

"And your aunt didn't come out, didn't talk to whoever came from the sheriff's office, didn't discuss anything with you—"

"She isn't . . . isn't well right now."

The car rolled to a stop. The headlights bored into the fog, made a smoky dazzle on the dark, a dazzle that reflected back into the car. He turned to face me, putting his left arm up on the steering wheel. His chin had turned stubborn. "This part about your aunt doesn't make much sense. She *had* to know. You shouldn't have taken for granted that someone must have told her about Perkins. She should have been in touch with her attorney, for one thing."

I put my hand on the door. "Please don't stop here."

"There's something you're not telling me," he insisted. "I can sense it. You're covering something for your aunt. Has she gone away for some reason and told you to keep quiet about it? Or what? And why? She's her own mistress."

"Please don't stop here." I sounded like a parrot, a deranged parrot. But the panic was rising, there was the feeling of being closed in here with him, too near to him, it was like being at the brink of something I couldn't endure, a smothering, and I had to escape. I yanked down the door latch.

"I'm trying to help. If I've said anything out of line—"

I opened the car door. The cold air struck my face. There was the edge of the blacktop a few feet away and beyond it gravelly earth sloping into a ditch.

He made some sort of exclamation under his breath; it sounded apologetic and self-accusing. "I'm sorry. I'm thinking like a bank. My idea was, since Perkins is your aunt's employee and was injured in some way on her property, she should be in contact with her lawyer."

I stumbled out of the car. I stood with the fog tumbling past me, colder than if I were wrapped in an Arctic blizzard, and I seemed a million miles removed from the warm interior of his car. And—hating it in some strange way—from him.

He leaned to look out at me. His eyes in the glow from the dash seemed contrite and anxious. "Please—I won't say another word. You can't stand out there."

I had to and I could. I wondered how far it was back to Larchwood. "I asked you not to stop." My voice shook and I despised it, and most of all the lostness inside me.

"I guess I wasn't listening. Please get back in the car."

"If I do, will you start the car right away?"

"Promise."

I got back into the car and he drove, and I sat shivering. He thought, of course, that he had offended me by insisting that Aunt Wanda must have known about Perkins. He had no inkling of the truth, and pray God he would never have.

The cemetery being on higher ground, a sort of knoll, the fog had blown thin here. There were even scattered shards of moonlight. I got out of the car quickly and switched on my flashlight and walked away toward Jim's grave.

"Wait for me!" He was hurrying after. I forced myself to stop and wait for him.

He put a hand on my arm, but gently, as if something told him I would bolt if he went farther. "Will you get mad if I ask you something?"

I didn't want to answer the question; I was afraid of what it might be. "I don't know."

It was surprising, though, to have him say, "What's the theory about why Perkins got hurt?"

"Someone struck him. It was obvious."

"Who?"

In my nervousness I clicked the light off and on. "Someone in the woods. Someone he might have followed there. Or who coaxed him there. Someone ugly and vicious." And again I was seeing Perkins, angry, staring at the tire marks in the grass verges of the drive. That image, and the one of Perkins fallen in the forest path, seemed tangled in my mind, each a part of the other.

We went on. He touched my arm now and then as if to reassure me that he was still there. I could feel the cold wetness penetrating my shoes. There was suddenly a feeling of empty tiredness in me, the thought that this was a trip I could have done without.

Ahead was the low marble marker with Jim's name, the scarred grass where the lettering had been burned. But nothing new. No waiting phantom, no toad with jeweled eyes. I was not going to discover an answer here tonight.

John Sutton said, "Could there be a connection between what's been happening here and—" He cut off what he was saying and we stood there facing each other; he was shadowy, spotted with the broken moonlight. I felt the wetness of my hair clinging to my face. "I guess that would be pretty farfetched. That there would be a connection."

I wanted to say, Yes, there had to be a connection. Somehow. What's happened here and what happened to Perkins are a part of the same ugly game, and perhaps Aunt Wanda's shenanigans with her household accounts were another item that belonged in the pattern—she was scared, she was saving up to get away.

"There's one person Perkins would go anywhere for, if she told him to."

What John Sutton said was true, only Aunt Wanda hadn't sent anyone anywhere, because she'd been shut in her room, drinking, all afternoon. To get hold of Perkins to send him out she would have had to leave the room, go down the big front staircase to emerge into the middle of the downstairs entry, or have gone down the smaller back stairs within sight of the kitchen and pantries. In the nervous, on-edge mood of that day, someone would have spotted her.

Objection, I thought. Aunt Wanda could have left the house without using either stairway. She could have gone out by using the tower. The tower was locked; Aunt Wanda had said it was unsafe and in need of repair, but she alone had the key and she alone knew how unsafe it was. It could be perfectly sound, like all the rest of Larchwood.

I found my attention picking up what John Sutton was saying. "Do you really think she is under some sort of pressure? An almost unendurable strain?"

"I don't think it has anything to do with you."

"Do you mean that it's none of my business?"

"I'm sorry if I gave that impression."

He was looking at Jim's grave. "Tell me what happened here." And when I'd told him what I knew, what Rye had shown me, he said: "The things that were done here were to plant the idea that your sister had buried the wrong person. Are you sure there wasn't a chance that—"

I broke in on this impatiently. "No chance whatever. Jim was an officer in a gunship, a helicopter, and they were struck by enemy fire. Some were killed, some wounded, but enough remained alive and in command to get the gunship back to its base. They were never lost in the jungle or in the midst of a battle, and there was never any question of who was who and of who was dead."

He moved moodily off a few steps into the fog. "I guess the meanest thing you could do to someone who has buried a soldier is to plant that doubt. Because if the one you love isn't in the grave, then there's the chance he's still alive."

It was true, he had seen to the heart of it all, the cruel misery that had been visited on my sister. I said, "We may as well go."

He came close to me and made a gesture as if he might lift his arms, perhaps put his hands on my coat, perhaps draw me close to him. I was incapable of moving, I was like a lump of lead, all thought dulled, the night and the whole trip here a waste, and what had I hoped to find, anyway? I'd been a fool. Perhaps if he had touched me then, pulled me close, I would have gone. But then he just said, "All right, we're leaving." And we walked together to the car.

The ride back to Larchwood was silent and swift. When he pulled in under the porte-cochere, into the yellow glow of the coachlight, he turned to look at me, not smiling, and said, "If you need me or want me at any time, just call."

There was so much I wanted to say to him, and I couldn't. Words didn't come. He was going to escort me to the door and leave this place and I was going up to my room alone, the room where I was an unwelcome guest, and this moment when I might have spoken would be gone, raveled into the past, never to be retrieved. He was waiting to see what I would do, and I wasn't going to do anything. I wanted to touch his hand on the wheel, in gratitude, perhaps in more than that—but I was the woman of ice, the spinster, who could not respond to what he was offering.

No miracle took place and no walls came tumbling down, and after another few moments he got out of the car and came around to open the door for me.

"Good night."

"Good night."

That's all there was.

Sixteen

I WOKE TO THE PEACEFUL SUNNY ROOM and for a little while I lay enjoying the softness and warmth of the big bed, and then something told me it was late for rising, and there was Rye to see to. I hopped out of bed and put on a robe and ran down the hall to my sister's room.

Rye was brightly neat and slicked up, her hair brushed and tied back with a ribbon, a bedjacket over her gown. A big silver tray with the remains of breakfast had been set aside on the bedside stand. The bed itself had been tucked up into a work of art.

Rye grinned at me. "Jealous? It was Martha and Mrs. Mim. Made me feel like a princess."

"How did Martha get here?"

"Bart drove into town for the maids. He's the kind you can depend on, Pock. And he's waiting downstairs to talk to somebody, and offer to do whatever he can, and all that. The Stryfes are coming over too —dying of curiosity, no doubt—and you've got to get yourself together and go downstairs and meet people. You're all we've got. Aunt Wanda won't show until afternoon—two or three o'clock, with a thundering hangover or whatever—and she won't sit and chat even then. You'll see."

"What's the news about Perkins?"

All of Rye's cheerfulness vanished. "Not good, I'm afraid. He's still in a coma. They're going to call a brain surgeon from New Orleans if there isn't a change soon. I feel such a fool, lying here with nothing really wrong, and there's Perkins, who's *really* hurt—"

"That's a silly idea." I bent and brushed my cheek against the soft hair above her temple. "Just keep your mind on your business. Outside of being guilty about Perkins, how do you feel?"

"Pampered within an inch of my life."

"So stay there. I'm on my way. The mistress of Larchwood. I should be wearing a morning gown with a train."

Rye's smile came back.

There was no morning gown with a train, of course. There was a green-and-tan cotton I had taught in for two years. Since I had lost weight it made me think of a balloon collapsed around a flagpole. I'm really skinny now, I thought. I ran a comb through my hair and brushed my mouth with a lipstick. I looked at that woman in the mirror. She was sick in some way, some helpless, inward, miserable way, and it didn't show; the eyes didn't seem scared, didn't hold the echoes of old memories or of future frights. No black thing stood behind me. I wanted suddenly to cry, but that didn't show either.

Bart was in the parlor with his own small tray: coffee, an uneaten crusty turnover, a pot of jam. He stood up when I entered, moving with that economy of motion, the litheness, that I remembered. His rusty-wheat stubble of hair had been brushed almost flat. He had a well-shaped head. In this early light, seams showed in the tanned face; they still didn't make him look old.

"Thank you for bringing the maids," I blurted without any polite preamble. Actually I was wondering if we couldn't have managed without the maids for a day or two. The splendor of Larchwood wasn't all that fragile.

"Nothing to it." He waved away any obligation. "I understood from Mrs. Mim that your sister is feeling better."

I remembered that he'd been thoughtful enough to phone ahead for us to the doctor's, and thanked him for that. He shrugged and went on, "Later I tried Potterby's office, but all the nurse would say was that Mrs. Parrish had been in and had gone home. So, I thought, I won't make a nuisance of myself. I missed hearing about Perkins until early this morning—a young officer came to the house, asking what I'd seen yesterday, late, anyone coming out of the woods—"

Hadn't Chris Warne said that he was going straight from Larchwood to the Stryfes', to Bart's place, yesterday?

"He said he'd been by before," Bart said, as if he were reading my mind, "and didn't find me home. Around twilight or later. But I'd gone on an errand to town, to the library, in fact. Again, missing out on the news."

He was still standing, waiting for me to sit down. I sat down, and as if on cue Martha came in with a fresh silver pot of coffee, a cup and saucer for me, another of Mrs. Mim's tempting pastries, all on a little silver tray lined with embroidered linen. Make-work, I thought. The little oval doily will have to be washed, starched, and ironed before it goes back again on the silver tray. Someone here should see how I'd gotten along in New Mexico.

"He didn't tell me what he had found before he got to my place. The proper noncommunicative young deputy. I've seen him around, I think he has a regular patrol in the district."

Martha was pouring my coffee, offering cream and sugar; I told her to leave it black. She went away silently, leaving me the coffee and pastry on the tray. I tried to think of something useful to say to Bart Linton. I was the chatelaine, the hostess of Larchwood, wasn't I?

Mute, awkward, disgraceful chatelaine . . . "I've met Officer Warne," I got out brilliantly. I found then that Bart had left his chair and was offering me a cigarette from his pack. He remembered from yesterday, then. A small but pleasant item. I accepted the cigarette and he brought a small lighter from his shirt pocket and snapped it into flame. The lighter in his hands made his hands seem bigger and stronger than ever. His wrists were thick but flexible, the manner of holding the lighter to my cigarette was deft. The clothes he wore, the denim shirt, corduroy pants, heavy shoes, were those of a woodsman. It occurred to me that he made a determined attempt to look like anything but a bookish professor.

I thanked him for the cigarette.

He sat down again. "What happened to Perkins doesn't make any sense." I remembered that someone else had said this, too. "What took him into the woods? There's nothing in there."

"There's concealment," I said, out of my memory of the forest in the twilight.

Bart's thick brows went up. "You mean he was doing something, meeting someone, he wanted to keep secret?"

"Perhaps he was trying to uncover someone else's secret."

I sipped nervously at the coffee to cover the inexpert pauses in my conversational efforts. Why couldn't my aunt suddenly appear, gracious, recovered, full of welcoming small talk? Why must Rye be withdrawn from combat? But I was thinking, too—there has to be someone inside the house who is working with the creep. Has to be. The wine, the broken flowers—suppose Perkins had been suspicious, had followed one of the maids or even Mrs. Mim into the woods?

It seemed too incredible for it to be Mrs. Mim. She seemed so kindly, straightforward. And there was Cindy, who was a darling.

I had no time to sort these ideas out any further because Mother and Child Stryfe arrived.

Mrs. Stryfe, who had summed me up as a poor relation, a nobody, on our first meeting, seemed disconcerted to find me as hostess. For a moment I thought she was going to reject me in the role, as I went to make them welcome; I thought she was going to push me away as she would a too-familiar dog or cat. But the two buns of gray hair framed a face that showed fatigue, or perhaps disillusionment and regret—something careworn shone from her eyes, and after an instant she took my hand limply. "So sorry to hear about Perkins. Is your dear aunt at home?"

"She's not feeling well." I let the hand go, gratefully.

"I don't blame her. An awful thing. Crime. In our woods, where no one's ever come to a bit of harm." She nodded over to Bart, who had risen from his chair. "You're there where the path comes out at our end. I don't suppose you saw anyone? Or anything?"

"If I had I would have told the police. How are you today, Angela?" His gaze on the daughter held a dry amusement.

Angela had remained tentatively in the doorway, as if uncertain as to whether she wanted to enter. The cornsilk hair was so perfectly arranged, so bouffant, tendriled, shaped, and curled that I began to suspect a terrible thing about it. Well, no, not terrible—a lot of women wore them now. Angela's silky dress was baby blue, and there were pearl earrings and a blue leather bag that matched her eyes and her dress. Her lipstick had not been put on in a hurry, as mine had.

She ventured in at last, not getting too close to me, and shivered daintily. "I wouldn't have slept a wink, last night, if I'd known. I don't believe I could even have stayed at the house. I would have made Mother go with me to a hotel in town."

"That's plain silly." Her mother stalked over to ram herself down upon a chair. "I keep a gun," she informed me and Bart, "and I'm well able to use it. Of course, we've never had any crime in this part of the country. This is a peaceful place. Unlike the mess down around New Orleans. I've always blamed that on the Mardi Gras mentality down there. At any rate, I wouldn't hesitate to plug anyone who came sneaking around."

Bart made some remark in defense of New Orleans—I remembered that he had recently spent some time there—and Angela found a chair for herself. Martha glanced in and left, obviously for more refreshments to offer. "What's being done for Perkins?" Angela asked, taking off lacy little gloves.

"He's in the hospital," Bart answered. "In a coma. If the police have any leads as to who hit him, they aren't saying so out loud. They have to be careful in that regard, you know."

"That's another thing, all this folderol about the rights of criminals. The entire Supreme Court should be impeached." But Mrs. Stryfe wasn't putting the old heat into it; she was just repeating something she had said before. She took a handkerchief from her big leather bag and dabbed some imaginary smudge from around her mouth. Then, still tiredly, she let her bomb drop. "I think I know what might have taken Perkins into the woods, though. I really do."

I could only think: She's telling us when she should be telling Chris Warne. Bart's smile had changed to one of skepticism; he was leaning forward in his chair to replenish his coffee and here was Martha again, two little trays this time, one in either hand. Angela was staring at her mother, literally drop-jawed, an expression that turned her doll's beauty into utter emptiness.

Mrs. Stryfe waved away Martha's offering; Angela didn't even notice it being set down beside her.

Mrs. Stryfe pursed her narrow unpainted mouth, drawing out the moment of silence. Then: "Trespassers!" The *s*'s made one long hiss. "I think we might have something like a motorcycle gang on our hands. They're sneaking through from around the cemetery."

"You mean *ghosts?*" Bart wondered, in obvious levity.

"Mother, if there had been motorcycles, we would have heard them."

"Mighty slim pickings in our neighborhood," Bart added, "unless they've come to press Angela to join them. Which she might find interesting in a way." He seemed to consider it, give some thought to Angela as a member of some outlaw gang.

Angela threw him a glance of poisonous warning, which he pretended not to see.

But I wanted to hear more of Mrs. Stryfe's theory, outlandish as it seemed. "You said *trespassers,* Mrs. Stryfe. Have you noticed any strangers around? Didn't Officer Warne ask if you'd seen any?"

Her blank gaze went right through me and she replied to Bart's remarks, not to mine. "When they come for one of us they'll get a bullet in their skulls."

I wanted to say, Get back to those trespassers. But she wasn't going to listen. I was just a poor relation rushed into service when everyone else had been incapacitated. I was thin and down-at-heel, shabby, and I didn't even know how to put on lipstick. Of course, I was a good example to display as a contrast to her daughter—though nobody could make Angela look bad. Mother and Child Stryfe looked much more at home in this room than I could.

Angela murmured, "Mother, remember, we were going to offer to help here, to do whatever we could—"

"Well, of course we'd do anything your aunt wished." Mrs. Stryfe's eyes were actually on me now. "We'd heard that your sister isn't well, from Bart. And now that your aunt is prostrated. . . ."

A good word, prostrated. It could cover anything.

"We felt we should come and see what could be done. We are highly familiar with the workings of Larchwood. With Perkins gone, you might need someone . . . uh . . . knowledgeable."

I was going to thank her when Bart said smoothly, "Oh, I think Miss Myles looks pretty knowledgeable herself. She must know something of running a house. A house is a house is a house, to overwork Miss Stein's observation. Even I, running my little place, know that all houses have certain things in common—they get dusty, crumbs have to be swept up, the carpets will fade if the sun shines on the same spots every day—"

"If that's all you know," Angela was saying with sweet poison, "then I'm sure that someday soon—"

But someday soon would have to be forgotten, for now we had a new arrival.

John Sutton stood in the doorway.

Seventeen

SOMETHING HAD BEEN SAID, a remark had been dropped during the conversation just passed; I should have made note of it, there should be more to the memory than the fact that it had come and gone as quick as a clock's tick . . . only now, I was busy with a tingling, breathless, aching suspense, waiting for John Sutton's eyes to settle on me. Thump, thump. *Thump, thump.* It was actually my lunatic heart, racing away inside. Over a man.

The woman of ice was going to crack.

But no, because John Sutton wasn't even looking at me; he was gazing at Angela, and she was gazing back as if John Sutton wore golden armor and carried a lance for her special benefit and had come to beg a scarf or some such to wear into combat.

What a fool I had become. They belonged to each other. He's all big and masculine and protective and she's a wide-eyed kitten melting with affection. In another minute she'll fall out of the chair and he can lift her swooning form in his arms.

And I didn't even exist.

Had I ever?

No.

Jealousy had a taste, all right. A bitter and tongue-stinging flavor, like a peach pit. Like that medicine you had to take when you were little, the dark brown stuff . . . it seemed for an instant that I could see my mother's hand reaching out with the spoon, the medicine mirroring the light, and the memory of retching seized me. I must have been awfully sick. But more than that, I'd been small, smaller than I'd been at the orphanage on that other day, the day of the dream. And I'd been at home, in bed, with my mother solicitously offering me the medicine. So what made sense?

I'll have to think about it later, I told myself. Right now I have to sort out how I feel about John Sutton, who has eyes today only for Angela.

Mrs. Stryfe's voice cut across the scene. I was neglecting my rôle of hostess; she would assume it. "Come on in, John. Not a happy time to meet again, I'm afraid. Are you here because of what happened to Perkins?"

It seemed to bring him out of his trance. "Well, yes, in a way."

"If you expected to see Wanda, she's prostrated."

He didn't agree that he needed to see my aunt. He gave Bart and me each an unfocused nod and then went and sat close to Angela, his heart's delight, who went first rose pink and then pale with ecstasy. "I guess that's to be expected," he offered to Mrs. Stryfe.

And what a fat lie that was, I cried inwardly. Aunt Wanda prostrated because of an attack on Perkins? Even this new Aunt Wanda had more spunk than that. I wished I could have told him this. I wished that my locked mouth would have let the words come out. But he was so enchanted now with Angela, so different from the man of last night; he couldn't even see me, and that filled the world for me at the moment.

Wretched fool. My nails dug into my palms and I was grateful for the pain.

Martha came to offer coffee to John Sutton, to replenish with fresh coffee any others that needed doing. She brought the tea cart this time, more muffins, butter, jam, honey, and for a while the air was fragrant with the new brew of coffee and the homey smells of baked things. Conversation was covered by the clatter of silver and china, and I could kind of get myself together.

John Sutton wasn't looking at me, but Bart was. He was studying me over a bite of turnover, then wiping his fingers on a napkin and sipping coffee, listening to Mrs. Stryfe but watching me. Pityingly—there was no doubt about it. But of one thing I was reasonably sure: the woman of ice hadn't shown her silly feelings to the roomful of people. The feelings were too far inside, and all means of expressing them had atrophied years ago. I met his sympathetic glances with a small smile.

Martha was fooling around, I noted, dawdling, making work to stay here within earshot. I told her briskly, "You may leave the cart, Martha, please. We'll help ourselves if we want anything more."

"Yes, Miss Esther."

Miss Esther . . . it was ridiculous. I was no more a Miss Esther than I was Madame Pompadour. I gave Martha a level stare to match the one from her rather lizardlike black eyes, while a voice inside me commented on how brave I could be to servants.

Mrs. Stryfe was back upon the subject of motorcycle gangs, and Bart was repeating his sly objections. Angela kept demure eyes on her cup, while John Sutton leaned close to her in what could only be masculine reassurance.

They were playing the game, and it was fun. But not fun to watch, so I murmured some inane excuse and got out of the room. They had refreshments and each other to talk to, and I couldn't stay there any longer. My day as a hostess was at an end.

I ran upstairs to my room, to the mirror there, and searched in dread for any visible signs of tears. There were none. The eyes were my ordinary eyes, set into my familiar face, the spinster's face from which all but a stony composure had gone. So thank God for small favors. John Sutton, nor Bart, nor anyone, could know how I had felt downstairs. I tried to orient myself by thinking back through the events of last night, the trip in the car; but something had become twisted, and what had seemed sincerity and warmth on John's part then, now in retrospect was just curiosity and patience. I had been no bargain, of course, full of cold panic, but I'd made a tremendous effort, and perhaps in time—

Time was gone. Run out. I had picked the wrong man.

I went to the windows. The morning had taken on a hazy, sunpuddled look, and I wondered if clouds were coming, if it might be going to rain. I feel like rain, I thought; I feel like being out in downpouring water and lightning, thunder too.

There was a sound behind me and I turned, my heart thudding. He wouldn't have followed me up here, of course, but for a dizzy instant there was the outlandish hope that he had—but this was Mrs. Mim, staring in at me from the open doorway. Her face was smeared with the overspill of tears and her mouth shook and twisted, trying to get words out, and she clutched the bosom of her neat uniform as if to hold, or to conceal, something unbearable inside.

I felt an electric alarm, a great jolt of fear, and for some reason I thought, *Cindy*. But in the next fraction of a second I knew, I didn't even have to hear what Mrs. Mim was trying to say.

"Miss Pocket, the . . . the officer is here. Waiting to see someone. It's Perkins." She covered her face with her hands.

"He's dead," I whispered, turning cold, not really believing it. Even the memory of Perkins as I'd last seen him, bloodied and unconscious, didn't help me to believe it. He seemed much more alive in my memory as the man in command of my aunt's home, too sure and too competent to be dead.

I went to Mrs. Mim and tried to comfort her. I led her to the chaise and made her sit down. "I'll go down in a minute. I just have to make myself understand it first." Tears welled now, real tears, tears for the decent and able person I'd known briefly. For a while we were together there, in silence, and Mrs. Mim's bitter grief betrayed a great sense of loss.

This would change everything, I thought. Aunt Wanda can't be allowed to lie hidden any longer. "We have to tell my aunt. Is there anyone else, Perkins' people maybe, whom we should contact?"

"He hadn't anyone here. He has a . . . he had a daughter in New Orleans. I think the police have already been in touch with her." Mrs. Mim's voice broke on a new burst of sobbing. After a little while she said in a half whisper: "We were engaged to be married. He'd wanted to marry me for a . . . a long time. And I put him off. I wanted to save up something for the future. And I felt a great obligation to your aunt. And now, because I waited, it's too late. . . ."

Too late. Terrible, tearing, brutal words.

I tried to think of something comforting to say, but what was there I could offer? I knew the depths of her loss.

Something else I understood, too: Since Mrs. Mim had been the woman he loved and hoped to marry, Perkins might have confided in her. He might have told her something about those tire marks on the grass, given a hint of his suspicions—suspicions that could have led him into those woods. Did I dare talk about these things now, with Mrs. Mim so distracted by grief?

It wasn't the right time. Questions would be an intrusion, heartless and tactless. And yet . . . I had come here to solve a mystery for Rye, and so far had accomplished nothing. If there was a link between what was happening at Jim's grave and what had happened to Perkins in the forest, a beginning had to be made. "Did Perkins ever speak to you of his suspicions of anyone?"

"Suspicions?" From tear-brimming eyes, Mrs. Mim looked at me in alarm.

"An . . . of an enemy." I was doing it badly, awkwardly. I hurried on: "Perhaps not an enemy of his own, but someone who was making trouble here, doing ugly small things, tricks with the wine at dinner, for instance."

It seemed that Mrs. Mim, crouched on the chaise beside me, had grown still. The slight rocking to and fro, the pressing of hands to eyes, the sobs, froze; and I sensed that the grief had been transformed into wariness. Her tone was low but harsh. "I don't know what you're talking about."

I knew that she was afraid, perhaps not quite knowing what she should be afraid of. "Someone's been playing cruel games. Games that are meant to hurt. I don't know how long they've been going on. I came here because the tricks had been extended to the grave of Rye's husband. Very unfunny little messages turned up there, telling my sister she had buried someone who wasn't her husband."

This got a new reaction: shock. Mrs. Mim's face was stunned, bewildered. Well, she hadn't known then what was going on at the cemetery. Rye had told our aunt, and if Aunt Wanda had confided in Perkins, he hadn't let it go any farther. One thing I was suddenly sure of, thinking back: Perkins hadn't been thrown off balance or rendered incapable by the repulsive trick with the dinner wine. He had remedied the affair smoothly, deftly.

Mrs. Mim put a hand on my arm. "I don't know of any tricks. Nor of any enemy of Perkins. He was a very good man. Kind, gentle. Firm when he had to be. He'd been here a long time. He knew that Mr. Barrod was lonely. A lonely old bachelor, and he was glad when Mr. Barrod got up his courage and took himself a wife and brought her here. I guess those were kind of difficult days, the first days after she came. I told you how the cook quit. There was a lot of grumbling and dissatisfaction, almost rebellion."

"Strange. Was Aunt Wanda overbearing at first?"

"No, not at all. She was a lot jollier then, in fact. And carefree. Full of fun. And there weren't any . . . uh . . . spells, like the one she's had now. It was after Mr. Barrod died, and she took on the whole weight of managing the estate, that she got so . . . so moody."

She started to drink, I translated. And how soon after that did she decide to start padding the household budget for getaway money? "She had Mr. Sutton's help, and Perkins ran Larchwood for her. I don't see how the burden could have been so terrible."

"I don't either, but it must have seemed so to her. Are you going to talk to the officer?"

"Yes. In a minute. I have to speak to Aunt Wanda on my way, give her warning. But first: If my aunt wasn't unpleasant to them when she first came, why did the servants almost rebel?"

"Well, I was new here, I didn't understand all of it, but my guess was, they'd had their own way a lot. Mr. Barrod would be gone—I suppose he was searching for someone to fill his loneliness. To love him. And while he was away, Perkins may have relaxed the discipline a little. Not as to the work being done. But maybe, since no mistress was here, there wasn't any . . . I guess the word I want is *formality.* A matter of doing everything in the polite and correct way."

"Yes, I see." Aunt Wanda had been a happy bride, enjoying her new dignity as mistress of Larchwood. And after the buffeting life had given her, the pinchpenny years, the wandering, the roistering, the homelessness, it must have seemed a heaven of luxury and security at last. "Perkins seemed most devoted to my aunt, to this house, to his responsibility here."

"He was a sincere, wonderful man." Tears welled from Mrs. Mim's eyes again; she bit her lips to stop their trembling. "If he had an enemy, it must have been a strange one. The main thing he hated was hypocrisy, cheating. That he couldn't stand." She made an effort to pull herself together, stood up, and tucked her uniform into place here and there.

"I'll go now." I also stood. "Please don't bother with cooking, with anything in the kitchen, for the rest of the day. If there is anywhere you'd rather go, than here, anyone you'd rather stay with—"

"Thank you. I will take the rest of the day off. But I'll stay here."

With a broken, haunted look, she walked from the room.

I believed her when she said that she knew nothing of any unpleasant tricks being played. Perkins had not confided in her. Perhaps he felt that in keeping things a secret between himself and Aunt Wanda, he had a better chance to spot the perpetrator. And certainly he had been too shrewd not to know that some of the tricks—like the one played with the wine—required an accomplice inside the house.

Perkins had been loyal and intelligent.

He had been angered at sight of the marks on the verges of the driveway; he had known the meaning of those marks. I remembered the look I had caught on his dark face, not one of surprise but of *knowing.*

Who had been the visitor, the unskillful driver, coming late under cover of the foggy night?

What business had brought him, or her, to Larchwood?

I was convinced that the visitor had come to see my aunt, and that she would lie if confronted with the question of the visitor's identity. There's something terribly wrong here at Larchwood, and Aunt Wanda is covering it up until she can collect enough of a stake to pull out, I told myself.

Would Perkins' dying bring anything into the open?
Well, it was time to see.

I knocked, and after a while there was a dragging sound, and Aunt Wanda muttered huskily through the door, "Who's there?"

"Pocket."

"Please go away. I'm sorry for what I said yesterday. But please, for now, just leave me alone."

"Something very serious has happened. You're going to have to talk to the sheriff, or one of his deputies. I'm sorry, but you can't stay in your room any longer."

After a long moment came the metallic scrape and click of the bolt, and Aunt Wanda peered out through the narrow space. Her face was puffed, bleary, and under the visible eye was a dark smudge. "What . . . what's happened?"

"Yesterday, for some reason, Perkins went into the woods. When Rye and I got home in late afternoon, the maids told us he was missing. They had no way to get to town. I took them home, and came back here, and went looking for Perkins. He was in the woods, on the path to the tenant houses, and had been struck down from behind and was unconscious."

Aunt Wanda brushed back the tumble of hair on her forehead. A look of apprehension seemed to be growing in her face. "Is he hurt badly?"

"He died this morning."

The face slid out of sight, there was only her shoulder, motionless, the hand clenched at the side of the door. The room beyond was almost dark. She had all the blinds drawn, and an odor that was stale and sick crept out into the air of the hall.

Inside the room she said at last, "He was murdered, then."

"Yes."

"All right. I understand. Don't worry about me, I'll shower and get dressed. I'll be presentable. Just ask the officer to give me . . . uh . . . twenty minutes or so. And send Lydia here if you see her."

"I'll tell the deputy you can see him in a half hour."

"Is . . . is Barbara all right? This hasn't upset her, has it?"

"We were visiting Mr. Linton yesterday morning when she began to feel ill. I took her into town to Dr. Potterby. He says she must stay in bed, rest, take care of herself. For her it's not easy."

"She must have needed me." The tone seemed muffled and far away.

"I guess she might have liked it if you'd been on hand."

Still not moving so that I could see her face, she said, "Esther—those remarks I made to you yesterday—"

"Forget that. If I have to find out the truth from you, in the way you'd tell it, I'd rather not know." It was cruel, I knew, hitting Aunt Wanda when she was down, groggy with hangover, but I wanted all the cards on the table. No more sniping, no more of mean little bits and pieces, no more of using the past as a weapon of spite.

"People would have loved you," she whispered from behind the door, "if you had let them."

"I know better than that." I walked away.

I saw Lydia in the hall and told her that my aunt wanted her. I went on down the back stairway. Those people in the parlor were going to have to look after themselves, until and unless Aunt Wanda could take over as hostess. There was no need for me to see John Sutton again. He had played his small game, and I'd fallen for it, a fool in spades, and probably he was one of those men who need to bolster their tiny egos once in a while with a conquest. And he had seen that the conquest in this case wasn't going to be worth the trouble, since he'd obviously gotten hold of some kind of freak.

Chris Warne was downstairs, outside by the flower garden. His official car was parked on the driveway. The sunlight was mottled by thin clouds, and the puddled-light effect I had noted earlier had increased. The air had lost some of its warmth. The young police officer had his cap in his hand, and he looked very businesslike, lean and shipshape in the neat trooper's uniform. "I'm sorry to have brought such bad news."

"When Mrs. Mim told me, I couldn't believe it. It's murder now."

"Yes, it is." His eyes on me were sober and studying.

I wondered if he expected me to come up with some new information. I felt awkward and inadequate with nothing to offer. "Are there clues leading to someone? Or perhaps I shouldn't ask."

"If we had anything, I couldn't tell you what it was. But I can say, so far there's nothing."

"What about the handkerchief? It was covering Perkins' face when I found him and later seemed to be missing."

"It turned up stuffed into his pocket. One of the ambulance men had noticed it and picked it up."

I decided I had to offer what I knew, though it was so little, so vague and inconclusive. "There is something I ought to tell you. Yesterday morning I came outdoors after breakfast, and Perkins was out here. He was staring toward the driveway. Someone had made tire marks, running off the gravel into the edges of the lawn. The wheelmarks were distinct. It seemed to me that something about those marks had made Perkins angry."

Warne was duly looking off toward the drive, where there were no longer any marks on the grass.

I was miserable with embarrassment, making a fool of myself as always. "I . . . I can't help wondering if someone had come here during the night and if something about the wheelmarks gave Perkins an idea of who had come. And if there might have been a connection between this . . . uh . . . incident—"

"And what happened to him later?" Well, I was not impressing Chris Warne. He was making a sincere effort to follow, to understand, but it amounted to so little. Just tire marks, gone now. And that Perkins might have been displeased.

All silly and trivial, and I couldn't go into the possible sequence, that perhaps this nocturnal visitor had been in to see my aunt, had harried and disturbed her to the point where she had to seek release in a temper tantrum and a drunk. I gave up the subject. "Would you like to come inside?"

He could wait for Aunt Wanda in her upstairs parlor.

"I do want to see Mrs. Barrod."

"She'll be with you inside a half hour."

"Oh." He glanced at his watch. "Well, in that case—"

"If you wanted to you could spend the time talking to Mrs. Stryfe and her daughter, and Mr. Linton. You might want to ask them a few additional questions."

He glanced at me thoughtfully. "Yes, I might as well talk to them while I'm waiting for your aunt."

He had much to do, obviously. But he would wait for Aunt Wanda since he could employ himself usefully with the visitors.

In the hall we met Martha, who had apparently gotten the news of Perkins' death, since she looked subdued and morose. She glanced somewhat apprehensively at Warne, and I told her, "Will you please take Mr. Warne to the parlor? He wishes to talk to the others there. When my aunt is ready to see him, please take him upstairs."

Aunt Wanda was not ready for any grand entry into the parlor, of that I was sure. She would want to see the officer alone.

Martha murmured an answer, and started off with Chris Warne following. All of my obligations seemed to have been filled for a while. I could trust Rye to stay in bed. The maids would look after her, rustle up a lunch for whoever was there and wanted one. I had to remember to tell one of them that Mrs. Mim had the day off and wasn't to be disturbed. Or perhaps, knowing how she and Perkins had felt about each other, they understood without my telling them. As soon as Aunt Wanda was showered and dressed, and out of her room, she was in charge here.

And I could go. I have to get out of this house for a while, I told myself. It was running away; that couldn't be helped.

I went back upstairs, listened at Rye's door, heard a radio playing in there, hurried on to my own room where I picked up gloves and purse and a sweater, and went down and outdoors again by the way I had gone before.

In the pantry was Pearl, sorting canned goods, sniffling with grief at the loss of Perkins, and I told her that Mrs. Mim was not to be disturbed.

The hazy light darkened the green of the forest. On many stretches of road there was nothing but the trees. I felt the isolation, the silence; but there was a feeling of release, of having escaped, in getting away from Larchwood.

After a while I became aware of the image in the rear-view mirror. I was being tagged, far in the distance, by what seemed to be a small sports car—not a big one with lots of power, but one of the small imports, one a lot like John Sutton's, for instance; and I put on speed, gunning the old car down a long incline and up to the top of the next rise. And the car in the mirror stayed with me.

My silly heart had started to pound.

I told myself, I won't let it overtake me. I won't.

An unreasonable panic settled over me, a childish feeling of having to outrace something that threatened me.

I tried for more speed, but the old car was doing all it could. There was no use overworking the motor, breaking something, stranding myself. The pavement rounded a curve, and out of the corner of my eye I saw the narrow side road, graded but unpaved, that dropped off down into the woods. I slammed on the brakes, turned with a lurch and a squeal of tires, crossing the road in an illegal maneuver, considering that this was just beyond a blind turn, and with a downward rush I was off the highway and down into the trees. The tires whipped through brush, and under the fenders breaking growth scraped and popped, and then suddenly I was past a twist in the road and out of sight of whoever had been in the rear-view mirror. I let the old car roll peacefully to a stop and cut the motor.

There was a great feeling of peace, and also one of letdown. The woods were around me like a safe green cocoon. I put my head on my arms, my arms crossed on the steering wheel. I shut my eyes. My silly heart was quieting. The minor crunch and rustle of growth disturbed by the car's passing gradually settled, and then there was utter quiet. Under the gray sky, here among the pines, I could rest and listen to nothing and perhaps even think.

It hadn't been John Sutton's car, I told myself. Get that silly notion out of your head. John Sutton was still in the parlor at Larchwood, playing knight to Angela's vaporous lady.

Perhaps it will be a while before I quit looking for him everywhere. But in the end, I *will* quit.

For the time, I had some hours of my own to do with as I pleased.

I must have dozed briefly, propped there against the wheel. I woke; there had been a sound of some kind, a rustling; and my heart began to thump again—with fear, this time. I was suddenly aware of how alone I was, and of what might appear out of that dense green forest, the phantom I had seen and didn't wish to see again.

Had Perkins glimpsed that same phantom?

The rustling turned to a scampering noise and I saw the squirrel, frozen to the trunk of a tree not too far away, regarding me in a funny, anxious way. In the glove compartment ought to be the remains of a sack of peanuts I'd bought on the trip out from New Mexico. I dug them out, tossed them one by one, and presently the squirrel grew curious enough to investigate. He kept a beady eye on me, though.

I started the car and drove forward cautiously. All at once I wanted out of these woods. If this unpaved track proved a dead-end, I might have to back up for the entire distance. But after about a mile I came to a paved road and turned into that. It ran east. When I came to an intersection, I headed north. So far since leaving the unpaved road I had passed one house, and it had seemed deserted.

I stopped to eat at a small town on the Arkansas border. A drive-in;

I had a sandwich and a glass of milk. Knowing that I was now in Arkansas gave me a feeling of exploring, of a new and different and perhaps alien place, though it all looked exactly like the northern Louisiana country I'd just left. At about two o'clock in the afternoon I came to a good-sized lake and parked the car and got out.

The overcast sky made the water dull and gray; there were a few little whitecaps tossed by the wind. This side of the lake was not built up with cabins. On the opposite shore were a small market and garage, some randomly parked house trailers, a pier, and a boat-launching ramp. Probably later in the summer the whole place would be quite busy. Right now it was quiet. I could make out a man in a rocking chair at the end of the pier, holding a fishing pole. His hat seemed to be down over his eyes, as if he were taking a nap.

I walked around. There was a smell like rain in the air, but no drops fell. I found a big rock near the water and sat on it, and after a while picked up a two-foot stick that had been in the water and was smoothed and bleached white and had a pointed end. And then I found myself drawing a map.

Here was Larchwood, this big square, with the driveway to the main road at one side, the driveway dividing, one part of it going out by way of the porte-cochere, the other directly from the garages across the lawns. Here were the gardens; I made scratchy rows for them. Plenty of flowers grew at Larchwood, though Aunt Wanda's florist bills were enormous. I made a small rectangle for the garages. I stabbed holes to represent the trees of the forest.

And here was the path. I found a small twig and stood it upright next to the square that represented Larchwood. This was Perkins, staring at the marks on the grass.

Someone had come to see Aunt Wanda in the middle of the night. I was as firmly convinced of this as if I had seen it happen. I too had been out in the middle of the night with John Sutton. Had the other car come and gone in the time of my absence? Somehow I thought not.

Rye had heard me come in from my trip but hadn't heard anyone else. Admittedly, she hadn't really listened.

Perkins had seen the marks of the tires on the grass. He hadn't been antagonistic toward me, hadn't connected the marks of tires with my car. He had been thinking of someone else. Someone whose identity he was sure of? Someone who just visited now and then, carelessly, at odd hours, and left Aunt Wanda in a state of frustration and fury?

Had he sensed my aunt's mood early, as Rye had—and gone out to see if there were any indications of a visitor because of that mood?

Somehow this seemed pretty logical.

I couldn't sell it all to Chris Warne, but I believed it. I believed in this sequence. I believed too that Perkins' suspicions, his surmises, out there by the driveway led to his terrible encounter in the woods. He had gone looking for someone.

The phantom?

There was danger in trying to find Aunt Wanda's nighttime visitor. More than danger: death.

The house should be locked up at night.

It wouldn't be, I knew. Locked up tight would go against tradition and custom in this crime-free part of the country.

I got off the rock, feeling very uneasy, and walked for a way along the lake's fringe, my shoes leaving a line of prints in the damp earth. A cluster of crows watched me from a lightning-struck bare tree, and let out a few half-hearted cries of warning. A jay scolded either the crows or me, and a squirrel scolded everybody from out of sight. I'm not popular here, I told myself.

I wasn't wanted at Larchwood, either.

Aunt Wanda wanted Rye there, but *not me.*

Is it because she senses my curiosity? Does she sense that I won't be put off, I'm not distracted as Rye is by pregnancy? And above all, why is Aunt Wanda so helpless, so frustrated, that she takes out her rage on her servants, and drowns it all in liquor?

Rye had said that there was no pattern to Aunt Wanda's angry moods, that they came at random.

Which must mean that the visitor comes at random. Comes whenever he, or she, feels like it. Comes for . . . *what?*

Could there be in Moss Corner someone out of Aunt Wanda's riotous and unconventional past? An old flame? A jealous ex-lover? Someone who possessed a hold over her? From what I remembered, my aunt had covered about everything west of the Mississippi. She'd been a restless wanderer, taking her living and her fun where she found them, sometimes in the money, sometimes practically penniless.

Into my memory flashed a picture out of another year, a long-ago year, of Aunt Wanda making an entry. My father had laid down his paper to answer the door, had returned with Aunt Wanda, she richly wrapped in a new fur coat, beneath it a dress that sparkled with sequins and beadwork, flipped with fringe—to my eyes at that age, a dream of a dress, incredibly beautiful—and with high-heeled pumps whose buckles also glittered, and on my aunt's head a feathered hat. Her arms had been stuffed with packages. Had it been Christmas? No, Rye and I had been playing on the front room rug with dolls, and there hadn't been any decorations in the room. The memory suggested that it may have been a Sunday shortly after the New Year.

Aunt Wanda had come flying across toward the two of us, while from a doorway to another room our mother cried out a happy, surprised welcome. Aunt Wanda had dumped the whole load of packages down upon Rye and me, a gesture of immense generosity, a showering of treasures. Rye had yelped because a corner of something had bumped her. Aunt Wanda had knelt, flopped down, instantly contrite and consoling. She'd thrown aside the coat, cuddled Rye, kissed the bump on Rye's arm. And all of the time crooning and half weeping. It occurred to me, after all these years later, that our aunt had been about three quarters gassed.

Then had followed the tearing of wrapping paper, the opening of boxes. Fancy dresses spilled out, bonnets, slippers, toys of every sort. I had gradually gone cold all over, with a feeling almost like terror. I had wanted to crouch small, not to be seen. The packages had been ripped apart, the contents exclaimed over, displayed to our parents, tossed aside . . . and all of it had been for Rye.

Suddenly Aunt Wanda had lurched back upon her heels and had stared glassily at me, and then laughed, and had snickered, "Well, look at our Esther! Sitting there with her nose out of joint!"

My father had risen instantly from his chair, with an angry exclamation, and our mother had said, in the instant of silence, "Wanda, how could you?" And my father was walking toward us with a terrible look, a look as if he might pitch Wanda and all she had brought right out through the door. But I was running. I fled to my room and shut the door, and since there was no lock on it I put a chair against it. For a long time I had sat on the side of the bed, not crying, but trying to control a kind of panic and breathlessness that was worse than anything I had experienced before.

Was that my first confrontation with nonlove?

Was it then that I began to doubt that my parents cared for me? That I began to believe that only Rye was loved?

Some time later my mother had come, bearing a small tray with cookies, milk, and a beautiful little ring in a jeweler's box, which she told me Aunt Wanda had brought. There had been something for me, after all. Aunt Wanda hadn't meant to hurt, only to tease.

I hadn't believed the story about the ring. I thought that in some way my father had hurriedly produced it to soothe me.

I had thanked my mother for the milk and cookies. I had drunk some of the milk, feeling that I owed it to our mother for her kindness. I had crushed the cookies and put them on the windowsill for the birds. I had never worn the ring, didn't even remember what had become of it.

Nor had Rye ever worn any of the dresses, bonnets, slippers, nor had we seen anything more of the toys. I had been protected, I supposed, in the only way my parents had known—by the removal of all the signs of how much more Rye was loved. And not a word was said. . . .

Were we fair, I thought suddenly, uneasily?

To be true, Aunt Wanda had been fearfully tactless and insensitive, grossly offensive toward a child who was waiting to see what had been brought for *her*—if anything. But here our aunt had come—let's look at it from her point of view, I thought—bearing lovely stuff for the kids. Toys and clothes for the smaller one. But I, Pocket, was now old enough to wear and care for and appreciate a piece of real jewelry. A beautiful and valuable ring, for such I'm sure it had been. Was that the way we should have looked at it?

Yes, I told myself, standing at the lonely lake's edge, that's how we should have seen it on that long-ago day. Out of our aunt's hopscotch life there couldn't have been many times when she had been so flush, so able to be generous. And though she had unwittingly spoiled the day for me, we didn't have to spoil it for her. There should have been a different way, a compromise.

People would have loved you, if you had let them. . . .

I shrugged. It was too late now. Much too late. And maybe John Sutton had wisely sensed it, and had intelligently switched back to someone else while he still had a chance. Probably Angela was loving enough, if a trifle shallow; or maybe he was showing me that he was freeing himself from me—it didn't matter.

Had Aunt Wanda sent Perkins on an errand into the woods?

I felt somehow that Perkins had gone on his own; and it was none of my business, either, unless it all tied in with what was happening to my sister.

Eighteen

Before I left the lake I scrubbed out my map of Larchwood with the toe of my shoe, picked up the twig that had represented Perkins, and holding it, facing the gray waters of the lake, I thought of the life ended now, a life given to service. A man of excellent taste, of integrity, loyalty—and he was gone. He had died, I was convinced, in an effort to help my aunt. I couldn't just toss the twig away, somehow, so I found a fallen leaf, one of last autumn's, and put the twig on it and set it afloat on the water.

I told myself I'd always been a kind of nut.

When I reached Larchwood I parked out beside the garages and walked back to the house. The afternoon was darkening fast, the clouds overhead were black, and a few big drops spattered and hissed on the gravel. I went indoors at the back of the house. The house was silent. I walked down the hall to the parlor, but the room was empty and unlit. Everything had been straightened and tidied, and General Lee looked down into the dim room with a thoughtful expression.

I went upstairs and now I could hear the murmur of voices.

I rapped at Rye's door and went in. Lamps were on in here, dispelling the gloom. Rye was in bed and our aunt sat nearby on a chaise. Both of them turned to look at me.

"Hello," I said, taking off my gloves and sweater.

"Where on earth have you been?" Rye cried. "You've been gone for hours and hours. I've missed you."

"I went out. I just drove around." I thought that my aunt looked better than I had expected. The white hair was neatly brushed back, caught with an ornate silver pin, some curls puffed above her temples. The makeup covered the exhaustion, the raddled illness of hangover. She wore a plain black dress. "I didn't see a soul downstairs."

"I sent the maids back to town," Aunt Wanda answered. "They

were depressed and gloomy over Perkins' dying. I told them I'd call them in a day or so. Meanwhile, Mrs. Mim and I will be going to Perkins' funeral. We'll drive to New Orleans day after tomorrow. I've called his daughter there and made sure that we would be welcome to attend."

If Aunt Wanda had cried over Perkins' death, there was no sign of it. But I acknowledged to myself that grief can be felt without tears following.

"You and Rye can hold down the fort," Aunt Wanda went on. "For a day. That won't be too bad, will it?"

"We'll be fine," Rye told her. "Don't worry about us."

I also murmured reassurances, we'd get by without difficulty, but I was aware of a touch of fear. Larchwood was a big place to be alone in.

"If anything comes up, anything at all, you can phone," our aunt was saying. "John Sutton will respond, bring anything you need, take care of any emergency."

Rye gave me a wicked glance. "There's another thing about Mr. Sutton. He wants you to phone him when you get home. That's *now*. He wasn't following you away from here, was he?"

"Why should you think so?" I tried to sound indifferent.

"I'm not deaf."

"You're not supposed to be keeping track of everything outside this room, either," I pointed out, and then relenting, I said, "I'll call him in a little while."

"I thought perhaps he'd coaxed you to make more suggestions about his house."

I gave her a stern glance. "I did not see Mr. Sutton on my jaunt. And I don't think you could hear my car, or his, from in here with the door shut—and the door was shut when I left here. I kind of think you've been up, snooping."

"I went to the bathroom," Rye said virtuously. "That's perfectly legal with Doctor. And I detoured just a teeny bit by way of the front balcony, to see the gloom outdoors. So I'd feel better about staying in bed."

"You're hopeless. You're sure you didn't also detour by way of the parlor to see who was down there?"

"Oh, I knew who was left down there."

Aunt Wanda put in: "I asked Mrs. Stryfe and Angela, and Bart too, not to stay. I wasn't rude nor crude. Mrs. Stryfe seemed to feel that she should fall to and make calves'-foot jelly, or something. She acted as if we had all been laid low here. And Angela could be filling icebags and bringing aspirin. Mr. Linton had more sense, of course. He took the maids to town and he'll come by later, or phone, to see if we need anything. I try to remember, Mrs. Stryfe means well."

"Oh, she's tiresome," Rye said impatiently. "She gets on political tirades. She thinks Angela's looks are going to take them both somewhere. Pock, didn't you and John Sutton really have a rendezvous? I shouldn't ask, but it's queer, his calling around noon, asking if you'd please phone him when you came in. Was there a slip-up?"

"Rye, why don't you just concentrate on your own affairs?"

She pretended to be shocked. "My, we're awfully stiff and standoffy all at once." She propped herself on one arm. "Are you really going to call him?"

Aunt Wanda was watching me shrewdly. I didn't like that look.

"There is plenty of time to call Mr. Sutton," I told Rye.

Aunt Wanda stood up from the chaise. Her eyes were now on a level with my own, but she didn't meet my glance. "I'll check up on what food we have, since I'll be leaving you here on your own. I know there's plenty, actually. Mrs. Mim keeps things stocked well ahead."

"Don't worry about us," I told her. And without any preliminary I asked, "Did you send Perkins into the woods yesterday?"

She seemed startled by the question; perhaps under the startled look was something more, evasion or fear. "Send him? What do you mean, send him?"

"He went into the woods, where he was hurt so badly that he's dead. Did you tell him to go there? Give him an errand?"

"Of course not. Perkins had no business in the woods. So far as I know, during the time I've lived here he never set foot in them. What took him there and why he was struck down are complete mysteries to me."

And still, she wasn't meeting my eyes, she was avoiding a direct look at me.

"He didn't tell you he was going?"

She seemed suddenly tired and haggard behind the carefully prepared façade. "No, not at all."

"Did Officer Warne suggest any theories today about the motive behind Perkins' murder?"

"If he had theories he didn't explain them to me." My aunt's tone was more and more guarded and defensive. "He asked when I'd last seen Perkins and I told him, perhaps at eleven or so, when I'd begun to feel . . . . to feel as though I couldn't endure any more sly remarks or any more . . . uh . . . disrespect—" She stumbled over the lie, the excuse for withdrawing into her room, and then for a moment she looked directly at me and that desperate, imploring expression swept across her. She seemed to be begging *me,* not Rye, for some sign of compassion or of understanding. And though I knew she was lying, I felt a great pity and sorrow for her.

"You were right," I found myself saying. "It was the best way to handle the situation."

Rye was staring obliquely up at me, a look that said, *Now, what on earth can you mean by that?*

Aunt Wanda's eyes grew shuttered and secretive again. "I had spoken to Perkins in the downstairs hall, calling his attention to some deliberate sloppiness on Martha's part. You two had been gone for a while. It was after you left that I . . . I felt that the maids were being rather sly and . . . mocking." She moved over toward the door. The silence in the room was awkward with what had gone unsaid, with what we all knew was the truth. "I have these times, Esther. Rye has told you, of course. I can't seem to . . . to cope. I have a terrible desire to just walk away, to leave everything, to go back to live the way I . . . I used to."

Well, I'd already guessed that. Aunt Wanda was building a nest egg for just that purpose.

"What seems to bring on these moods?" I probed.

She put a hand on the doorknob. "Just . . . just nerves, I guess. Tension. The weight of responsibility. I'm so afraid I'll do something wrong, something to ruin it all."

She was baffling me. How could she ruin anything here? It was all too smoothly geared, too well organized, between John Sutton and Perkins. There was a desperate, miserable truth in the background somewhere.

"Is there anyone living around here whom you knew in days past?" I asked pointedly.

"Oh, no!" Her face blanched under the makeup; I'd come too close to the truth. "No one! No one at all!" Fear looked nakedly from her eyes, a fear like that of an animal's when it sees a trap closing. And again I was stirred to pity.

"It was just a thought, Aunt Wanda. I don't know where it came from."

Rye hadn't been fooled, though. She was giving the oblique, doubting glance to our aunt now. It was plain that Rye wanted to ask some questions of her own, but Aunt Wanda's open distress kept her quiet.

"If you did have someone," I amended, "like an old friend with whom you could relax and be yourself, you might find it a great comfort."

But I was making things worse, not better. Aunt Wanda was shaking her head almost fiercely. "There isn't anyone like that at all. I left everything behind, everyone I knew, except Barbara and you. A clean break. Like being reborn. With your parents dead . . . who was there to care anything about?" She gave us a strange, broken smile. "Well, I'm on my way to check supplies." It was an excuse to get out of the room and not to listen to any more of my questions.

She went out, and then came back and stuck her head in. "If anything should happen while I'm gone, if some emergency should come up, just call John Sutton. He isn't really the . . . the ogre I've made him out to be."

She didn't explain why she had made John Sutton an ogre.

She wanted us to wonder about it, no doubt, and to leave those other ideas alone.

"What was that all about?" Rye demanded.

I sat down on the chaise and dropped the sweater and purse and gloves. "Nothing much. I was just fishing around."

"You scared her out of her wits. And that bit about an old pal out of the past? What brought that on?"

"It just occurred to me to wonder if anyone around here could be a person Aunt Wanda had known in her roughneck years. She covered a lot of ground."

Rye sat up. "You mean, a man? Some secret love? Pock, you're dreaming!"

"So, I'm dreaming," I agreed.

"I bet I know something else you think," Rye said. "You've decided that the things that happened at Jim's grave, the nasty little messages, have something to do with what went on in the house. And with what happened to Perkins."

"Rye, I'm not a superbrain. I can guess a little, but I can't prove anything."

"No, but you can think. And getting back to this old friend out of the past—"

"Look," I said impatiently, "there has to be a reason for it all. A motive. It springs out of *something.* Nobody sets up a mean little plot, tricks, hurtful machinations, for nothing. You could say, perhaps, Aunt Wanda stepped on a few toes when she first came here, gave orders too freely, insulted the cook so that he left, made the others resentful—but I can't believe that for such a motive, things would be done like those that have been done. It just has to go deeper. And deeper has to mean the past. She's made somebody so raging mad that he, or she, will torment her in any way possible. And I think she's given someone, perhaps the same person, a hold over her. She sits still for what goes on, she wants you to keep still too, and she plays at ignoring it all and perhaps it will go away. She doesn't even show any grief over Perkins, though you would think she'd really be broken up over him."

Rye flopped over, brushed hair from her eyes, the tangled red curls like the color of flame. "And you think—"

"I have a big fat suspicion that Perkins stumbled into a part, or perhaps all, of Aunt Wanda's secret. Aunt Wanda's private skeleton in its hidden closet. And Perkins wasn't the kind to sit still and do nothing. He was too loyal. He wasn't afraid, as the phrase is, to get involved. So he went after somebody. And that somebody murdered him."

"She can't keep silent after that, if there *is* a connection. If she knows there is."

"She knows. And she's still going to keep still. You saw what happened a minute or so ago when I asked my few questions."

"What about Mrs. Stryfe? Doesn't she have a motive for being angry? She was kind of heir to all this, to Larchwood, before Mr. Barrod married Aunt Wanda. And Aunt Wanda cut her out."

"Maybe she is angry. Maybe she feels cheated. But I can't see that what she's doing, if she's doing it, is going to get her in here as mistress of Larchwood. Even if Aunt Wanda just walked away, as she threatened to do, the place wouldn't go back to Mrs. Stryfe. She's been permanently sidetracked, and there's no way it can all revert to her."

"Maybe Angela had hopes. Maybe she had an eye on Mr. Barrod

herself, a May-and-December thing, and then when Aunt Wanda stepped in as the unexpected bride, she went psycho."

"So what hold does she have on our aunt, that Aunt Wanda won't even talk about it? And by the way, you're not to thrash around and sit up. Lie down flat."

"Mother Pocket speaking. You exasperate me." But she dutifully turned over, stretched out. "I'm really kind of sorry I came here. And even sorrier I got you into it. This might be a kind of dangerous place."

"Yes, it could be."

"Are you sorry you came?"

"No." Well, not entirely. Let's leave John Sutton out of it, I told myself.

"Have you been to Jim's grave since that first night you came?"

"Yes. Nothing new and ugly has been done." I won't think about that shape in black, my mind is covering it the way scar tissue covers a wound. My thoughts go around it, circle it, and I don't even try to visualize the face behind the hood any more.

But the malice behind it all—that remained.

"Would you get me some orange juice, Pock?"

"Delighted."

I took my purse and gloves and sweater to my own room, and then went downstairs. The house was gloomy, and silence lay thick. No lights had been lit, though the dark afternoon was drawing into rainy twilight. Aunt Wanda was in the kitchen. She stood in the middle of the floor, rather as if stranded there in a web of misery, obviously trying to figure something out. Perhaps a way out of her difficulties. I went close to her, but there was no word of greeting. I put a hand gently on her arm. "If there is anything at all I can do for you, please tell me."

My aunt started to draw away and I thought I saw a flicker of dislike in her eyes, her usual reaction to any approach by me. But then, rather hesitantly, she put a hand on mine. "Thank you."

"I'm sorry for . . . many things."

There was a sudden glisten of something like tears, which were quickly winked away. She said softly, "I, too. Many things."

The years were there with us, in this room, all of the long past in which we had known and disliked each other; only now, perhaps, some small change was taking place. I couldn't be sure.

I said, "Don't think about leaving Larchwood. It belongs to you and you belong to it. You are the mistress here. Don't let anyone or anything make you forget that."

For once she seemed to turn toward me as a friend, and I was aware of her not as an enemy, someone ready to heap hurt and ridicule, but as a person related to me, a part of my life from its beginnings, someone to whom I owed loyalty and love even as I owed them to Rye. "Oh, Esther, be careful how you live. The past *isn't* dead, *isn't* forgotten and buried. You have to live with your mistakes forever. God doesn't let them die."

"God does. Man doesn't." I waited, anxious that she should go on. I wanted to say: Who is it? Who came into your life here, out of the past?

"I was drunk," Aunt Wanda said, and her voice hoarsened into its barroom contralto. "I was drunk when you came to talk to me yesterday. Drunk and cruel."

"Well—I *am* an orphan." I tried to make it light and uncaring. "And so is Rye. Since our parents are gone. I can take it like that, until you want to talk about it further."

But the look of hope and reconciliation was fading. Aunt Wanda found herself, plainly, on dangerous ground. She wasn't ready to be confiding and honest. She removed her hand from mine and stepped away. "When I get back from New Orleans, we'll talk. I'll have time to think of what I ought to say. There is so much . . . so much you might not understand. So much you might not even forgive. I don't want to take anything away from you, Esther. Promise me you'll always believe that."

A strange request, and the wording of it made me very apprehensive. What had I that she could take away?

"I literally own nothing." I have memories, of course, like the one of being led from the orphanage into the unfamiliar street. Could she take that away?

"Just remember what I've said." In the gloom of the kitchen, my aunt's eyes seemed masked, almost as if she were looking through me at some possibility of danger, danger that must not be openly acknowledged, must be kept hidden. The frost of her white hair was the only brightness in the shadows. "Just remember, Esther."

For a moment as we remained facing each other, I thought: I've a million things to say and I don't know how to say them. Time has turned me mute. I could begin by thanking her for the lovely ring she gave me all those long years ago, the beautiful and expensive thing she had paid for out of some uncommon fluke of fortune. I could beg her forgiveness for my ingratitude, but I don't know how to sound loving and grateful to my aunt.

So instead I said, "Rye wants some orange juice."

She went to the refrigerator for a bottle of juice, took down a small tray from a cupboard, a glass, and a small starched doily from a supply in a drawer. In short order Rye's thirst-quencher was ready.

"When Barbara and you are ready for dinner, don't hesitate to fix whatever you want. It was very good of you, Esther, to tell Mrs. Mim to take the day off. I'll see that Cindy has her meal."

The storm was pelting past the window, and the room was suddenly darkening. As if seized by an afterthought, Aunt Wanda went to a drawer and removed a ring of keys and handed them to me.

"We may leave earlier than day-after-tomorrow. Mrs. Mim may want a hand in arranging Perkins' funeral. You may as well have the keys now, while you're here. And so that I don't forget to give them to you."

Keys were not used at Larchwood. Was she also handing me a warning? I went out with the tray and the keys, leaving my aunt alone with her thoughts.

Nineteen

I TOOK THE ORANGE JUICE TO RYE. "Aunt Wanda gave me the house keys. I'm going up to the belvedere to watch the storm."

"Don't fall off," Rye warned.

"Thanks for the vote of confidence. I'll get my coat and a scarf."

A few minutes later I was up there on top of the house, the vast slopes of the roof all around me, the slates running with water under the last of the twilight, the storm beating in in sheets under the small eaves of the belvedere. Low clouds and rain and the beginning of darkness cut off the near distance; this was a narrower world than I'd seen from up here with my aunt. In spite of the coat and scarf, I was chilled. The smell of rain filled my lungs.

Lightning twitched against the dark, far away, and then without warning a great brilliant fork of it spread downward from directly overhead, so that I felt caught and pinned in that blue-green explosion, and in the instant of greatest brilliance I saw something—or someone—at the edge of the woods beyond the garages. Was it at the point where the trail came out of the woods? I couldn't be sure. The light was gone in the next instant and then came the enormous bump, bump, bump of thunder; I actually seemed to feel the floor of the belvedere rocking under me. I couldn't see any trace of the figure, or shape, or whatever it was. I'd thought in that fugitive moment of someone in a raincoat, one of those lightweight and light-colored garments made almost alike for both women and men.

I waited, standing well back to shelter from the driving rain. Who was watching the house? And *why?*

Or am I seeing things?

Could Aunt Wanda have hurried out there, checking up on something? It would scarcely seem that she'd had time. Could it have been Mrs. Mim? Somehow that was even more unlikely.

I willed the lightning to come again, but there were no further flashes close enough to lighten the dark perceptibly, and after a time of waiting and of growing more and more chilled, I finally went down into the house. Passing the dark nook where the stairs ended, the door to the tower, I whispered to myself, "Why not?"

I slid the key into the lock and it turned without squeaking; the lock was not unused, not without oil. I pulled the door open and was met by an odor of dust and disuse. There were windows here, tall ones that faced west, and these let in the last of the dying light, without really illuminating the interior. I felt beside the door for a light switch and clicked it on. A lamp came to life in the center of the circular room, a small lamp on a table piled with papers and books. Around the walls were various trunks and boxes, apparently stored stuff. The air was stale.

I walked to the table with its lamp and felt a slight give and shiver of the floor under my feet. Aunt Wanda had said that the tower was unsafe, and now I believed her. I hesitated, then got busy looking over the stacks of papers—they were mostly receipts for stock feed and nursery equipment, lumber and cement, all stapled together according to month and year of payment, and going back in the main about four or five years. A film of dust covered papers and books and the dull green cloth that covered the table.

Against the far wall was the bannister of the stairs leading to the lower room. I went to the stair opening and looked down. The stairs, I made out, followed the curve of the wall and were narrow and graceful, with the wrought-iron railing painted white, carpeted in dark blue plush. I tested the top step with my weight, expecting some give and shuddering, but the tread seemed firm enough.

I went down carefully into the gloom.

This lower round room also had tall windows giving a murky half light. It seemed a little larger than the room above, perhaps because the tower widened by a few feet at its base. I crossed to the light switch beside the door opposite, and as soon as I touched the switch a small, elegant chandelier shone brilliantly overhead. I saw at once that this room showed no signs of neglect, nor of clutter or dust. This room was ready for occupancy.

Two blue-velvet loveseats faced each other across a round marble-topped coffee table in the middle of the room. There were matching chairs, with scattered occasional tables, on the outskirts of the room, and a raised white-brick fireplace stood against the inner wall. The hearth was clean of any ashes, and materials for a fresh fire had been laid. The circular rug was a thickly tufted one of various shades of blue and violet; the walls were paneled in a bleached wood of some sort. It was a tiny parlor, beautifully arranged, neat and cozy, markedly different from the room above.

I shed my damp coat, went to the coffee table, and explored a box of inlaid brass. It held a supply of cigarettes and I took one and lit it from the matching brass lighter. I sat down to think over what I'd found here. This was a room where people met to talk and to consult regularly. It was a very private place, unlike the big parlor, for instance, or Aunt Wanda's little offices, or any other room in the house. It was as if alone and separate from the rest of Larchwood.

It could be the room, I told myself, where my aunt entertained visitors who came at odd hours—like the middle of the night—and whose business concerned her alone.

I noted that this room had two doors. With the stairs, there were three ways of getting in and out. The door to the right of the fireplace must lead out into the big cross hall of the lower floor, the hall whose opposite end gave on the porte-cochere. The door near the windows would seem to lead to the veranda, not far from the spot where breakfast was served on nice mornings.

There was no creaking and no give to the floor down here. It was as solid as stone.

I leaned forward to tap the cigarette into a bronze ashtray, and something hard nudged my hip from beneath the cushion at the end of the small couch. I tapped out the cigarette and ran an exploring hand under the blue-velvet cushion. What I found was a gun. Not a small gun either, but big and businesslike, with a blued steel barrel and a worn ivory grip. An old gun, a well-cared-for gun that had been expensive to start with. I knew enough to break it open and look into the chamber. The chamber was full of bullets.

I put the gun back where I'd found it. There was a kind of natural recess there where the webbing and springs joined the arm of the loveseat under the cushion.

Well, I thought, I know where to lay my hands on a gun if I need one. The gun could belong to my aunt and be where it was, hidden in the small couch, for some reason known only to her, or it could have belonged to Mr. Barrod and have been left there by him before he had died, forgotten. Just one point bothered me. If Perkins had known about the gun and had known he was walking into danger, wouldn't he have taken the gun with him?

So Perkins hadn't known of the gun, or hadn't realized his danger.

I got up and took the ashtray to the fireplace and carefully disposed of ashes and cigarette behind the wood laid there. I wiped out the ashtray with a stray tissue I found in my coat pocket, put everything back the way I'd found it, picked up my coat and turned out the light, and went back upstairs. The floor creaked a little as I crossed it to turn off the lamp, but I decided that Aunt Wanda's warning had been on the strong side. The tower was far from ready to fall down. With her telling you in advance that the whole thing was ready to collapse, you naturally exaggerated every hint of wobble and quiver.

Clever Aunt Wanda.

No, not clever enough. Not nearly clever enough to outwit what was tormenting her.

Rye was bored and restless and not interested in dinner. I fixed the two of us a bowl of soup apiece, canned split-pea soup, and made scrambled eggs and toast. I saw no sign, in the kitchen, of my aunt or of Mrs. Mim or Cindy.

"It's going to rain all night," Rye said accusingly when I came in with the cart.

"Well, I hope it stops before morning. I'll admit, I don't like to wake up to rain clouds. I've made us soup and sandwiches. That dumb-waiter idea is really pretty cute."

"I'm really not hungry."

"You ought to eat anyway."

"You make me feel like an egg ready to hatch," Rye grumbled, but she let me fix the bed tray and lay it across her knees. "Did you call John Sutton?"

"I forgot."

"Pock, you aggravate me. He took out after you in his little car. I know I wasn't supposed to be up, but I heard you pussyfooting in the hall, listening at the door to make sure I was being good for the doctor, and then I just had to go look as you were leaving, and it was gloomy and I enjoyed standing there feeling terribly sorry for myself, and then lo and imagine if Mr. Sutton didn't leave too, dashing grimly away in his sports car. Didn't he catch you on the road?"

"I managed to lose him." I dipped into the soup. Grimly.

"I know you want me to keep my mouth shut," my sister persisted, "but I'm going to talk anyway. Isn't there, someday, going to be a certain someone? I know that sounds tacky." She giggled. "But isn't there?"

"I don't know." I considered it highly unlikely. The sound of rain made a sudden spatter at the window. "Maybe not."

"But why not? You're beautiful and you're intelligent. I'm *not* saying it because you're my sister. You *are*. Well, they always blame these things like . . . uh . . . being unresponsive—"

"Frigid."

"I hate that word. And you're not. But they blame it on when you were a kid. You couldn't learn to love because you never saw anyone having a loving relationship. Like parents. But that isn't true about you. We grew up together in the same house—"

"Part of the time."

Rye was abruptly silenced. She laid her spoon down slowly, and as I watched I thought that the spoon would never reach the tray, Rye would never finish the gesture, the slowly descending hand would go on descending forever. What on earth had made me say what I had?

Rye's tone was scratchy and uncertain. "What's that supposed to mean?"

"Oh, nothing. I don't know."

"Yes, you do."

I couldn't control my miserable voice; it shook. "Didn't it ever occur to you that I don't resemble anyone else in the family? That I'm the odd one and always was? The freak? You and Mother and Dad were of a pattern. Aunt Wanda, too. You made a . . . a bunch of people who belonged together. But I was just a . . . a—" I shook my head angrily, dismissing the rest of it. And willing that Rye should let it be.

"Are you trying to tell me something crazy?" Rye had actually turned pale.

"There's a place I dream about sometimes. An orphanage. It's just too real to be nothing but a nightmare, made of nothing."

"I won't let you do it!" A pulse was beating in the side of her throat. "You're saying that you're not my sister. You're someone else, someone strange. But I won't accept it. I'm not letting you out of this commitment, this being here because I need you. Whatever it is, the meanness, the criminal rottenness, we can face it together."

"I didn't mean that I wanted out of *that!*"

We were yelling at each other, the way we'd done when we were children.

"So shut up!" Then, more quietly, Rye added. "And I'll shut up about John Sutton. Okay?"

I didn't answer. I was eating my soup. I was remembering that Aunt Wanda had said she wouldn't willingly take anything away from me, and I'd thought there was nothing to take, and now I knew better.

And Rye was looking me over now as if toting up all those unlikenesses I'd been talking about and that she hadn't noticed before. Aunt Wanda didn't have to take my sister from me; I was doing the job myself.

"Take a good look."

"Are you going to shut up?"

"Glad to. Just stop staring at the freak."

"I know what you mean. You think I'm staring because of what you said. But I'm not. I'm not trying to see what color your eyes really are, nor if your head's the wrong shape, I'm staring because all at once—" She choked over it, and I realized with a twinge of grief that she was trying not to cry. "—all at once I'm seeing my sister, you, and knowing how p . . . precious you are to me, and always have been, and how awful it would be if—"

I set aside my tray and went to the bed, picked up Rye's hand, and laid it against my cheek.

"But you can't just love *me,* Pock. There has to be a man somewhere, a man for you as Jim was for me, a loving and good man, a companion, and I want you to find him."

The very words froze me, but I couldn't tell her that. The spinster had been too long in control. "Some girls get into a lot of trouble trying to run down a man. You ought to be glad I'm taking my time."

"I just hope that's what you're doing."

I turned on lights in the long hall, ran the tea cart down to the little cupboard where it was stored, where the dumb-waiter had its little door in the wall. I sent down the dishes and trays and then went downstairs and turned on lights in the pantry and washed up. While I was putting away the last of the dishes I heard a car outside.

I turned out the lights quickly and waited in the gloom. The sound of the car came closer, as if it were being driven through the porte-cochere, then on toward the rear of the house. Through the noise of the rain I could hear the crunch of gravel; and then the car went on, must have turned out toward the garages, and I relaxed. Aunt Wanda had been out on an errand.

I'm *not* thinking of John Sutton, I told myself.

I realized that the car was coming back; it had circled out there, the big loop at the garages, and had come back through the porte-cochere and was again at the rear of the house.

And now had stopped . . .

This was no casual, tentative caller. I sensed authority here. I went out into the lighted hall and on to the rear entry, and here was Chris Warne, his big cap in his hands, his hair wet with rain. "Miss Myles?"

"Do you want to see my aunt?"

"I was just passing. Checking things. We haven't got anyone yet in this murder case, and I thought I ought to stop. Someone else will be by during the night. But meanwhile I wanted to ask you to lock up. Just a matter of precaution."

I felt like telling him that there were too many doors to Larchwood and that probably a lot of them have locks that haven't been tried for years, and if anyone wants in, how about all the windows? But I said, "Thanks for reminding us. I'll see what I can do."

"How is your sister? I hope that this trouble hasn't . . . uh . . . caused any complications. Or anything." He was nice in his shyness.

"No, she's fine. Thank you for asking."

"I took the liberty of turning on a light out at the garages. I suggest that you turn on other outside lights, too, at least one on each side of the house."

A single light on each side of Larchwood wouldn't be much, but I agreed it was a good idea—providing I could find the switches for doing it—and I said, "Are you sure you couldn't use a hot cup of coffee or something?"

"No, thanks. I'm going off duty now, I'll eat at home."

I thought: He's married and his wife is waiting dinner for him, baked ham and sweet potatoes and a chocolate meringue pie—

As if to correct what he knew I was thinking, he added: "My brother and I share an apartment. He's the cook. I clean up. I can't say he's a terribly good cook, but then he isn't too awful, either."

I told him he was lucky.

Someday, I thought, watching Chris Warne walk away in the rainy night, he *will* have a wife and there will be a chocolate pie. And kids, nice kids. And when he comes home to them out of the wet and the dark, into all that warmth and gladness . . .

I had come up against a wall, a wall of ice, and I was the spinster who could catch a glimpse but never really know life as it should be, and who knows it will never happen to her.

I found light switches for the verandas, north and west, and turned on the coachlight in the porte-cochere, and a big bulb over the rear entry, a light so bright that I could even make out Aunt Wanda's flower garden. I locked up as best I could. All locks seemed to be in order. The fastenings on the French doors to the verandas seemed the most vulnerable. A good prying tool should do the job in less than a minute.

The house, as I walked through it, was completely silent. Dimly, as from far away, came the whisper of rain at the windows.

In the upper hall I could suddenly hear a phone ringing; and then it stopped, and so Aunt Wanda must have answered in her bedroom. While I hesitated with my hand on Rye's door, my aunt came out into the hall. She wore a loose robe, her hair hung limp and white, and she seemed in a way much older and tireder than when I'd last seen her in the kitchen.

"Esther, Mr. Sutton wants to speak to you. He's on the phone now. Why don't you take the call in my office?" She motioned toward the door down the hall where I'd done my small burglary, if you could call it that.

Was this the moment of decision?

Could I go now and talk to John Sutton? And what could I say? How is Angela? Have you set the date? And other such female-jealousy nonsense? I didn't have it in me, and the spinster didn't know the words nor the maneuvers. The game was unfamiliar.

But was this the time I'd look back upon later and say, that's when it could have been one way or the other, I could have answered John's call, only I didn't? I turned my back to him for the last time. He had tried to get hold of me all day to tell me something, he followed me from the house, he left a message to phone him, and I didn't, and now he's making a last attempt.

I shivered. Yes, this must be that kind of moment, that kind of time.

Poor John Sutton.

Poorer—much poorer—me.

"Aunt Wanda, please tell Mr. Sutton that I've gone to bed early and can't be disturbed now."

"Esther—"

"Please do." I opened Rye's door and went into the room.

Twenty

I GOT OUT OF BED in the gray, rainy light and found the note stuck in at the bottom of the door.

DEAR ESTHER—

We are leaving now, 4:30 A.M. I decided not to wake you to say goodbye. Mrs. Mim wants to drop Cindy off at some relatives' place, and this involved a long, roundabout detour. It's not that you and Barbara couldn't have cared for the little girl. Mrs. Mim had already planned for Cindy to spend most of the summer with her cousins, where she'll have other children her own age to play with. And this is a good chance to get her there.

Thanks for locking up last night. I should have thought of it. If you need help in any way, call on John. I'm sorry you refused his call last night. I know it's none of my business, but you could be making a mistake. I know that I talked about him as if he were some kind of money monster, but that was just a pretense on my part. He isn't like that. And I'm sure he likes you very much.

I'm not sure just when I'll be home again. I may stay for the funeral, but if it involves a wait of several days, I may not. It just depends.

I know that you will see that Barbara obeys the doctor's orders. I put all trust in you.

AUNT WANDA

So she put all trust in me, did she, leaving all things in my hands? For some reason I resented the tone of the letter, I felt it was patronizing, though she may not have meant it to sound so. Prickly old Pocket, I jeered at myself, always looking for insults and rejection and belittling.

I showered and dressed and went down the hall to Rye's room. Rye was in her nightgown, standing at the window. She gave me a frowning, disgusted look and said, "It's going to rain all day. It's that settled kind of drizzle that doesn't quit. And I'm bored."

"Rye, please—"

"I know, I know. Chin up. Be brave." Rye went to the bed and flopped on it. She pulled the coverlet up under her chin. The room was comfortable, warm, well lit. "When we were little, Mother made up all kinds of silly rainy-day games for us. Do you remember? We had contests. We had raindrop races on the windowpane. We made paper ducks that we could float." She rubbed her head discontentedly into the pillow. "Life is easier when you're a kid."

"I guess so."

"Oh, I forgot. You weren't a member of the family. Mother never paid any attention to you. You never made paper ducks."

I stood perfectly still just inside the door. "If you say."

"I know just how horrible I'm being. How cruel and nasty. And how much I need a good pop in the chops."

"I didn't come here to fight with you. I know you're edgy and short-tempered. You always were, in bad weather. What do you want for breakfast?"

Rye rolled over on her face and cupped her eyes with her hands and began to cry. I sat down on the edge of the bed and waited.

After a while she said, "It's been forever since Jim died. I've been caught in a kind of limbo. A nowhere place. I'm not a wife any more, I'm in between being a wife and being something else, and I'm in between being one person and two people. I'm a thing that's going to hatch, only not yet. I have to wait. I can't be anything nor do anything that's new and fun."

"Do you mean that you don't want your baby?" I asked quietly.

"Are you out of your mind? Of course I—I—" She twisted to face me.

"I wish I could comfort you, Rye, but what can I say? That I can change things? Or that you can? It *is* a time when you simply have to endure. Endure being a widow, being pregnant, and all I can do is be here. To stand by."

Rye curled on her side and rubbed away the tears. "I know. Really I know. It's just there all the time, the miserable knowledge of the fix I'm in. I'm sorry I came here to Larchwood. I thought, you know, the beautiful big home, being here with Aunt Wanda, no problems, servants to wait on you. . . . Why don't I see the good things any more?"

"You're tired." I felt helpless and baffled.

"I tried to knit," Rye wept, "and the stuff I knitted, you wouldn't put in a rag bag. Awful things. I let Aunt Wanda buy it all, the baby's things, the little sweaters and booties and things. It all came out of a damned s . . . store!"

"And probably just as well. Won't you try to eat something? I don't want to nag. But you should."

Rye cried for a little longer over the failure of the knitting, and then let me coax her into wanting a little breakfast. I told her about our aunt's early departure, the note under my door, and this took her mind off her own miseries for the moment. She was no doubt picturing the horrible drive in the pouring rain.

As I was leaving, she called after me, "Call up that nice cop and see if they've caught whoever killed Perkins. I woke up in the middle of the night to worry over it."

And so did I, I wanted to answer; but I kept still. Downstairs the night lights burned along the halls, and there was an eerie sense of emptiness. The kitchen was gloomy, so I turned on lights to make breakfast by. The refrigerator seemed stuffed with food.

I was aware of being completely alone down here. Rye was far away upstairs. And there were just we two. With silence ringing around me, I felt a moment of near panic.

I forced myself to get to the business at hand, and I was buttering toast when the phone rang. The extension here was on the wall above the counter; I reached for it. I'd thought of Bart, offering his services, or of Chris Warne. But this was John Sutton. I said, "Hello," and he said, "Pocket." And then my tongue clove to the roof of my mouth, literally, and I was voiceless.

"It is Pocket, isn't it?"

"M . . . my aunt isn't here," I got out, choking over it.

"I know. She phoned me late last night. I want to come over there. Now."

I was possessed in that moment by a bitter and childish spite, and wanted to say, "But Angela isn't visiting now." Only what I managed to say was, "Why not?" I sounded stupid.

"I wanted you to tell me Yes, come on over—and that you wouldn't run away from me again."

I stood with the phone against my ear, and I was dizzy with fright, my heart thudding. "Don't . . . don't—"

"There was some misunderstanding yesterday. I guess I was trying to be clever. A false hope in all cases, as far as I'm concerned. Can't I tell you about it?"

I had to say something. "You don't owe me any explanation at all."

He waited a moment, as if thinking. "What you're trying to tell me is that you don't want me to feel that I owe an explanation. You want me to shrug everything off. You want to pretend that there is nothing between us and so my little act with Angela didn't matter. Isn't that right?"

"What am I supposed to say then?" I was driven to ask, feeling silly and childish, and aching to hang up and not to listen to his voice.

"I guess I wished that you care a little. About me. I guess I wanted you to remember our trip to the cemetery . . . not a romantic place, really. But since I went there with you, it seemed romantic to me. When we were there, the two of us, all alone in the night, I wanted to hold you. I keep thinking about how much I wanted to do that."

There was nothing I could say to this.

The house was completely silent and I felt very alone, pinned down here, held by his voice, a bright light overhead, rainy gloom outside, breakfast half prepared. He was hoping I'd say that I too had wanted him to hold me.

"I was afraid," I stammered.

"Not of me."

"Yes." Let the truth come out, and let it scare him away, or open his eyes to the freak he thought he was beginning to fall for. I tried to say, "I am just a congenitally—" Was that the word I wanted? "—frigid woman. There are some, you know. Congenitally frigid. Frozen solid. Loveless and always alone, except for a few safe people like very close relatives." It was a sensible speech, inside me where I rehearsed it; but it wouldn't come out, it wouldn't become vocal. It remained in there tied in my throat like a lump. And finally I made a noise like a croak, and hung up.

It took a minute or so to get straightened out, to get back into the business of getting breakfast. I finally got it all upon a big tray, took the tray to the pantry and got it into the dumb-waiter, and ran upstairs and put the tray on the cart up there. Then I stopped for a moment. My mouth was dry, and there was a dull ache inside me. There was a terrible feeling of having done something irreparable. A hollow emptiness; I'd thrown away something I could never get back.

But after a short time I forced the feeling away and took the cart down the hall to Rye's room. And as I came in, Rye lifted her head and cried, "You've been crying! And what an ugly beast I was."

"Nothing to do with you." I began uncovering our food.

"Who, then?"

"Just something I need to think about."

Always think about a thing when it's gone for good.

My sister gave me a long, frustrated stare but didn't ask any more questions.

While I was doing dishes in the pantry, the big sheriff's cruiser came into view outside the window, circling out by the garages, then came to a slow stop just at the edge of the space I could see.

I drew the night bolt at the rear door and asked Chris Warne inside, and wondered why I wasn't so tight-frozen with him, and decided that it was because he was a cop and that the uniform removed him a little from those with whom I had to be afraid. He was very big, there in the dimness of the hall. I asked if he would like some coffee and he said Yes, that would be fine. He was carrying a single irislike flower in one gloved hand. Unexpectedly, he offered it to me.

The stem felt hard and cool in my hand. The flower was beaded with rain, a purple bloom with yellow stamens, giving off a hint of wild odor.

"There's a bouquet on your brother-in-law's grave," he said. "It wasn't there last night. I went by, I checked after leaving here. Nothing. Now this morning there are flowers. No message, nothing ugly. Just the bouquet and some fern, making a fan shape. Sort of pretty."

For some reason, in that instant I thought of the handkerchief spread over Perkins' face. What was the connection? I couldn't explain the possible link, even to myself. A gesture of gentleness coming after savagery? It might be.

"No footprints?" I offered. "Anything to show whether the person came by road or by the path?"

We'd gone into the kitchen and he was putting his cap on the tiled counter and was stripping off his gloves. "It's all too wet. Grass springs back, earth's turned to mud."

"Let me get your coffee."

I put the flower into a water glass, ran water in, and stood it on the windowsill. Chris Warne leaned against the counter to drink his coffee, refusing my offer of a chair; he said he was tired of sitting, that being in the patrol car kept him sitting most of the day, and it felt good to stretch. "When will your aunt be back?"

I was putting away the last of the breakfast things and didn't try to hide my surprise. "You knew she was gone?"

"She called the office last night and wanted an eye kept on the place here. But of course we were doing that anyway. She seemed especially concerned about your sister." He gave me an uncertain, lopsided smile, and his eyes were suddenly shy. "I don't suppose she wants to see anybody."

"Rye? Wait, let me ask her."

When I ran up and told Rye that Officer Warne wanted to look at her to make sure she was all right, Rye laughed. "Give me my mirror and makeup. You'll have to work on my hair. Oh, for Pete's sake, why can't I stay neat and pretty in bed? I'm a cow."

Chris Warne seemed even bigger, more masculine and out of place in the fluffy bedroom. He accepted a chair, a gilt-and-white chair with a brocade seat, and the three of us exchanged banalities about the horrible weather, and he told us that of all the states Louisiana had the highest average rainfall. Rye quizzed him about his background, and it turned out that he had come to Louisiana from Minnesota when he had been about fifteen.

"That's why you don't have the local accent," Rye told him.

"I'm getting it. Slow but sure, creeping in about the edges. You hear it all the time, you can't help copy it. I'll sound like a native after a few years."

"You intend to stay here, then?"

"Well . . ." He hesitated, the look of shyness returning. "My plans aren't entirely set. A lot depends upon what the . . . the future holds, I guess."

"Do you have someone in mind?" Rye teased, and he turned scarlet. Well, that was Rye for you. She knew all about the game and she could play it, pregnant and flat on her back in bed.

I didn't say anything about the fresh bouquet on Jim's grave and neither did Chris. He was interested in Rye, and Rye knew it. Perhaps on his part it was a matter of chivalry, rare these days, the wish to comfort and befriend someone his own age who'd gotten a rough deal, or perhaps it was that here was a man who could comprehend that a woman wouldn't forever be newly bereaved, grieving, and pregnant. If this last were true I had to give him a lot of points for uncommon insight.

He rose and made his farewells after a decent interval, trying to give the impression that duty—as imposed by our aunt—had been satisfied; he was an officer, doing what was expected of him, and Rye's teasing could make him blush but didn't obscure the official correctness of it all. I wanted to laugh.

I took him downstairs and saw with a start that someone stood in the lower hall, a little past the kitchen doorway where light spilled into the gloom. Coming closer, with Chris's massive presence right behind me, I recognized Martha. She wore a dark raincoat, and her hair was hidden by the attached hood. "Miss Esther, I need to see Mrs. Barrod," she said without preamble.

"My aunt isn't here."

"In that case I'll leave a message for her with Miss Barbara."

Chris nodded to Martha and to me he said, "I'll let myself out. And I'll be back again today."

"If you want to, you may leave the message with me," I said. Martha's eyes seemed brilliant and piercing instead of what I'd thought of as a sullen and secretive look. But she shook her head.

"I'd prefer Miss Barbara. No disrespect intended. It's just that I've known her longer and I'd feel freer in what I have to say."

I sensed some unpleasantness in her manner, a hint of anger. "I can't subject my sister to any kind of scene."

Martha's mouth grew prim. "Nothing at all like that."

"Very well." I led Martha back the way I'd just come with Chris Warne. I rapped at Rye's door, and Rye called to come in.

Rye said, "Why, hello, Martha." She shook her head as if over a puzzle. "How did you get here?"

The question deflected what must have been a prepared speech. "I borrowed my sister's car, miss. I *do* drive. I came to leave a message for your aunt."

"Couldn't it wait until she gets here?"

"No, miss. Or rather, I don't want it to wait. Please tell Mrs. Barrod that I'm quitting my job here. My reasons have to do with family matters—my family. I won't be back, and she can mail my last check to my house in town. She has the address."

Martha's dark face was tense and determined; her hands clutched her handbag to her bosom as if it were a shield. I saw that she exuded an air not so much of anger as of decision, the reaching of a turning point. "Tell Mrs. Barrod it won't do any good to come into town to talk to me, or to ask me back. I won't come back. Ever."

"Does this have anything to do with what happened to Perkins?" I put in.

She must have known the question would come; she snapped her reply quickly. "Nothing at all. Please make it plain to your aunt."

"How about the other girls?" Rye asked. "Lydia and Pearl?"

"For all I know they'll be back when Mrs. Barrod wants them. This is just me. And I'm quitting."

"There has to be a reason, Martha," Rye said, sounding sympathetic and coaxing, and I could see the effect on Martha, the slight thaw in her manner.

"I've felt for some time that I was being blamed for things that happened here, and that I didn't do."

Rye nodded. "Of course, when Aunt Wanda's in one of her spells—"

"Pardon me, but I didn't mean that," Martha interrupted. "All of us know that your aunt has a . . . a problem. We excused this because most of the time she's a very nice lady, a nice person to work for. No, this wasn't anything to do with her moods. And anyway, it hasn't anything to do with my leaving. That's family."

"I'm sure that if you change your mind, Aunt Wanda will be happy to see you again."

"That won't happen." Martha walked to the door. "I wish you all of the best, Miss Barbara. A beautiful baby and a happy life. Please take care of yourself and do what your doctor orders." She glanced over toward me, and her attitude visibly cooled. I was the interloper, of course, unwelcome here. Or was it more than that? Had I somehow come too close to the truth? All unknowing? I couldn't imagine how. To me she said, "Goodbye, miss. Don't see me out. I know my way well enough."

With a nod of farewell she opened the door, walked through, and shut it firmly behind her.

Rye's brows went up and she started to speak, and then stopped. We waited a couple of minutes; then I quietly opened the door, looked out, and walked softly to the corner where the two halls crossed.

When I returned Rye said, "I can't figure it out. 'Blamed for things I didn't do.' I would have sworn she was the spy and troublemaker."

"So would I."

"Maybe it's a matter of pride, a case of 'I'll quit before she can fire me.'"

"I don't know. It seemed as if something had built up in her, she'd thought about it for a long time. Maybe I wasn't very tactful—I figured her for the spy, too, and maybe she sensed that."

"She *did* listen and snoop," Rye insisted. "I've even halfway caught her at it."

I remembered Martha's dawdling in the parlor yesterday morning. "Now I sort of wonder. Perhaps she felt she was being blamed and wanted to find out the truth." And I wished she had shared what she knew, I added to myself.

The subject was one that could only make Rye uneasy. I told her I was going to do a little work around the house, dusting and so forth, at which she hooted, knowing my abilities as a domestic.

By noon the house looked in apple-pie order to me. Admittedly my standards were not those of Perkins, nor of Mrs. Mim, but on the surface all seemed tidily straightened up. I'd even gone out in the rain for flowers, let them dry off in the kitchen, and had replaced withered blooms in the bouquets. I left lights on in the important rooms, the big parlor, the kitchen, my own room, and in the halls, to dispel the gloom caused by leaden skies.

And face it, by my own apprehensions.

I wished now, irrationally, that while I'd been standing with Aunt Wanda in the kitchen last night I had told her of the phantom in the graveyard. In those moments when our old animosities had been put aside, when there had been almost a feeling of closeness between us, she would have listened. She would have believed me.

I was downstairs making a last survey of dark spots that should be lit, when a call from outside took me to the rear entry. Here was Mrs. Stryfe in a raincoat and waterproof hat, carrying a basket.

She came in shedding water and stamping her black boots. "Ugh. Horrible day. I'm a drowned rat. Came through those woods. That path you wouldn't believe. But I had to get out, cooped up so long, and Angela's out with John Sutton again, rain and all. He must be crazy." She handed the basket to me. Did she also take a sharp glance to see how I took the news of Mr. Sutton? I had my mind on other things, however; I was staring at her off-white all-weather coat, a fabric coat treated to shed water and to shut out wind. "Something for the mother-to-be." Mrs. Stryfe pulled off black cotton gloves and yanked the wet hat from her head. The gray buns over her ears made me think of earmuffs. "Let me drop these wet things off in the pantry."

She opened the pantry door and hung coat and hat from a hook, and her actions showed her familiarity with the house. She shucked the boots and left them under the pantry sink. "Now!" she said.

"Did my aunt call you last night?"

"Wanda? Call? I'm afraid not. Did she intend to? Forgot?"

"I just wondered." Aunt Wanda had alerted the sheriff's office and John Sutton to her absence. But not Mrs. Stryfe. Mrs. Stryfe was not to be considered a protector; but here she was. I lifted the lid of the small wicker basket she'd handed me and found myself looking at a pie in a foil pan.

"It's a pie," she said unnecessarily.

I agreed, it did seem very much like a pie, and I thanked her for her trouble.

"Deep-dish gooseberry, I've made them all my life, learned how as a child in Baltimore. Just stick it in the 'fridge, it'll keep. I know you're supposed to bring an invalid something soft and silly, like corn-starch pudding. But I'll bet your sister is tired of stuff like that."

"Rye isn't really an invalid, and there's nothing wrong with her appetite. I think she'll enjoy your pie very much. Let me put it away for now." I put the pie into the refrigerator and the basket on the sink counter. "Will you have lunch with us? I was just trying to think of something to fix. Aunt Wanda isn't here, but she seems to have supplied us with just about everything."

The news of Aunt Wanda's absence didn't raise a brow. Had John Sutton spread the news? Somehow I thought not. And I remembered the figure keeping watch on the house.

"Well . . . why not?" Mrs. Stryfe rubbed her chilled hands together and grinned, showing crooked teeth.

"Have you always worn your hair like that?" I asked, not knowing where the question came from but struck with an alien sense of familiarity, and a deep feeling of unease.

The gray head came up sharply. "My hair? I . . . well, really, of course not." She licked her lips, staring at me, then forced a smile. "When you're younger, you know—and styles change all the time. I haven't always been an old gray hen. Or goose. Or whatever." Under the bright lights of the kitchen her face took on a carved look, the middle-aged flesh seamed by a tool. "An old gray goose," she babbled on, watching me as if wary. "Yes. Say, I'm kind of half frozen. Does your aunt keep brandy in here? Or should I ask—"

I told her I'd been stupid not to offer her a drink right away. I thought of the keys upstairs. Would the liquor supply be locked up? "Do you know where the brandy is kept?"

"There's always a bottle in the dining room sideboard. Why don't I just go and bring it?"

"Fine. I have to run upstairs for a minute. I want to tell Rye you're here and ask what she wants for lunch."

As I hurried upstairs to Rye's room I tried to pin down the impulse behind the crazy question I'd asked Mrs. Stryfe. What did it matter, how she might once have worn her hair? Of course, it wouldn't always have been arranged in funny buns over her ears. It must once have hung free, cut shorter, ungrayed, a frame for a more youthful face. And why should I care?

When I came back down to the kitchen I found Mrs. Stryfe there with a decanter and a couple of snifter glasses. One glass sat on the counter with a drink poured into it; the second was in her hand. Her back was toward me as I came in; she faced the sink, leaning across to stare out of the window—or so I thought in that first moment. Then I saw, just before she jumped back and turned to face me, that what she was peering at closely and intently was the flower in the water glass. The flower out of the bouquet Chris Warne had found on Jim's grave that morning.

Mrs. Stryfe gestured jerkily with her snifter, sloshing the brandy around in it. "Well, cheers! I brought a glass for you, too, off the sideboard."

"Thank you." I waited, expecting some comment about the flower on the windowsill, but she busied herself pouring a little more brandy from the decanter. I took a sip of brandy from the snifter she'd set out for me and then went on to the refrigerator.

Rye had expressed a desire for fish, and so we were to have clam chowder and lobster salad—both chowder and lobster from cans—topped off by the gooseberry pie, about which Rye had expressed great curiosity. "Who would have suspected that the elder Stryfe could cook, Pock? It's a miracle."

"Perhaps a calamity."

"She somehow isn't the cooking type, I mean, not motherly and plump with flowered hands and a gingham apron. You know what Mrs. Stryfe always makes me think of? An institution!"

"You mean *she's* an institution?"

"No, no. She belongs . . . belonged . . . to an institution. She's a retired grade school principal. A head nurse in a hospital. Or she ran a girls' reformatory. I can't explain it, but she's been something like that."

Something like that . . .

I went to the pantry for canned soup and lobster. Mrs. Stryfe was working valiantly on the brandy when I returned. I stopped to sip again at my own. "Your aunt's gone to see about Perkins, about his funeral, is that it?"

"Yes." I manipulated the cans into the electric can-opener. Now my bafflement as to why I'd asked Mrs. Stryfe if she'd ever worn her hair different was mixed up with Rye's conviction that she might have been a kind of female warden.

"Where are the maids?"

"She sent them away until further notice."

"She thought they might be in danger here?"

"I don't know. I doubt that she thought that."

An odd blankness had settled in Mrs. Stryfe's eyes. "I don't get it. She's left the two of you to shift for yourselves? And your sister laid up?"

"We're well able to do for ourselves. She won't be away for long. We'll hold down the fort. It's no great thing."

Mrs. Stryfe stared into the glimmering light reflected in her brandy. "They could have held the funeral here. This is where he worked for so long, for Mr. Barrod."

"His relatives are to the south."

"It's as if she rushed away," Mrs. Stryfe muttered. "Sent the maids, then went herself. Are you sure you aren't the least bit nervous?"

Twenty-one

I WANTED TO SAY, Yes, I'm not a fool and of course I'm nervous. Who wouldn't be? But I just shrugged and put three eggs into a pan, ran water to cover them, and put them on the range to hardboil for the lobster salad.

Rye and I would be alone for a couple of days. We weren't stranded or helpless. It was just—when you thought of Aunt Wanda leaving us here for that length of time, alone—kind of queer. As if Aunt Wanda had washed her hands of us.

But of course she hadn't.

Of me, she might. But never of Rye.

"You've been left to your fate," Mrs. Stryfe muttered into her brandy.

Nice fate, I told myself. Beautifully kept big house, warm, well lit. Pantries and refrigerator stuffed with food. So who was naked and starving?

There was always the phone and John Sutton, or the police. Only now John was out with Angela in the rain, tucked in together in his little car. Cozy. I found myself cutting lettuce as if I were slitting Angela's pretty throat.

The woman of ice was a witch all right, I told myself. I'd better watch her. She'll have me doing things completely out of character. "Do you ever come through the woods," I heard myself asking Mrs. Stryfe, "and just stand there and look at the house? Just look, and then go away again?"

She at first seemed dumfounded, incredulous, and then laughed with embarrassment. "Well . . . you've seen me! You must have thought what a crock I was! But yes, I do get restless, and sometimes I come over this way, and I do just look. This house *is* good to look at. You know, once upon a time I dreamed that Larchwood was going to be mine. Mine, to leave to Angela. During the years I worked, and we moved here and there—I was widowed, you know. . . ." She took the brandy down by a hefty gulp. "It didn't turn out that way. Does anything we dream about ever come true? Not really. Anyway, your aunt married my cousin and came here, and I'm glad it happened, because what would I have done, playing at being the mistress in a place this size?"

Was it wistfulness, or bitterness, that looked out of her eyes? I would rather have seen hatred than the befuddled acceptance of defeat.

"Aunt Wanda wasn't exactly born to the role."

"No. But she's done a thousand times better than I would have. Even though I was born right here in Larchwood. Umpteen hundred years ago." The embarrassed laugh came again, and there was a brandy hoarseness and a brandy carefreeness about it. "I *was* born here. Like a princess. No, more like a mislaid serving wench. And we stayed for a few years. Imposing on the Barrods, really, though they were kind enough. I can remember a little of it. When I was five or so we went to Baltimore, where my father had found a job with a railroad."

"And you learned how to make deep-dish gooseberry pie."

"Yes, that. Just think. Five years old." She remained quiet for a moment. "How far back do *you* remember?"

For some reason the question frightened me, though I'm sure that my face betrayed nothing. At the same time I was reminded vividly of that scene on the steps of the orphanage, facing the unfamiliar street. And I wanted to say, "I remember the orphanage. Were you there?" And is this the secret, my adoption—but it made no sense. My being adopted could have no bearing on what was going on at Larchwood. The one who had found Aunt Wanda here, or whom she had found out of the past, the persecutor and tormentor, had been someone Aunt Wanda had known in the dim wild years, someone with whom she'd shared a wild disreputable episode, a shameful or even criminal caper.

Don't get Aunt Wanda's past confused with your own past, I told myself grimly.

"Most of my childhood memories are of things I shared with Rye," I told Mrs. Stryfe. "She's the younger, and yet it seemed when we were little that she was always comforting me over something or other. I was always a prickly, easily offended kind of child, and Rye was always lovingly trying to smooth things over."

"Nice to have a sister like that." Mrs. Stryfe gave herself a generous dollop of brandy. It was excellent brandy, but if Mrs. Stryfe didn't eat before too long she might have trouble telling the soup from the salad.

"Do you have brothers and sisters?" I asked.

"I had a brother." The statement was cut off sharply, and I sensed some worry or grief. "My father being with the railroad, we traveled a lot. Moved around. We must have been in Baltimore five or six years. After that, it seemed we moved almost every year. We lived all over. My schooling was interrupted—I was lucky to get through high school. I took nurse's training, over a year of that. Didn't graduate, got married instead."

I put the canned soup on to heat and ran cold water over the boiled eggs to cool them for the salad. "Did you marry a railroad man?"

"How'd you guess? Bill Stryfe was an engineer. Made good money, but we had the same kind of life I'd always had. Angela was born in El Paso. Had her first birthday in Los Angeles. Her father died before her third birthday. Heart trouble. We were in Chicago."

"You must have had a hard time, making a living as a widow."

"That I did." She emptied the glass and poured a new drink. She was making quite an inroad on Aunt Wanda's brandy. "All alone, with a small child to support. Not many places where you can work and keep a child with you. Not many like that." She looked at me with what I could only describe as drunken meaningfulness.

As if we shared a secret.

"I think everything is about ready," I told her. "Would you get down one of the big trays in the cupboard there—" I motioned toward the cupboard doors above her.

She put down the brandy rather uncertainly, reached to open the cupboard doors, and pulled recklessly at the stacked trays. I saw that I had made a mistake in asking her help. I'd wanted to take her mind off her memories, which seemed unhappy ones, and now the whole stack of trays, some of silver and some japanned and lacquered, began to move ponderously outward, like rimrock weakened by rain. There was a metallic grating, the prelude to avalanche. Mrs. Stryfe was now trying to push them back into place on the shelf, but their progress was inexorable. She screamed. Then, even as I was darting toward her to help, the whole mass came thundering down. Mrs. Stryfe tumbled to one side, slipped, and fell. The trays spread, some clanging on the tile counter as they went down, others bouncing and thudding directly to the floor. A lot of other odds and ends came down with them, and the noise made my ears ache.

Mrs. Stryfe picked herself up, looked dazedly at all the wreckage, and began to weep. She covered her face with her hands and sobbed loudly and brokenly.

I touched her arm. "Are you hurt?"

Still sobbing, rocking to and fro with misery, Mrs. Stryfe shook her head.

I picked up the trays and tried to arrange them in their original order, big ones on the bottom. Some of the broken mess I swept up with a broom from the pantry.

"Your poor aunt and I—" The words came out choked and muffled, and I stopped sweeping to listen. "We're the unlucky ones. It all has to happen to us. The bad things. The no-way-out things. And nobody giving a damn. My brother shouldn't have driven my car, bad tire on the front, tread gone. And in the snow, the storm. I should have remembered to tell him, be careful. Then when he went over the edge at the bad turn, he had to lie trapped there and freeze. Freeze to death. Just bad luck. My fault, only not entirely—" She clung bent to the counter, arched in misery and regret.

I put the broom aside and went close to her and tried to speak gently. "I'm sorry about your brother. It's a terrible thing for you to have to remember all this while. But perhaps the way he drove had something to do with what happened, and it wasn't entirely your fault. What did you mean, the thing you said about my aunt?"

"All bad luck . . . . unlucky people. We didn't deserve it."

"What didn't my aunt deserve?"

"None of it. She's a good-hearted woman."

"What happened to her?"

The bent figure twisted; I thought that Mrs. Stryfe stole a glance at me through her fingers.

"How should I know? It was her affair." She took her hands from her face and turned, and stared at the floor, as if surprised that the wreckage had been cleared so soon. Her brandy snifter had been among the casualties, so now she simply took a water glass from a cupboard and poured brandy into that, and got it down. She blinked at me with watering eyes. "Don't mind me, don't pay any attention to my babblings. I'm kind of drunkie. A li'l bit drunkie on Wanda's brandy."

Her face was blotched, puffed with crying and drinking, and her eyes were evasive. All at once I was seized with a conviction, with an unquestionable knowledge. Mrs. Stryfe was the one who had driven over here in the middle of the night. Half gassed, the way she was now. It was she who had swerved in the drive, crunched off woozily upon the neat grass verges. I didn't know how I knew, but I was utterly convinced.

She and Aunt Wanda shared some memory of the past.

No. I had to admit, this wasn't what Mrs. Stryfe had said. What she'd said was that she and Aunt Wanda had both had bad luck. Undeserved disasters.

They shared, in separate ways, old wounds that wouldn't heal, haunts that never went away.

I said firmly to the puffed, half-frightened and yet sly face: "You want to tell me about my aunt, don't you? This old trouble she had, this bad luck. It needs to be explained. I need to know, so that I can be properly helpful and understanding. Isn't that right?"

As if to choke back any inadvertent words, Mrs. Stryfe put her hand over her mouth. She shook her head solemnly. She made me think of a middle-aged lying child. Suddenly she blurted, "I won't eat lunch after all. Must get home. Rain. Dark in the woods. And you know what happened *there*."

"Was it you who put the bouquet this morning on Jim's grave?"

An explosion of fright seemed to take place behind the watery eyes. In spite of the flush from the brandy, Mrs. Stryfe paled. She chattered some incoherent denial, or plea, and then ran from the kitchen, and I heard her briefly in the pantry getting her raingear. Following, I found that she had run off without her boots. I took them and ran after, but from the back door I could see her almost out by the garages, and running like a deer. She was buttoning the raincoat with one hand and holding the hat on her head with the other. I put the boots back under the pantry sink and locked the rear door.

I fixed the tray with our lunch, took it to the pantry, and went through the now familiar routine with the dumb-waiter to the closet upstairs.

Rye wanted to know where our guest was, and I told her about the brandy, and the accident with the trays, and let her think that Mrs. Stryfe had left out of embarrassment, which cheered Rye up and made the lunch a brighter occasion than it might have been.

The afternoon dragged its rainy and gloomy way onward. Rye fiddled with her radio, made a list of things to be bought for the baby, did her nails, read. I was as restless in my own way, and tried to find things to do around the house. I puttered in the kitchen, aware that I was trespassing on Mrs. Mim's territory. I tidied cupboards and mopped the floor, and without wanting to, I found my thoughts returning to what Mrs. Stryfe had said. And had not said.

Mrs. Stryfe admitted that she prowled the woods; it had to be Mrs. Stryfe I'd seen in the lightning flash.

Could have been, I amended.

Had Mrs. Stryfe's admission of coming to look at Larchwood been too quick, too pat? A coverup for someone else? Angela? I couldn't imagine Mrs. Stryfe covering for anyone but her child.

And yet Angela, of the perfectly arranged hair and marshmallow makeup, didn't seem the type to be wandering in the lightning-lit dark.

I found myself forgetting to move the mop.

Perkins had gone into those woods after *somebody*. After Mrs. Stryfe? I tried to imagine Mrs. Stryfe as a murderer, lying in wait. She was skinny, active, energetic. If Perkins had been taken entirely off guard, could Mrs. Stryfe have dealt the blow that killed him?

And then, later, had come to cover his face?

That return trip didn't jibe. Didn't make sense. Murderers don't come back to kindly cover the face of the dying. Or did they? What did I know about it all, the spinster schoolteacher, isolated in icy misery? The freak?

I mopped in circles, unseeing.

It seemed that there had to be two parts to what had happened to poor Perkins. Two people had been involved, and covering Perkins' bloody face had been the act of the second, a confused but compassionate one.

Like the placing of the simple bouquet on Jim's grave.

Angela coming along, conscience-stricken, after Mother?

I found myself staring at the blossom in the glass above the sink. Behind it the pane ran with water, and in the distance the skies looked black.

Mrs. Stryfe must be the one out of Aunt Wanda's past. There were coincidental alikenesses—she'd been a widow, had traveled around a lot, skirmished for a living here and there. She'd known Aunt Wanda somewhere, and she held the sorcerer's grip—and still there was the crazy note of sympathy and the attitude of shared bad luck, of commiseration.

She too had something terrible in her past, she'd loaned her only brother her car, and the car had had a bad tire, of which she'd failed to warn him. And thanks to the lack of warning, perhaps, he'd lain dying in the freezing cold. Mrs. Stryfe couldn't forgive herself. Nor forget. And in spite of her denials, her slyness, she knew of Aunt Wanda's trouble, whatever *that* had been.

She had come over very late at night, drunk enough to let her car wobble on the grass verges, perhaps drunk enough to let her emotions slop over too. She'd begged sympathy of my aunt—or offered it—and had left Aunt Wanda in a mood to do some drinking of her own.

Could Aunt Wanda, in some shared moment of remembered misery, have *told* Mrs. Stryfe of her troubles in the past?

I leaned on the mop handle. Try as I might, I couldn't picture my dear aunt, drunk or sober, telling Mrs. Stryfe of her past mistakes. The image wouldn't come. Neither the new nor the old Aunt Wanda could be so big a fool.

Mrs. Stryfe was a danger, I thought. She was going to get drunk enough someday to tell everything she knew. It might occur to someone that her mouth ought to be shut.

I should have run after her, made sure she got safely home.

I'd better go now, I told myself.

I can take her the boots she forgot.

This was such a crazy and nonsensical impulse that I stood rooted for a moment in sheer disbelief that I might act on it. The next minute I was looking through the storage pantries in the rooms next the kitchen for something to wear out into the rain.

To whom was Mrs. Stryfe such a danger, that I had to make sure she hadn't been killed in the woods? It seemed she might be an awkward embarrassment to my aunt if she spilled some old indiscretion. That was all.

But in some idiotic way I had to follow and make sure that she'd reached home and wasn't lying face up, bleeding and being rained on in the woods.

In a cupboard I found a plastic raincoat with an attached hood, an old one of Mrs. Mim's, probably, and I put it on and rushed out the back door.

The rain was coming down in sheets and the air was cold, though this was the beginning of summer. I ran past Perkins' station wagon, which waited there to be disposed of, and on into the forest. The trees gave off a muted howl of their own, and concentrated the falling rain into huge drops. I skidded on the muddy path, caught myself, and tried to keep to the edges where fallen needles gave a foothold. The path twisted and turned, new vistas opening wetly ahead, the earth of the path shining in the gloom, the trees a dark tangle, and nothing alive here but myself.

Even before I had expected to, I came out upon the road.

The rain had suddenly lightened, though the black clouds moving northward seemed lower and blacker than ever. I turned my face to the wind, and felt the promise of June weather when the storm was over. I stood there hesitating, and a voice spoke.

"Hello, Looking for somebody?"

It was Bart Linton in a dark green raincoat, almost invisible against the heavy brush. I said, "What on earth are you doing out in the rain?" My usual ill-thought-out blurt, I told myself. I felt myself go red with embarrassment; I must have sounded a fool. Wasn't *I* out in the rain?

Under the narrow brim of his weatherproof hat his eyes gently mocked me. "I won't ask what you're doing, since it seems you must have been looking for someone and hadn't found him."

"Mrs. Stryfe." I ignored the mischief in his voice and I tried to sound like a sensible woman. A woman with her wits about her. "She left Larchwood in such a hurry. And I was worried about her."

And I'd also forgotten to bring the boots, the original excuse for coming after her at all.

Bart made a wry mouth and said, "It seems to me she flitted by quite a while ago, so your worry must have a long fuse, so to speak. Won't you come to my place for a drink? A hot toddy? Or something as innocent as tea, perhaps?"

I sensed that he knew all about Mrs. Stryfe and her half-whacked condition; and that perhaps he had expected me to be likewise. I wanted to turn and to run back to the safety of Larchwood and the company of the only person I was at ease with, my sister. I could feel the ice stiffening inside. But I forced myself to say, "It's good of you to offer." And I went with him, on down the road to his house.

He stepped ahead and opened his gate with that economy of motion, the flexible grace, that I had first noted about him. In his house he helped me out of the raincoat and put it into a closet by the door and said, "I wouldn't run about looking for John if I were you. I think Angela finally has him hooked. It seemed to happen, improbably enough, in your aunt's parlor yesterday morning. For the first time he seemed to realize that Angela was a living creature and not a doll."

"They all amuse you very much," I ventured to say as I sat down. "Perhaps I should correct that—*we* all amuse you." The room was warm with lamplight, a cheerful and casual place. "I didn't come running for Mr. Sutton, though. There was a detail or two I wanted to discuss with Mrs. Stryfe." I felt safe here in this room with Bart, I realized; and the storm seemed far away outside.

"A detail?" He had removed his coat and hat and wore a dark turtle-necked shirt and corduroy pants, far from new. He went past me toward the corner cupboard where drinks were kept, and took out a bottle of rum and one of brandy. "A detail about poor Perkins?"

"I . . . I don't know."

"What sort of hot toddy would you prefer?"

"Rum, with lemon and sugar."

He left the bottles out and went off to the kitchen, presumably to heat water and to get sugar and lemons. "Well, a detail about John's unaccountable behavior, then," he said on coming back.

"I have nothing to do with Mr. Sutton's behavior. He can behave as he pleases." I was almost enjoying this exchange with Bart, perhaps because he made it seem a teasing and lighthearted game that neither of us must take seriously. "I know you think I'm funny, but I suddenly had to find out if . . . if Mrs. Stryfe had gotten safely through the woods."

"If she hadn't, what would you have done?"

His gaze was still mocking, defying me to make up some response that would sound ironic. But if I'd found Mrs. Stryfe in the path as I had found Perkins, there wouldn't have been any irony about it. "I took a chance," I said, forgetting the game, and perhaps I looked a little haunted and sick for a moment, because he went away tactfully to make the hot toddies in the kitchen.

We sipped for a short while in a companionable silence. I thought of his life here, the settled professor, surrounded at home by woodsy silence, a nice break from the busy hours on campus.

He must have been remembering that it had been I who had found Perkins, and perhaps laid my sudden lack of small talk to it, for he said, "Away with gloomy thoughts. This is a day to enjoy pleasant company in a cozy room."

"I am enjoying it. I was thinking how comfortable you are here. Have you always lived in this part of the country?" I couldn't recall for the moment what history of Bart Rye had told me.

"No. I was away at school. I managed to get a scholarship to a college in Maryland. Then I taught for a time in Maine. I liked the East Coast, and the winters, but finally I'd had enough and I came back here and applied for a teaching job at the college, and got it. And now I'm rooted like one of the pines hereabouts. The story of my life." He laughed wryly.

"Your people lived here?"

"Yes. Down the main road a way. Across from the cemetery, as a matter of fact. There used to be a church in the cemetery grounds. But the congregation sort of melted away, and the church fell into disrepair."

"Do you then own the land across from the cemetery?"

"Oh, no. The land had belonged to Barrod for years before he married your aunt."

I felt a deep uneasiness stir in me, and I said slowly, "That was your family's home, the house that . . . that's all—"

"Fallen to ruin. Yes, it was our home."

"Mr. Barrod bought it, allowed it to go to ruin?"

"Well, what he did was, he advanced money for a mortgage. My father had gone crazy over horses. Thoroughbreds. Some fellow came along with breeding stock and a lot of glamorous stories about racing life, and they formed a partnership, and needed money. My father felt that he was on the verge of making a fortune. He borrowed on everything he owned. I believe he would have mortgaged me in some way if he could have managed it. And it's an old story." Bart spoke in a slow, drawling, half-amused way, as if the story bored him. "It's also a quick way to get rid of all that you have in the world."

I sat in silence, sipping at my drink, remembering the old house with its ghostly and vacant windows, its walls swayed out of line, the barn or outbuilding behind it falling beneath the weight of creepers. For some reason I felt torn with sadness. A house should not go like that. "You told Rye and me the other day that Mrs. Stryfe would have been Mr. Barrod's heir if he hadn't married my aunt."

"I should have said, *might* have been. Who knows what he would have done with his property if he hadn't married? Mrs. Stryfe isn't so close a relative that she would have an ironbound claim under the law. It wouldn't be, if he forgot her, the same as cutting off a child with a dollar. Or so I imagine. I'm not an attorney, of course."

"Mrs. Stryfe doesn't seem to hold any ill feeling."

"Oh, I'm sure not." His hands, holding the heavy cup of toddy, had the calloused and workworn look I'd noted before. They were rough and scarred and in contrast to the intelligent, wryly mocking face and the grace with which he held the cup. "She knows she doesn't belong in that house as its mistress."

For some reason the remark annoyed me. "How do you know she wouldn't have done at least as well as my aunt has? And how can you be sure that my aunt has done well at the job at all?"

He shrugged and smiled. "I don't listen to gossip, if there is any. So far as I can see the place is run well enough. No lack of care and polish and all of the nice things." He gave me a mock frown. "What would you like me to say about your aunt?"

"How does the saying go? The ignorant talk about people and the more intelligent talk about things, and the real brains talk about ideas? Isn't that it?"

"And here we are, being utter boobs," he chided.

Our conversation went on into more conventional channels. I had found Bart, on this rainy day, strangely easy to talk to. No witch, unseen, laid a freezing hand on my heart nor turned me mute because he was a man and practically a stranger. Shut in by the rain in his comfortably shabby professor's house, I was almost at ease. Or as much at ease as I was ever likely to be. He warned me of the real steaming heat to come, the days of July and August and September. He admitted that at times the isolation palled and when that happened he headed for a brief stay in New Orleans.

Wind blew the clouds on northward and a wan light shone in at the windows, and a bird sang unexpectedly outside, close to the house. I thanked him for his offer of a second drink but said I'd best be getting back to Larchwood and to my sister. My questions for Mrs. Stryfe would have to wait.

He helped me into the raincoat and saw me to the gate.

Twenty-two

As I ran back through the dim and dripping woods, it seemed that the apparitions of the past ran ghostlike at my heels. So much of what is gone lies all about us here, I told myself, brushing a spray of water from my cheek. The old Army sign, for instance, that John Sutton had found built into his house, wood brought from an encampment of Union or Confederate soldiers, more than a hundred years ago, from where men waited a trumpet's call to rise to fight; and then there was that old falling house across from the cemetery, Bart's home and whose every empty room must live in his memory. And how did he feel, passing the ruin every school day to get to his teaching job in Moss Corner? Did specters stand at the windows to watch him on his way? And how about Mrs. Stryfe, staring through the rain at Larchwood? Didn't she see a small child playing there still, a child that had been herself?

But now there was Rye, waiting for the future.

And me, I thought, trying to keep from skidding in the muddy path—me caught in a web of the past somehow, caught more tightly and more frighteningly than most—a web of my own, a web of dreams. Mostly a dream of an orphanage, a day of strangeness, a day of beginning. For I knew that it had been a beginning, going out upon the top of the steps with my mother and father and looking down upon the street, seeing the figure in the distance, the statue of the woman above the portico with a shield against her knee, one arm upraised.

A woman of bronze who could give love no more than could I.

O day of long ago, I whispered to myself, which made my life. Which brought me my cold heart and polished it as stone. And I brushed away drops that were not rain. And so running and half blind, I tore headlong into the one who waited on the path.

John Sutton.

He caught and held me.

"Don't . . ." I was instantly my old self; I turned rigid as steel. "I have to go. Rye's been alone too long. Please—"

"Listen to me." He grip was tight. He wore clothes I hadn't seen on him before, a plaid raincoat, an old hat. His eyes seemed unfamiliar too. They were as hard, as piercing as a stone arrowhead. "I have a right to be heard. I'm telling you something that you need to know."

"There's no time. I shouldn't have gone off without telling my sister."

"She's fine. When I couldn't raise you, I went in and I saw her, and we'll be back with her inside five minutes. But right now—"

I stepped back and tried to force free of his grip, but couldn't. "Please don't keep me here." Panic was rising, the kind of panic that had made me get out of his car to stand in the dark at the side of the road.

"I've been talking to Angela," he went on, determined to hold me and make me listen. "She finally got over the swoons and the eye-battings enough to answer some questions sensibly. Questions about her mother."

"If you're about to tell me that Mrs. Stryfe knew Aunt Wanda years ago—"

"Yes." I had surprised him. For an instant there was the sound of dripping trees, nothing more.

"And that she came back, hours and hours after she and Angela had had dinner with us—she came, and I think she and my aunt talked about old times . . ."

He shook his head, and then surprisingly he released me. "You're right. We shouldn't be talking here. Let's go to the house."

I rushed past him and took a dozen steps or so, and then not hearing him I paused to look back. He was standing where I'd left him.

A flicker of dread crossed my thoughts. In some way I sensed what was coming.

"Aren't you going to wait for me?" he asked quietly.

And there it was, the last question of all. The last chance to want him, to have him. I could run away now and it would be finished, it would be over and he wouldn't bother me again in any way but a strictly business one. Because a man like John Sutton has his limit; and even a cold heart like mine knew it.

I stood trembling, wanting to run. He didn't move, and the only sound was the continuing drip, drip, drip from the wet trees.

"I know it isn't easy," he went on in that quiet tone. "For a long time you've told yourself you didn't need anyone, didn't want anyone. And didn't care."

True. All too true. But how did he know it?

I felt the cold wetness seeping up into my shoes. In the gray light John Sutton looked sturdy and masculine, able to take care of himself, not terribly handsome nor graceful but very attractive anyway. His eyes on me didn't waver.

"For a long time, well, ever since I was a kid, I've had a hobby of taming wild things. Birds, mostly. I don't have one right now. I haven't been out at the place very long. Well, yes, in a way I guess I do have one, there's a jay that's been getting friendly. But don't get mad because you think I'm comparing you to a bird. It's just that I've acquired a sense of patience and of knowing when something is afraid. I knew you were afraid of me long before you told me."

Surprise jerked the words out of me. "You did?"

He didn't answer my question, he just waited with the air of willing himself not to frighten me away.

"Wh . . . what do you do with your birds, once they're tamed?"

He smiled a little. "Nothing. Oh, I keep feeding them as long as they care to hang around. I don't pop them into a skillet, if that's what you're thinking."

I took a single step toward him. "I can't understand why you want . . . why you want—"

"That's probably the heart of the problem, Pocket, my love. You can't believe that I could want you. To you there's no possible reason why I should. And so you tell yourself, *he can't*. And then you turn away because unraveling the truth might be pretty painful."

"But . . . but I could try."

His glance was skeptical, as if saying, Yes, you could try. But not very hard. And suddenly I was getting angry.

Was this the way his birds felt?

I even stamped my foot, squelching mud. "You could come *half* of the way."

He laughed, and he began to stride toward me.

That night the dream came again, more vivid than ever, stranger, beginning far before it had in any previous time. Beginning with walking *into* the orphanage . . .

The morning light threw our shadows ahead of us on the marble steps. To our backs—in the dream I knew this—was the busy street, traffic, pedestrians, and in the distance the statue of the woman above the portico of the large, official-looking building. The three of us stood together at the top of the steps, facing the big carved-oak door of the orphanage. My father put out a gloved hand and pushed a button on the wall beside the door. My mother breathed out something half weary, a sigh, and words like, "At last . . . at last."

And in the dream I, small Esther, knew that this had been a thing long in coming, a thing whispered about for weeks, a newness, a change, and I was afraid. I was terribly frightened.

A woman in a uniform, not exactly a nurse's uniform, opened the door for us, and shut the door carefully when we had entered. The hall was wide and clean and smelled of soap and polish. Sunlight shone in through windows set high in the walls and made gold squares on the wall we faced. From far off came the tinkly notes of a piano playing a marching song. I clung to the hem of my mother's coat, but now the woman in uniform had taken my other hand.

"How would it be," the woman was saying in an artificially jolly tone, "if your little girl came to the morning kindergarten class with me while you talked to Miss Olson? She'll be able to enjoy the games with the other children. Time will go faster for her."

I didn't understand all of this too well, but I got enough sense out of it—out of the words spoken in a strong southern accent—to know that the woman meant to separate me from my parents. I clung tighter to the coat, and my heart almost choked me.

My mother bent and put a hand under my chin and said, "Would you go to the kindergarten? You'll be able to play there. If you stay with us it will be long and boring for you."

"No, it won't."

My mother couldn't see my terror, and I couldn't express it.

"Esther darling, we have to talk to a lady."

What she meant was: We have to talk to Miss Olson, the woman who sits behind the desk and wears the biscuit of pale hair on top of her head.

My father touched my shoulder gently. I turned to look up at him, to find his eyes full of loving kindness behind his glasses. "For us. And just for a little while."

My father! I almost cried the words aloud in my sleep, and almost woke. A great bubble of warmth and comfort seemed to enfold me, a great wave of loving and knowing; and it had been true as he had said, I had always belonged to them.

Always. So why—

The near-waking had made the sequence of the dream wobble and I lost something of the interval; I was walking now with my hand in that of the gray-uniformed woman. We went a long distance down the hall, my small legs hurrying to keep up with her stride, our footsteps almost silent on the brown polished linoleum, our shadows flickering along the walls. The sound of the tinkly piano grew gradually louder. We turned a corner, where I tried to balk. The woman wheeled me onward, and then to the doorway of a big room with a lot of toys and chairs and small tables and about a dozen children. The children were all girls with their hair done in identical pigtails, and they all wore pink-and-white pinafore dresses, white socks, and brown shoes. They were walking with stiff-legged solemnity in time to the piano. For an incredible moment I was sure that the scene was that of a store window, a display like those at Christmas, things being moved around by a kind of puppetry, and that the pink things must be dolls.

Standing by the door, fixed by all the eyes, still wearing my coat—which the woman was now taking off—faced with the terrifying mechanical pinafores and pigtails, I began to scream.

The woman first spoke softly. Then she put my coat on a chair and ran back to me and began to shout. She shook me.

I tried to run, to fight free and away. I slid down through the skinny grasping arms, my clothes dragged almost over my head, my breath filled with sobbing wetness, screams tearing out at the face bent above me. I scrambled around on all fours, and some of the pink pinafores jumped up on chairs as if I were a mouse. I collided head-on with a piano leg next to a human leg in nylon, and a second disapproving adult voice joined the yammerings of the first.

I crawled all the way through under the piano, while the two pairs of women's legs circled it madly, and then they had me corraled in a corner where a vase of flowers sat on a low table flanked by some books standing up with the covers ajar, inviting one to look, a sort of primitive culture center. The table and I, the vase of water, and the flowers along with the books all became an amalgamated mass from which the woman in gray seemed to extract me piecemeal.

I was carried bodily into the hall, struggling to get down, convulsed but not screaming, probably turning blue. There was a lot of hurry, a lot of adult fright that I sensed, and this part of the nightmare was too terrible to be endured.

No wonder it had never been a part of the regular program.

The woman got me away from the room, the pinafores, and down the hall, and in condition finally to stand alone. She stood gripping my shoulder, sucking breath into her lungs in great gulps. She kept whispering, "Oh, my God!" over and over, and now, after all these years, I could understand that it had indeed been a prayer. After getting her breath and adjusting her own uniform, the woman began to straighten my clothes, and now for the first time in any of the dreams I looked directly into her face.

When my clothes and hair had been adjusted, when one of the mechanical pinafores had appeared carrying my coat at arm's length, I was led on into an office where my parents sat facing a desk. My father rose at once. This was the part of the dream that had always seemed to be an introduction, being presented to strangers, and sure enough, it *was* an introduction, because I was being presented to my parents as a very naughty little girl. In the dream I was vividly aware of being offered to them as something they surely weren't going to want.

My parents didn't seem overly disturbed, though, and I was picked up at once and placed on the Lap. The Lap that I'd dreamed of over and over, and it was just my father's lap, nothing strange about it, though I felt odd and new with him because I'd been brought back in such deep disgrace.

Then I became engrossed with the woman behind the desk, the woman to whom my parents were talking, because the woman began to say all those things that had seemed so disturbing in the other dreams, especially about this child being brought in by an unknown woman.

Presently, as in all the other dreams, we were out upon the steps, this time facing the unfamiliar street. In the distance was the statue of the woman above the portico. The windy sunlight, the street, the images of the people, were shattered into crystals by my tears. Nothing would ever be the same again. All had been changed. I was no longer their small one, their most-loved one, because though my father held my hand in his, in his free arm he carried the new child, an infant wrapped in a pink blanket—everything that came out of that place would inevitably be pink—and he and my mother had paused to peer fascinated into the new baby's face.

Why had they taken me along that day? Why hadn't I been left at home, where it would seem I belonged? Had I been considered too small to remember? Or had my parents planned to make explanations afterward, explanations that never came?

Because I never asked?

Because in my fear of that day's mystery and terror, I'd never dared to question them?

In the end, of course, they had simply thought of Rye as their own.

I was awake, free of the dream, at last, and I lay in the dark of my bedroom listening to the rain at the windows. I had wanted my parents to love me, I thought, and all of the time they had . . . they had, and I was too stubborn and too determined to be rejected to see.

I had created my own grief and my own not-being-loved simply because I hadn't understood the events of that long-ago day, and the mystery had seemed a disaster. When the dreams came, they'd been a garbling of what I had remembered, and what I'd feared, and of new difficulties that had intruded as I grew up.

I threw aside the bedding and put on a robe and stood for a while at the window to the balcony, opening the French window a crack to let in the smell of the rain and the night. Gradually my thoughts settled from the confusion of the dream and I could sort some of it, the new things. There were gaps to be filled yet.

After a little while I shut the window, turned on a small lamp, and put on slippers. I let myself out into the hall.

Night lights burned dimly here and there. By their glow I went downstairs to the small office, let myself in, and shut the door. Since my aunt was away, there was no need for secrecy; I turned on the lights and walked directly to the gilt-and-white desk. I pressed the carved rosette, and the top of the desk slid smoothly to one side. In the velvet-lined interior I saw the legal-looking folders tied with tape. There were four of them.

I took them out and spread them on the white-leather top of the desk.

For a moment I hesitated. I was prying here into something that was truly no business of mine, and what I found could destroy lives. To myself then, I made a promise: I would never reveal what I found here unless it were absolutely necessary, unless there was no alternative whatever.

I opened the first packet. Here were deeds and legal agreements pertaining to Larchwood and other properties; I returned them quickly to the folder. The second folder held documents signed by Mr. Barrod, the dates were those of some years past, and nothing here had anything to do with current affairs.

In picking up the third folder I noted that it seemed different from the others, the surface felt worn under my touch, and the color seemed faded. On my opening it, the papers inside gave off the smell of age.

These were personal papers of my aunt, I soon discovered—intensely personal. There were a few letters, some folded documents, what looked like contracts. Among the legal documents were a marriage license and a divorce decree, both dated over twenty years ago, and issued in Seattle. My aunt had been married, a fact I'd never known. To judge by the dates on the documents, the marriage had been a very brief one.

The letter that I read in full was, like most of the other papers, yellowed and brittle with age, the folds wearing apart.

> HEY WANDA,
>
> I was so glad and flabbergasted to hear from you—finally! How many years has it been since—well, you know! A long time, honey, isn't it? But I haven't forgotten a thing of those old time days. And of course I'm still your friend and always will be.
>
> You can bet on that as we used to say in Reno. God, didn't we have the wildest times?
>
> It's true, as you say you read in the paper, that I've been appointed to the Adoption Board of St. Luke's. It isn't me that's appointed, baby, it's Fred's checkbook. He's such a good guy. And they know a sucker when they see one. You know how respectable we are now if you read all that stuff in the paper.
>
> In the Adoption Board we don't match parents and children or anything like that. All such matters are handled by our professional staff, headed by our Miss Olson. And you should see *her!* But I do have a certain amount of influence, thanks again to Fred's checkbook, and I'll be glad to do anything I can

for you. You didn't explain the problem, but you can do that when you get here.

Will Tuesday at three o'clock be all right?

Love,

TOOTS

There was no accompanying envelope for the letter, nor any other name nor address on the letter itself.

The *Toots* of those twenty years past and more was completely and safely anonymous.

But certain conclusions could be drawn.

A conversation had taken place on that faraway Tuesday at three o'clock. Something to do with St. Luke's, where, obviously, children were placed for adoption. A favor had been asked. A child was to be left at St. Luke's without the mother being identified. In violation of all the rules, a child was to be placed for an unknown woman. A woman whose marriage, brief as it had been, was now broken and whose life was too chancy an affair to be encumbered by an infant.

The child was to be taken from St. Luke's by a couple already chosen by the mother. All of the social-work organization, the investigative procedures, of St. Luke's were to be bypassed, with one important exception. A record would be kept of the placing of the child, an iron-bound documentary proof against any question. If in years to come there should be an investigation, any need of proof, the trail would lead to St. Luke's, to the eminently respectable Miss Olson or her successor, and stop there.

Thank God, I thought, for Fred's checkbook. And for Fred. And for Toots . . . and most of all for Wanda, my aunt, who'd given me my sister.

I tucked the letter and other papers into the folder, tied the tape, put everything away, and closed the desk.

At the door, lights out, I stood for a moment. I would go back to my room now and think. There were a lot of lonely questions that had suddenly acquired answers. Some questions had only surmises, devious and perhaps evil conclusions, and these had to be considered too. But when I was upstairs again, I turned instead toward Rye's room and slipped inside.

This was better than being alone.

I crossed to the chaise and sat down silently, put up my feet, and stretched out. The dark, the whisper of rain, Rye's sleeping presence, was eerie and comforting at once, a strange combination.

I felt no more anger toward my aunt. True, she'd given that mean little stab about my being an orphan. Unworthy of her, but understandable. I was an orphan, my parents gone, while Rye's own mother still lived to protect her. After the long years of pretense, of denial, of separation, seeing her child in another family, calling another woman Mother, and accompanied always by a sister, a stiff-necked, prickly older child whom Rye adored—the moment of lashing back in triumph had been something she couldn't resist.

But the hurt was gone, for me. I felt only pity for my aunt.

God only knew what agonies of indecision had preceded her giving away her child. And then the years had passed, the years of wandering, of being mostly broke, making a living by whatever means she could; the years had gone, and then a miracle had happened. Wanda had married Mr. Barrod. She'd become overnight the mistress of Larchwood, truly a Cinderella enchantment. And almost immediately came much more—with Mr. Barrod's death, she had the power to make her own will and to pass the property to Rye's child. Her child's child. What a sweet victory it all must have seemed!

And then like many examples of Paradise, here had come the serpent. The matron who had taken me in charge at the orphanage had known all about the baby. She was a part of the staff. She had without a doubt attended to the admission of the baby, brought there by the unknown woman. Unknown, but seen. Remembered.

Under the supervision of Miss Bun-on-Top Olson she would have taken charge of the baby as its mother relinquished it.

And so it had turned out that she was here, in this most unlikely place, she had returned from the years of working here and there, come here with her own child, and become the serpent.

Mrs. Stryfe, of course.

Twenty-three

Rye's voice out of the dark, soft as it was, made me jump. "Pock? How long have you been here?"

"Not long."

Some silence then, thinking going on. "Did you have one of your nightmares? You know the kind I mean."

Inwardly I kicked myself for having ever mentioned those dreams. "Yes."

"Was it terrible this time? Did it scare you?"

"No." I forced my tone to be casual. "I guess I've been looking at those dreams all wrong. They don't mean exactly what I've been thinking. I might have seen a movie years ago, when I was little, and got things in the movie mixed up with something I'd experienced. It's hard to explain, but I can see some unreality there I'd never noticed before."

"Good. That's the best news I've had in a long time." Rye moved around with a faint rustling of the bedclothes. "Is it still raining?"

"We're still in Louisiana. I'm afraid it is."

"Who was it told us about the average rainfall?"

"I forget."

"You had John Sutton downstairs in the parlor this afternoon. Late. I didn't quiz you about it, but I'm curious. What were you talking about?"

"Aunt Wanda. He's worried about her."

"Why should he be?" Rye was punching her pillow; I could make out dimly the shape of her tousled head.

"Oh . . ." I was at a loss, how to explain John's theories about Aunt Wanda. That our aunt was being blackmailed, driven to the wall. Of course she was being blackmailed—the deepest secret of all had come right home to roost. The secret Rye must never know. "It's about her household accounts," I finished lamely.

"All fouled up, huh? And all that about Mr. Sutton being an

ogre and a money monster was just a fable? She made it up to cover the fact that she couldn't keep her accounts straight?"

"Something like that."

"You're not telling it all. You're thinking, poor ol' Rye, she's so preggie, mustn't upset anybody like that—"

"Rye—"

"I'm *not* going to get nasty. Not with you. Never again. I'm just kidding, and if it weren't dark in here you'd see me smiling. The funny Mrs. Parrish. Preggie and funny. You like him, really, don't you? John, I mean?"

"Yes."

"You might even consider—and I can feel you shying away from over here—but you might think someday about even marrying somebody like John Sutton. My God, I'd have a brother-in-law!"

"If it happens, it'll be a long time from now." But to myself, I had to admit some uncertainty. John Sutton seemed to have made up his mind, firmly and rather quickly, about our possible future.

"Of course. But he's so nice and he'd be so kind to you. He's not stuffy and self-satisfied and a nincompoop. You'd never have a worry in the world."

"Thanks for marrying me off," I said dryly.

"You must wait, though, until after the baby comes and I can get my shape back to be matron of honor—"

"You're incredible!"

"Did he kiss you down there in the parlor with General Lee looking on?"

"Yes. What are you, a peeping tom?" But I was suddenly tingling at the memory of those kisses of John's.

"Psychic is all." Rye subsided, probably with visions of a sugarplum wedding dancing through her head. Next she'd ask me to wait until the baby was old enough to be ring bearer. Or flower girl. Let's get everybody into the act.

"I wonder who that is downstairs," Rye said suddenly out of the silence.

I think every hair stood straight up on my head. "What do you—"

"Listen. Someone's very quiet down there. Tiptoeing around. I think they came in from the veranda. Or from that direction somehow. Didn't you lock up down there?"

My mouth was so dry, my pulses pounding, that I could scarcely speak. "Yes, I locked everything."

"Those French windows to the veranda wouldn't be much to pry open," Rye whispered. "Do you think we have a burglar?"

"Are you sure you're hearing something?"

"My ears always were better than yours," she reminded me. It was true.

"I was down there earlier. Maybe—"

"I heard you. This is somebody else." Rye was sitting up, her figure blurrily visible against the gloom. "Could it be Aunt Wanda home again? Not wanting to wake us?"

Aunt Wanda wouldn't have crept in by way of the veranda. Aunt Wanda would have let us know that she was home. She and Mrs. Mim wouldn't have tiptoed . . .

Suddenly I heard it too, a sound from below us, from the direction of the front hall or of the parlor. It had been a soft sound, a faint scrape or bump as if some piece of furniture had been touched, moved inadvertently, tipped and caught and set straight again. The sound was followed by intense silence, as if someone down there waited to see if he'd been heard.

Or if she'd been heard.

Gooseflesh had come out along my arms. "I heard something then."

"What shall we do?" Rye's voice was dry with apprehension; I knew suddenly how scared she was. "Just wait 'til it comes up here, or what? Turn on lights? Gather things to throw at it?"

"I . . . I have to go after something."

I have to get that gun—

The knowledge struck me like a blow. What a fool I'd been. The gun should have been up here, at hand, ever since our aunt had left. I shouldn't have gone into the woods without it. No, I saw now, I should have left that gun with Rye and asked Chris Warne for another one for myself, and I knew somehow he'd have gotten one for me.

"Go where?" Rye whispered. "You aren't going down there to *look,* for God's sake!"

"No, and I'll be back right away. The thing is, I want you to lock the door after me."

"I don't think it locks."

"Put a chair under the knob, then."

"Should I turn on the light?"

I thought about it. Would the intruder enter a lighted room, expose his or her identity? Why not, if he was wearing that black garb I'd glimpsed in the cemetery? What was to fear with his face masked? "Don't turn on the light. Most especially, if someone comes in here in the dark, don't suddenly turn it on."

"Pock, you sound as if you *know* something," she accused. "You came in here tonight to think over something you know. Is it . . . is it about who was putting that stuff on Jim's grave? Is that what you've figured out?"

"No."

I stood up in the dark.

"Are you sure? And what about the things going on here at the house? The little mean tricks? Was that Martha, after all?"

I couldn't tell Rye that John and I had concluded, during our talk in the parlor, that Aunt Wanda herself was guilty as far as the stunts at the house were concerned. It was she who had doctored the dinner wine, had half destroyed her own bouquet, and had done whatever else had been done here and had fooled Perkins in the bargain.

"The tricks at the house," I said, heading for the door, "were meant to distract everyone's attention. To keep people watching each other —the way a magician makes you notice one thing while the real sleight-of-hand is going on somewhere else."

"That doesn't make sense."

"We'll talk about it later. Come and put the chair under the doorknob."

Across the dim hall I headed for my room, for the house keys on the dresser top. I was in and out of the room with not more than a whisper of sound. I stood still to listen. But there was only the blowing, murmuring wetness from out of doors against the walls and windows of the house.

At the end of the hall I found the door, felt along the lintel for the lock, and fitted the key into it. The lock turned with a metallic rasp that seemed to me as loud as any thunderclap. I swallowed my fear and waited; heard nothing from downstairs; and opened the door. Across the circular room the windows let in a dim gray light. I searched my way past the furniture to the stairs that led to the room below.

Down in the lower room the sound of the rain was unexpectedly loud, and there was a chill in the air, as if a door to the outside had been opened. I felt my way to the door that must open upon the veranda and found the reason for the chill, for the noise of the rain. The door was open a little way. I shut it silently. This was the way the intruder had entered, which meant that he, or she, had a key to the outer door.

But was this so strange? Hadn't I known, on first finding this room, that it was a secret place and used for secret business? Like the handing over of blackmail?

Yes, I'd known that.

My eyes were adjusting to the dimness. I ran to the loveseat where the gun should lie hidden beneath the cushion, sat down, and ran my hand between the velvet armrest and the end of the seat.

And found nothing.

I almost cried out in that moment of fear, of realization. The intruder had beaten me here, had taken the weapon I needed to defend Rye and myself; and for a moment I was simply unable to move. Then a hope occurred to me, I was disoriented or I'd misplaced the gun in putting it back.

In frantic, numb-fingered haste I searched under all of the cushions, felt along the carpet, then turned to the tables and the other furniture. But the gun was gone.

There was someone loose in the house who had to be stopped, though. I sat with my head bent, arms tight across my bosom, hugged together, afraid, and I tried to plan. The imperative thing was that Rye not be harmed nor frightened. At all costs I must protect my sister.

If I could reach a phone I could call John and he would come as quickly as possible, or I could summon the police, who would come roaring up with sirens. The trouble was, we needed protection now, at this instant. Before the intruder could go upstairs.

Stop and think, I told myself, trying to bring order into my chaotic head: Whoever's here could have come on an ordinary, easy-to-explain errand and mean no harm at all.

Correction, cold common sense answered: Only Rye and I had any business in this place. Anyone else was an intruder, didn't belong, and had nothing but bad intentions.

I stood and walked through the dark to the door that led into the lower hall. I reached to touch it, and it moved. It moved toward me.

I was caught in a moment of freezing fear, but some instinct flattened me against the wall to one side.

The door opened, and the night lights from the hall beyond showed me what stood there, tall and black-robed, masked.

My phantom of the cemetery.

He should have heard my hoarse breathing; he couldn't have helped hearing my heart thud. He looked into the room with his head bent forward under the black hood. It was not until later that I understood that the hood interfered with his hearing, and to a lesser degree with his sight, which must have been adjusted to the dark by now, as mine was.

For some reason he neither heard nor saw me, rigidly pressed to the wall not more than two feet away. In turning back to the hall he moved so that he didn't face in my direction. Otherwise, I am certain now, he would have killed me then.

I heard his footsteps fade away on the carpeted hall floor. I just stood where I was like a mouse, like a rabbit, when the hunting fox has prowled past.

But I had to go after him. I had to reach a phone, even if it meant someone arriving here too late . . . and I had to get between him and Rye's door, and die there if I had to, whether it made any difference in the outcome or not.

He had left the door ajar, and I slid through the opening. The hall held a ghostly dimness but no tall waiting figure. In my fright, the dimensions of the place looked distorted to me, the ceiling bulging far away and the walls anchored at odd angles. Most of the night lights had been disconnected, I noted; a few were left, enough for him to see his way.

There was a telephone in Aunt Wanda's little office, where I'd been earlier—but how did I know he wasn't there? I decided to try for the kitchen.

But then another idea intruded: Why not turn on the lights in the parlor? If he weren't in there, if I could light the great room, have the glow blazing and completely visible from the road, wouldn't any passing car, hopefully a sheriff's cruiser, take note and come in?

If I could turn on the lights in there, then shut the door and get to the phone in the kitchen, wouldn't I have two things going for us? Two signals for help?

I put a nerveless hand on the light switch in the parlor. I braced myself to find him standing there in black, facing me, when the lights came on. I pressed the switches, all of them, and the room sprang into brilliance, into glorious brightness.

And it was empty.

I backed out swiftly and shut the door, and so well were Larchwood's doors fitted that no rim of light displayed itself around the lintel. I slipped without sound all the way down the hall to the kitchen.

The telephone line was dead.

Twenty-four

I THOUGHT OF THE KNIVES.

Mrs. Mim kept them in a drawer, each in its slot; they shone with whetting, with sharpness.

Could I . . . I shivered. Could I really use a knife on another human being?

I decided that if the other human being meant to harm my sister, I might be able to. Only the moment of final action would tell. I didn't have the gun; I wasn't sure I could have used that either. But a knife was different, more repulsive. It meant the actual cutting and stabbing of flesh. For a moment, there in the dark of the kitchen with the useless phone hanging in my hand, I almost rejected the idea of taking one of the knives.

But I did take one, finally, a medium-sized knife with a solid grip and a well-sharpened blade that I tested gingerly against my thumb. Not knowing how else to conceal the knife, I slipped it up my sleeve.

I went back out into the hall, and now something was different. The last of the night lights had been disconnected. I was lost now in the dark. I would have to feel my way to the stairs, to the door of Rye's room where I would make my stand.

But cold reason warned me not to play the game his way. I remembered the switches on the wall near the kitchen doorway—they controlled lights all the way to the front entry, where there was another duplicate set of switches like these. I put out a hand. The switches, five or six of them, were in a row along a metal panel. The metal was cool under my touch. I flipped the switches up, one at a time, and the ceiling lights spread their brightness the length of the hall.

And the hall was empty.

Somewhere he waited, laughing. Or she waited. Mrs. Stryfe? Why not? Who else would know Aunt Wanda's secret?

I ran. I turned to mount the stairway to the upper floor, to Rye's room, and something behind me moved, or made a sound . . . at any rate, stopped me there a third of the way up. I looked back.

A door was moving, the door to Aunt Wanda's little office.

I can't explain how I felt at that moment. I knew that the phantom was here, in the house somewhere, the black thing that had caught me alone in the cemetery—and yet because it was my aunt's office door that was opening, in a great surge of irrational relief I felt that *my aunt* was coming out.

Aunt Wanda was coming from her office to tell me . . . what? That this was another kind of dream?

I felt the knife slipping around inside my sleeve and almost threw it away, almost tossed it over the bannister. The door moved very slowly, and then stopped for a moment as if the person inside had realized that all of the lights were on in the hall. I waited, it seemed not even breathing, caught up in a wild hope.

Then the door opened fully and a man's figure emerged.

No black phantom, no hood nor robe. He faced me across about twenty-five feet of space. He wore the raincoat but he was bareheaded, and the wheat-stubble of hair was frosted with damp. He looked boldly and curiously at me. "I think you have a prowler in the house somewhere, Miss Myles."

I was trying to orient myself to the idea that this wasn't my aunt after all. It was Bart Linton. An old friend who'd been told that we were alone and that he should keep an eye on us.

Hadn't he been one of those Aunt Wanda had talked to?

I couldn't remember.

"I went into the office," he continued, "because your aunt was supposed to leave some papers for me. They have to do with my house, with repairs and so on. It was while I was in there that I realized you had an intruder."

"This is a strange time to come for papers of that kind."

He shrugged. Nothing changed in his unwavering weighing of me. What was he expecting? That I might launch myself at him from the stairs, begging protection from the prowler? "I couldn't get to sleep tonight and so I thought I'd come for the papers, I'd be careful not to disturb you or your sister. It turned out not to be a bright idea. And I'm sorry."

"What are you going to do about the intruder?"

The silence settled while he thought about it. "I think the intruder has gone. All of these lights, the stirring around, people being awake—"

"Aren't you a kind of . . . of an intruder yourself, Mr. Linton?"

He smiled a little. "Wanda wouldn't call me that."

"But she would suggest, in view of the time of night, that you left now. Wouldn't she?"

He folded his arms and leaned against the edge of the doorway. He seemed completely at ease. "I guess you intend to tell your aunt I was here. Late like this."

I felt myself on such uncertain footing. What would my aunt expect? She'd always hated my prickly staidness. Was I supposed to be friendly at this hour, under these circumstances? Friendly and welcoming? Common sense said not. "Why shouldn't I tell her?"

He searched through his pockets, pushing the damp raincoat aside, and took out cigarettes and got a smoke going. "The thing is, Wanda might be annoyed if she thought I came here so late and sort of inadvertently disturbed anyone. Oh, not you. She doesn't care what happens to you. But the one upstairs, Barbara—" His voice had died to a husky whisper; he seemed almost on the edge of laughter. And his eyes were busy, searching out my feelings.

I went up a step or two. "You want me to promise that I won't tell my aunt about your visit."

"Now you're getting the idea."

"You'd trust my word?"

He gave me a glance of mock surprise. "Shouldn't I?" When I said nothing he added, "Does your sister know that anyone's down here besides you?"

"No," I lied quickly.

"I think Mrs. Parrish must know that there is an intruder. I think I'd better get her promise, too, not to tell."

"But you aren't the intruder, and we're—" I almost choked over the words. "—we're grateful you came and chased him, or her, away." He stepped erect, away from the edge of the doorway, and I added, "You can't see my sister."

He pretended to be astonished. "What do you think I am? Some kind of beast? All I want to do is to explain to Barbara why I was here, how thoughtless it was of me to come late like this, and how she might save everyone a lot of trouble if she promised, as you have, not to mention my visit here tonight."

Had I promised? I couldn't remember promising not to tell of his visit. I backed up two more stairs, and he came to the bottom step.

I tried to crowd down the sudden fear, tried to figure out what was the important thing, and I decided that getting him out of the house was most important. There was a black thing waiting for me, the phantom of the cemetery—or was there?—but right now my instincts told me to deal with Mr. Linton. "Will you let me go and talk to Rye and get her promise for you?"

He seemed to think it over. I think he pretended to consider it. He smoked, standing at ease at the foot of the stairs. He'd been in Aunt Wanda's office for something, and I wondered in that instant if he knew the secret of opening her desk.

He sighed. "Well, no, I guess I couldn't. There are some pretty important things at stake here, and I couldn't afford a misunderstanding. I don't want your aunt angry or upset."

She might do more than just get drunk. . . .

Was this what he was saying?

I blurted out my thoughts. "You want to keep her secret and to share that secret. Not to reveal it as you've threatened to do. Because by keeping it you can go on blackmailing her forever."

I turned and ran to the top of the stairs, and turned again to face him. He said, "What ugly words you use, Miss Myles. I've never threatened your aunt. I've sympathized with her, tried to help her come to terms with the past. I've lent her my shoulder to cry on."

"It wasn't Aunt Wanda who cried on your shoulder. It was Mrs. Stryfe, when she was drunk."

How clear it all seemed suddenly, what had been going on here before Rye had come, while our aunt had been alone as mistress of Larchwood.

He exhaled a long plume of smoke and came up the stairs, not hurrying, taking one tread at a time, watching me, pausing about halfway up. "Well, Mrs. Stryfe does have her problems. And so do I. And I have to see your sister and ask her as a favor for her silence."

"You'll have to leave Rye alone."

"Sorry."

There was a gun in his hand. It seemed to have appeared as if instantly. The cigarette had been tossed away, and he'd taken the gun from the raincoat pocket in one smooth gesture. Even now, putting one foot soundlessly on the tread above, he had the economy and tautness of movement I'd always noticed about him. But it was the gun that held my eyes. This was not the gun that had been hidden in the couch in the tower room. This was a shorter, uglier weapon. In his fist it was squat and dangerous, and the barrel was fixed on my heart.

He could kill me now, of course. I had no recourse. Only if I could lure him into some enclosed area—and we were close enough—but I wasn't sure that even then I'd be able to use the knife.

I backed away into the hall. "You're spoiling it for yourself."

"No, I'm not. I'm simply going to ask your sister not to tell your aunt I was here. But the thing is, you're in my way—I don't like to threaten you and I don't know how much your aunt would care if I went ahead and shot you. I really don't."

"No doubt you talked about her feelings toward me, as well as toward Rye, in that tower room. And she told you what a nuisance I'd always been.

"You're being a nuisance now."

He was close enough so that I could read clearly at last the expression in his eyes. There was no real humor, no ironic repose, no assurance. There is whatever is left after years of frustration and the thirst for vengeance. There was what remains after the year-by-year passing of an old home, driving by it with the feeling that the outraged ghost of your father stares at you from its shattered windows. While in your mind's eye you see the house of long ago, the rooms full of familiar things, clean with your mother's care, all of it abandoned to become a broken ruin. In Linton's eyes were memories of unendurable things, a life broken like the house itself.

He motioned with the gun for me to move, and I said desperately, "I haven't told you the truth. Rye isn't in her room. I hid her safely before I went down to look for the intruder."

Was he going to believe this?

The point of the knife was in my palm, held tight against my flesh by my fingers. There was no way that he could know I held a weapon, no hint that could betray I wanted to lead him into a place where I might have a chance at close quarters. I would be quite at his mercy, even as I was now; but he might also be at mine.

If in that crucial moment I would have the courage to act . . .

The test would come. Right now I had to lead him where I wanted him. So instead of backing toward Rye's room, with a defiant stare I stepped between him and the door to the tower and the belvedere.

For a moment he must have sensed the trick; he glanced toward Rye's door and then swiftly at me and the gun leveled and steadied.

To distract him I had to keep his mind on something else, so I said, "Mrs. Stryfe told you about the orphanage. But that's nothing, there was no disgrace involved. My aunt had been married. Why shouldn't her sister and her sister's husband adopt her baby?"

His face stiffened. "Mrs. Stryfe came to my house one day and drank my whiskey and cried over her troubled memories. Her brother, for one, whom she seems to think she killed. And other things, such as Angela's not finding a husband, beautiful as she is. I think Mrs. Stryfe had some weird idea I might fill a need there. But never mind. And true, she told me of the orphanage. But I sensed that there must be much more to the story than the simple one of the adoption. I made a quick trip to Seattle and hunted around and what I found was so much uglier—" He shook his head over the memory of his discoveries. "You wouldn't believe it. I'm not asking you to. I want to see your sister. Now."

"I can't let you face Rye carrying a gun."

I backed, as if unwillingly, toward the doorway to the tower stairs, the entry to the belvedere, and my heart was hammering with fear that he wouldn't believe me, wouldn't follow.

I went on: "Don't you see what you're risking? You've got a good thing here. A nice income, to top what you make as a professor."

For a moment he looked at me in disgusted incredulity. "Do you think that's what I want? The little handout? The nickels and dimes from the small budget? No, no, my dear. . . ." His sudden wide grin mocked me. "In time—" He looked up and down the dim upper halls of Larchwood. "In time this will all be mine."

That was it, I thought. And the day might well come when Bart would be master here, when my aunt would be dispossessed, driven out by threat of a scandal she couldn't face.

"Let's go up and see your sister," he said, his tone pleasant, almost sane again. "I hope she's well wrapped against the weather. The belvedere, isn't it?"

"I can't let you . . ."

"Lead the way." *Or be shot.* There was sudden indifference in his expression; he actually didn't care, for the moment, how things turned out. The years gone by cried for vengeance, for violence, and I was here to be used as he chose.

I backed up the stairs to the belvedere. All of the doors had been unlocked. I passed the open door to that upper tower room; I wondered if some black shape waited inside, though I knew better. I knew my phantom now, wherever and whenever he had shed his black robe, and put on the raincoat.

We were, it seemed without any warning, up there in the rain and wind, my hair was blowing into my face, and under cover of dark I was letting the knife slide down out of my sleeve into my hand. He might shoot me, but if I could I'd keep him from getting back down out of here.

He came close and put the gun against my breast.

"I wasn't fooled for a moment, poor Miss Myles. Or may I call you Pocket? I wasn't fooled, but it occurred to me that before I pushed you out upon that roof I might have a little fun with you. You may not believe this, it's only fantasy, but if under different circumstances I'd been master of Larchwood, you would have been its mistress if you would have had me."

He put a hand to the neck of my dress.

I thrust out with the knife but the fabric of the raincoat turned the blade as if it were made of butter. It slid past the mark; I think he believed that I'd tried to push at him.

"Don't fight. We've only a little time. It won't be love as you think of it, but while you're trying to cling to those wet slates it will give you something to remember. Briefly."

I gripped the knife tighter. I had to get the blade in under the coat. The wind lifted my soaked hair, and he was so close now that I felt the heat from his body. His hand, opening my dress, was cold, but I was colder where he touched me.

A gun spoke in the night. In all the noise of wind and rain the sound was still unmistakable, and for a moment I thought he had fired, perhaps recognizing at last what I meant to do to him. But this gun had been fired from the other side of the belvedere, from the opening to the stairs.

He sagged against me and I flung myself aside, and for a moment I looked out upon long reaches of wet slate, dim under the night sky, a slide to death.

Aunt Wanda's voice spoke out of the dark. "Come, Esther. Leave him where he is and . . . hurry."

He was trying to get his feet under him, clinging to the railing of the belvedere. I heard the gun clatter off down the roof as I ran to the opening of the stairs.

Fools get down stairs in different ways. I fell down these.

It seemed only the next moment that I opened my eyes and found all the lights on in the upper hall. Someone was carrying me. Surely not my aunt . . .

No, this was John Sutton.

John Sutton followed Aunt Wanda and laid me on the bed in my room, where the lamps glowed, and in the gentlest way possible he began to refasten the front of my dress. Under the gentleness was an air of fury, not directed toward me. My aunt came swimming into view above me, all out of focus, and bathed my head with a cloth that smelled of spirits of ammonia or some such. It took a while for my wits to clear—I'd banged something pretty hard on the way down—but I had a most important question to ask.

"What happened to you?"

John Sutton was battered, bloody, mad, and his clothes were mud-smeared. "He chopped me down outside. He was waiting, and I was a fool."

"Is Rye all right?"

"Just dying of curiosity," Aunt Wanda whispered.

"You came back so soon."

"I took Mrs. Mim and Cindy as far as her cousins' place. Then I came back. Not here. I'd decided to do what I should have done in the beginning: turn to John for help."

I saw that Aunt Wanda showed the exhaustion of long hours of driving. Her hair was mussed and flattened. How long had she been in the house? How much had she heard of the conversation between Bart and me?

"He's going to come down out of that belvedere," I warned the two of them, hazily, my sight fogging up again.

"When he does they'll stick him into an ambulance," John told me. "And he'll go away with Chris Warne."

"You saved my life," I croaked to Aunt Wanda, and she bent and kissed me, and I felt her tears on my face, and she said, "I would have died for you, Pocket. Anytime. From the beginning."

And this I had to believe.

Chris Warne came in to look at me and to say hello, and he looked big and businesslike and smelled of rain and the northern Louisiana countryside and his car, and I thought dazedly, I'm looking at Rye's future husband. She's going to get married again.

Dr. Potterby also showed up and did various things. Bart Linton was removed and was going to have to have surgery and was lucky to be alive to need it because it seemed Aunt Wanda was a good shot from way back. She had even managed to shoot him in such a way that if the bullet had emerged from the other side of him it wouldn't have hit me. Aunt Wanda the sharpshooter.

Aunt Wanda, my aunt.

It occurred to me that a whole new relationship lay ahead. She was *really* my aunt. She could boss me as a kind of surrogate mother, and I could sass back. We didn't have to keep up this sort of armed vindictiveness any longer. We could be our true selves: repulsive.

I found myself looking forward to it all in a perfectly natural way.

And then, of course, there was John.

He was getting patched up for the time being but he was going to come in here again, and this time he wouldn't be buttoning my dress and full of fury at Bart Linton. He was going to have new ideas entirely. I tried to stiffen up that spinster, the woman of ice I'd depended on for so long, the one who kept all involvement at an arm's length, but it seemed she'd gotten tired of it all and had left me. I was new and raw, and I knew that when John Sutton got here he was going to put his arms around me and kiss me, the way he'd wanted to that night in the cemetery—unromantic place—and that after those kisses things weren't ever going to be the same again.

When he finally came in I managed to stall him with a question. "What about that black robe he wore?"

"An idiot thing." John Sutton did as I'd expected, he bent and lifted me and put his mouth on mine. After a while he added, "He'd left it in your aunt's downstairs office. What a getup. He must have looked like a spook."

"He sure did."

Then there wasn't time for conversation, because we had each other, and when you love someone it's all new, it's a brand-new dizzy, melting sweetness that tastes like honey and makes you drunk as wine. If Larchwood had blown away on the rain and let us alone in the forest I don't think either of us would have known a thing about it.